SHOTS ON NET

SCU HOCKEY: BOOK ONE

J.J. MULDER

Copyright © 2024 by J.J. Mulder

All rights reserved.

No part of this book may be reproduced in any form or by any electronic or mechanical means, including information storage and retrieval systems, without written permission from the author, except for the use of brief quotations in a book review.

The story, all names, characters, and incidents portrayed in this production are fictitious. No identification with actual persons (living or deceased), places, buildings, and products is intended or should be inferred.

This book was not written with AI. Without in any way limiting the author's exclusive rights under copyright, any use of this publication to "train" generative artificial intelligence (AI) technologies to generate text is expressly prohibited. The author reserves all rights to license uses of this work for generative AI training and development of machine learning language models.

ISBN: 9798320681252

Book Cover by Ivanna Nashkolna.

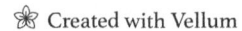

❀ Created with Vellum

For Mom

1

Zeke

I'M COLD, wet and miserable as I hurry to my appointment, which, incidentally, is also the way I would describe the weather. It's raining today, just as it had been raining yesterday and the day before. Just as it would likely be raining tomorrow. By the time I make it to the house on Walnut Ave, I'll be soaked. My spirits, already low, plummet further. I should just call and cancel, really. Carter Morgan III will take one look at my bedraggled self and shut the door.

But I can't cancel. Not only because I've come this far already, but because this is, quite literally, my last hope. I've been scouring advertisements for roommates for weeks; at the beginning, I'd been picky and only chosen to reach out to the ones that actually sounded good. Now, I wasn't quite so discerning. My only requirement at this point is a roof over my head. Beggars cannot be choosers, as they say, and I am way beyond begging.

As I pass under a street sign for Walnut Ave, I nearly cry.

No crying, you're wet enough, I tell myself firmly, and hasten toward number 840. Standing on the covered porch, dripping, I lower the hood on my useless raincoat and attempt to get my hair out of my eyes. I need a haircut—something that is immediately apparent now that it's plastered to my forehead and tickling my eyelashes. Taking a single deep breath in, I knock.

Nothing.

I knock again. And again. I stop at kicking the door, but it's a close thing. Checking my phone, I note that I'm exactly on time and that it is, in fact, the agreed upon day. *I swear to all that is holy, if Carter Morgan the fucking Third leaves me standing on this porch, I'll...*

The door swings open. I try not to stare. I try really hard to make my grandma proud and *not* stare. Unfortunately, I am not having a great day, and subtlety is not my strongest attribute. The man standing in front of me, whom I assume is Carter Morgan III, looks like the kind of person who would rob Carter Morgan III at gunpoint.

I had been expecting a polo-wearing, boat-shoe type of guy, which goes to show that one should not create expectations in their mind. Carter Morgan is wearing athletic shorts and what is probably an artfully ripped muscle shirt. A shirt which shows off two full sleeves of tattoos that cover his arms from wrist to shoulder, and snake their way up to his neck. His blonde hair is shaved on the sides, but left longer on top and pulled into a bun at the back of his head. He has a silver hoop through one nostril; I can count on one hand the number of men I have seen with nose piercings, and I wouldn't even need all five fingers. To top it all off, his blue eyes are filled with an unmistakable look of annoyance that almost has me stepping backward and away. This is what I get for answering ads on the internet.

"Can I help you?" Carter Morgan III asks rudely.

"I'm Zeke Cassidy," I say, even though I can tell it's futile. He's forgotten. Either he found another roommate and forgot to cancel our appointment, or he's just plain forgotten because clearly Carter Morgan III has more important things to do with his time. *God, what a waste of a day.*

"No," he says, and I stare at him, probably looking as forlorn and unkempt as a stray puppy. "Please tell me that wasn't today."

Sorry, buddy, today was the day and yes this is me. Sorry for the letdown. "Sorry."

He throws the door open wide and I wince when it hits the wall with a bang. "Don't be sorry, Jesus fuck, I'm the one who forgot. Come in, did you swim here?"

I step inside barely a moment before he flings the door closed with the same amount of force he used to open it. That poor door is never going to survive. Looking down, I watch as water begins slowly pooling under my feet onto his hardwood floors. I think the best thing for me would be to find a deep puddle on the way home and drown myself.

"I'm sorry," I say ineffectually, still looking at my soggy shoes.

"Whatever, it's fine." A towel is thrust under my nose, and I grasp it. Looking up, I lock eyes with Carter Morgan's navy blue ones. He doesn't sound pissed but he sure looks it. I start to kneel, meaning to use the towel to dry the floor. He makes an irritated tsking noise.

"That's for you." He grabs the towel, pulls it roughly from my fingers, and flings it around my shoulders like a cape. "Follow me. We can talk back here."

Without waiting for a reply, he turns and strides off. There is a deep V of sweat soaking the back of his shirt and the faint aroma of sweaty man is in the air. I follow him, and make a mental note to check his name against police reports. Those look like the kind of biceps they make in prison. He leads me to a massive kitchen, where he promptly ignores me in favor of making a smoothie. I wait, dripping water and using the towel to try and dry my hair as best I can. Once the smoothie is finished, he gulps half of it down before once more remembering my presence.

"Don't you want to sit down?" he asks, as though it was strange for me not to invite myself to do so in his home. I definitely want to sit down, though, so I do. Squelching over to the island, I slide onto a barstool and clutch the towel around me. The water has become a different sort of nuisance now—I'm freezing.

"Thanks. Sorry to interrupt your workout." Technically, his workout interrupted our scheduled meeting, but who am I to split hairs.

"Dude, stop apologizing. I should have set an alarm on my phone, I'm sorry I forgot."

He sounds sincere, which is surprising. He also didn't give me an excuse, which, again, is surprising. I'm not one to hold a grudge, and I'd already decided to forgive him even without an apology. "No worries. It happens."

"You want some soup or something? No offense, but you look like a corpse."

"Full offense, but you look like someone who deals weed to middle schoolers."

Carter Morgan snorts, but doesn't smile. His gaze is appraising as he looks me over, trying to get a measure of me. I hope he finds something he likes. If not, begging it is.

"So, here's the place." He holds his arms out wide. "I'll take your best offer on the spare room."

"My best offer?"

"Yeah. Whatever you want to pay for rent."

"Uhm, well, right then." Scrambling, I eye the vaulted ceilings and the large, open floor plan. This is a *nice* house. Chances are the bedroom is big and so is the electricity bill. The ad said I'd have my own bathroom. "I'd say $400 would be fair for base rent, as long as I'd have access to the kitchen and living room as well, not just the bedroom. Plus, half of whatever the monthly utilities are, obviously. I'd buy my own groceries, and help with the household chores. I don't have a car, so you wouldn't have to worry about me needing room on the driveway or in the garage."

He sips his smoothie, leaned casually against the opposite counter and staring at me. I'm coming to realize that the expression I had thought was annoyance earlier, is actually just his face. He doesn't seem to have another expression.

"That's a fair offer," he says, and I nod. It is fair, which is why I said it. But it's also more than I was hoping to pay. I'd been expecting to rent a room in a shithole, not a nice place like this. "How about you just share utilities and we call it a day?"

Pushing away from the counter, he throws back the rest of the smoothie and places the cup in the sink. Flinging the refrigerator door wide, bottles clinking together alarmingly, he bends over and peers inside. Eventually, he emerges with a Tupperware, which he holds up to show me.

"You good with leftovers?" he asks, and then starts heating up a bowl before I have a second to answer. *This guy is insane.*

"Uh, Carter? Morgan?" *What the hell do I call him?*

"Jesus, one or the other."

Right. "Carter, I don't think I understand what you're saying."

"Venmo me half of the utilities every month and the room is yours."

"You just told me my offer was fair, and you counter with an *unfair* offer?" I don't know why I'm arguing, except for the fact that none of this encounter has gone the way I'd planned and it's got me off-kilter. He pulls the bowl of soup from the microwave, drops a spoon in, and pushes it over to me.

"An unfair offer for me, maybe. But a good deal for you, I'd say," he counters, crossing his arms and looking menacing. Inmate turned soup kitchen chef.

"Okay, but..." I make a disbelieving noise and shrug my shoulders. "I mean, I'll take the room, obviously, but it doesn't make sense."

"My dad owns this house and everything in it, including me. He doesn't need your money, ergo, I don't either."

"Oh." There really isn't an appropriate response to that, so I employ silence. Carter is a little intense, and I'm not entirely convinced I'm making the correct decision here. This is what happens when you are forced to make a decision based on need. "Well, okay, thank you. I'll do more than my share of chores, to make up for it. I can do your laundry."

The look Carter gives me is acidic enough to peel paint from walls. "You're not my maid, dude, what the fuck. My laundry is rank, you don't want anything to do with that, trust me. Eat your soup and I'll give you a tour."

The soup has done more to warm me up than the towel, and was so unexpectedly kind that I'm still grappling with it. Carter Morgan is a fucking weirdo, that much is clear. I finish the bowl in record time, stopping just short of licking it clean.

It joins his smoothie glass in the sink and he waves me after him as he leaves the kitchen. Like earlier, he doesn't wait to see if I follow. *Keep up, or don't,* his long-legged strides seem to say, *either way it means nothing to me.*

He leads me down to the basement first, which is completely unfinished. Carter has taken it upon himself to build a gym: padded mats on the concrete floor, a heavy bag hanging from a chain, weights scattered about the space, and various machines pushed against the walls. It smells vaguely of sweat.

"Gym," Carter tells me unnecessarily. "Use whatever you want. I'm down here a lot, between classes and practice. But I can share."

He does not, in any way, look like someone who knows how to share. I'll take his word for it. "Practice?"

"Hockey," he says, and his tone changes marginally. He looks a fraction less angry.

"Oh, cool, I didn't know you played hockey." I know nothing about him at all, except that he lives on Walnut Ave. Hockey tracks, though. I've heard it's a violent sport, and Carter looks like he might eat nails for breakfast. "What position do you play?"

"Net. Do you follow?"

"No, sorry. I'm not much of a sports guy." Not much in this case meaning not at all. I couldn't tell you anything about hockey except that sticks, pucks, and big men are involved. Carter grunts, expression tightening back into moodiness.

I follow him back upstairs. He points things out as we go, such as closets, bathrooms, and other shared spaces. When we get to the upper floor, he walks through an open doorway and I'm inside before I realize this is his bedroom. Halting, I retreat to the doorway and try not to stare at the pair of boxers flung on the bed.

"This is my room. If the door is open, feel free to come in."

"Oh," I say, because this is both a generous and strange offer. Obviously, Carter doesn't care about privacy at all—I've been given free rein to his entire house, including, apparently, his bedroom.

He shows me to the spare room and the bathroom that will be mine. Both are larger and better equipped than any space I've ever called my own.

"This is great. Thank you."

He shrugs my thanks off, and puts his hands into the pockets of his shorts. His shoulders have crept up toward his ears, and I wonder if he's cold, in that sleeveless shirt.

"When should we get your stuff?" he asks, and correctly interprets my silence as confusion. "Your clothes, and shit. Do you want to move in now?"

"Yeah, today would be fine, but you're not—"

He leaves the room. *Oh boy.* Sighing, I follow after him, pulling the damp towel off and folding it as I walk. I peek into Carter's room, assuming this was where he went, and am treated to a half-dressed visual. He's shirtless and curled over, abdomen clenched as he pulls off his athletic shorts. Slapping a hand over my eyes, I back up and hit the doorframe.

"Sorry! I didn't realize you were...the door was open, and you said—"

"Chill. I'm just changing."

Peeking through my fingers, I see Carter shoot me a look and walk over to his closet. He's wearing his boxers and nothing else. And yes, those tattoos do indeed climb up the back of his neck and crawl all the way down to his waistband.

It's hard not to stare. I can't tell what the tattoos are, except for a large one on his shoulder which is a mask of some sort.

"All right, let's go."

Ready for him this time as he leaves the room—fully clothed, thankfully—I follow close so as not to be left behind. He's slipped on a pair of black sweatpants and a black, long-sleeved shirt. It's tight enough to show the muscled arms beneath. Covering up the tattoos has done nothing to make him less frightening-looking—now he only looks like a burglar. I speed up to walk beside him, my shorter legs already burning in the effort it takes to keep up with him.

"You don't have to take me to get my things. Really, it's completely unnecessary."

"You don't have a car, you said."

"I don't. I was going to rent one."

"That's stupid." He flings open the door to the garage, and the handle bounces off the wall. Not once today has he opened a door with an appropriate level of force. I'm surprised the walls of this place aren't riddled with holes. "Just get in the car."

Feeling that it would be both childish and foolish to disagree, I climb into the passenger seat. He drives some sort of SUV, and when I peek behind me, I see the back seats are already folded down as though he was expecting to move furniture today. There is a faint stale odor that I can't place, and no less than five air fresheners hanging from the ceiling handles and rearview mirror.

"Sorry if it stinks," Carter says, sounding not an iota sorry, "my pads and shit can get pretty disgusting."

"Oh, you have a lot of pads?"

"No, I just block pucks naked and hope for the best."

Okay, Carter, no need for snark. "It's possible that I've never seen a hockey game before in my life. Or football. Or baseball."

"Coming to SCU home games is a requirement of living with me. We'll get that cherry popped."

"Oh boy." I'm picturing an entire team of Carter Morgans. Thugs on ice.

"What's your name, anyway?" he asks, and my jaw actually drops.

"Zeke Cassidy, I already told you that," I remind him, a little bit hurt that he's already forgotten.

"No, like what's your full name." He looks over at me, a flash of blue between shockingly dark lashes. "I remember your fucking name, I'm not an idiot. But that's a nickname, right? Zeke?"

"Oh. No, that's my name."

"Weird."

"Whatever you say, Your Majesty, Carter Morgan the Third, Baron of Walnut Ave and King of the Hockey Court."

Carter makes a choking noise that I tentatively identify as a laugh. I've never seen anyone laugh without smiling before. It's a little impressive.

"You're a smartass," he says, not sounding mad about it. "Zeke. I like it. Better than Carter, anyway. Fucking white bread name."

It would be rude to agree, since we've only just met. But he's right. Carter Morgan III is the most posh name I've ever heard. And totally unfit for him. I wonder if he did that on purpose—modeled his aesthetic around what people expect him *not* to be.

I direct him as we drive. These streets are as familiar to me as the back of my hand; I didn't go far from home when I left for college, but it was just far enough to make me feel independent. And close enough that I was only an Uber away if my grandma needed me. The closer we get, the more nervous I become. I hadn't thought through the fact that if my new roommate helped collect my things, he'd also be seeing where I was collecting them from. I have a feeling Carter is about to see a side of South Carolina he hasn't seen before.

"Number 14C," I tell him, and am ashamed of how small my voice is. I shouldn't be embarrassed. Lots of people live in trailer parks, and it's nothing to be humiliated about. He doesn't say anything, but turns the vehicle around so he can back carefully into the space beside my grandma's car. Resigned, I push open my door and meet him at the back of the car.

"Want me to wait out here?" he asks. He'd rolled the sleeves of his shirt up while he drove, and the tattoos look stark against his skin in the outdoor light. We're being treated to a lucky break in the rain, which probably means we need to hurry and load up the car before it starts up again.

"Nah, you can come in. It's just my grandma here."

I knock three times, pause, and knock twice more in quick succession. Using my key, I push the door open and call out. As I knew it would, my grandma's voice calls back from her sitting room. Holding the door open for Carter, he makes a production of wiping his shoes off on the mat and tugging his sleeves down. He looks uncomfortable.

"Hey, Grandma." I lean over her favorite chair and give her the best hug I can, with her seated. She beams up at me, eyes clear beneath a cap of white hair. I just saw her this morning before I left to meet with Carter about the available bedroom, but her age and frailness is always reminding me just how little time I have left. I feel like I need to treat every minute with her like it's our last minute. Lots of hugs and lots of *I love you*'s.

"Hi, sweetie. How did your appointment go? Is it a nice house? Was he a nice boy?"

"Everything was really good, it's going to be perfect. Actually, Carter is here to meet you and help me move my things." I wave for Carter to shuffle into view. He's got his sleeves pulled down and clenched in his fists. It's futile—anyone can see the ink scaling his neck and the silver nose ring glinting in the light. He looks precisely like someone you wouldn't introduce to your grandma.

"Hello, ma'am. I'm Carter." He holds up one of his clenched hands, waving it a bit. I bite my lip so that I don't laugh.

"Oh goodness, well, hello there." Grandma climbs out of her chair and approaches him. Carter looks like he wants to retreat, but remains steadfast. He's at least a foot taller than her, and twice as wide. I've never seen anyone look so frightened of someone so harmless. Grandma wraps a hand around his wrist, pulling it toward her and patting his hand. "Carter, is it? What a nice name for such a lovely looking boy. Come on with me, Carter, let's get you something to eat."

She keeps ahold of his arm and pulls him into the kitchen. He looks over at me and I grin, mouthing *lovely looking boy* at him. His wide-eyed look turns to one of squinty-eyed annoyance. Something clicks into place between us; I think I'm going to enjoy living with Carter Morgan III.

2

Carter

Zeke's grandma looks like a stiff wind could blow her away. She tells me I can call her grandma too, if I want, and then deposits me at the dining room table. There's a half-finished puzzle on the table and the chairs are all mismatched. I've never felt so out of place as I do right now, in my black sweats and too-big-for-this-house body. Everything in here looks breakable, including Zeke and his grandma.

"Do you like coffee cake, honey?" She brings me a plate with a piece on it before I can answer, setting it down in front of me and placing her hand on my shoulder. It startles me, and I flinch. People *never* touch me, and certainly not little old ladies.

"Uh, yeah, coffee cake is good. Thank you." I try the cake. It's dry and decidedly *not* good. I'm fucking starving though, so I eat the whole thing while she chats and have half a mind to ask for more. I don't know where Zeke went off to, but I hope he comes back soon. His grandma left a glass of juice in front of me too, so I gulp that down as well. "Where did Zeke go?"

"Oh, he probably went to his room to pack, I'll show you the way. Give you a tour, shall I?"

She links her arm through my elbow, like I'm escorting her to a Ball. I hope she can't smell how sweaty I am, since I worked out and didn't shower before coming. I hope she hasn't noticed my tattoos, peeking out around my shirt. *Thank god I put on something that had sleeves.*

She walks me through the house, pointing things out and telling me stories. There are dozens of pictures of Zeke: baby pictures, elementary school pictures, band pictures, and pictures of him playing chess. There's a picture of Zeke doing fucking *everything*, like I'm walking through a shrine. It makes me feel faintly ill, being slapped with so much blatant love. There's not a single picture of me in my parents' house; my mom would laugh herself silly if I asked to see family photos from when I was growing up.

It's a relief when we get to Zeke's room. There is a helpful sign on the door proclaiming *Zeke's Room* that looks like it's been hanging here for a decade. It's probably something I should make fun of him for, but my throat feels a little tight and everything in this house makes me feel awful—holding up a mirror to my own childhood home and revealing what was wrong. I want to leave.

His grandma knocks on the door. "Sweetheart, your friend is here to help you."

The door is pulled open before she even finishes speaking, and there is Zeke, the fucking deserter. "Thanks, Grandma. Get him all fed up? He was working up a sweat before we got here."

"All taken care of. I'll pack you up something for the road.

You kids have fun." She pats my arm, smiles at me the same way she was just smiling at her grandson, and shuffles off down the hallway. The hallway is lined with more photos of Zeke, and lots of framed art that was done by a childish hand. I hate it here. I really fucking hate it here.

Feeling inordinately sweaty, I push past Zeke and enter his room. He shuts the door quietly behind me, and walks over to his bed. Open on the mattress is a shabby suitcase, half filled with clothes. There's a desk pushed against one wall; I pull the chair out, flip it around, and straddle it.

"Make yourself at home," he tells me.

"Your grandma is nice." Literally the nicest person I've ever met. Nobody is ever as nice to me as she was, which probably says more about her than it does about me.

"She called you *lovely*," Zeke reminds me, and grins. He's folding his clothes carefully before putting them in the suitcase.

Scowling, I kick a foot against the leg of the chair. "So what?"

"So nothing. She's never wrong, though. If she says you're lovely, then you're lovely."

"Stop saying lovely." I wonder if he'd think I was lovely if he knew I'd once set my uncle's house on fire. "Can you hurry up? I want to go home."

He looks at me, brushing his hair out of his eyes. He's got dirty blonde hair that's in desperate need of a haircut, and light blue eyes. There's no trace of facial hair, and he's got the sort of skinny face that looks born of missed meals and not genetics. I have no idea how old he is, but with the baby face and his small stature, he looks barely older than fifteen.

"Sorry," I say, shaking my head. "I don't know why I said that. Take your time. Also, how old are you?"

Zeke is still staring at me. I don't know what the fuck he's expecting to see, but he needs to focus on packing and not on my face. He gives a startled laugh when I ask his age and I glare at him.

"Uhm, I'm in my junior year. I'm twenty, but I'll be twenty-one in a couple of months."

"You look twelve, or something."

"And you look like someone who breaks kneecaps for the mafia," he retorts.

He almost gets me on that one—I can feel my mouth try to smile but bite it back. "Less talking, more packing."

Finally, *finally*, he looks away from me and goes back to packing. I snoop around his room as much as I can from where I'm seated. There are band posters on the wall for groups I've never heard of, and a well-used chess set on top of a bookshelf. Squinting, I try to make out the titles of the books. I don't recognize anything except for *The Hobbit*, which is probably embarrassing.

His room is as threadbare as the rest of the house, but also has a lot of character. It's the sort of bedroom that speaks of someone who knows what they like and are comfortable displaying it. It's as unlike my own bedroom, in my parents' house, as it's possible to be. This is the room of someone allowed to be themself; mine is a room bland enough to be used for guests.

"Do you play chess?" Zeke asks, zipping up his suitcase. He crouches down in front of the bookcase, pulling out a few books and tucking them carefully into his backpack. He glances over at me when I don't immediately answer.

"No." *Do I look like someone who plays chess?*

"Maybe I could teach you! We can play together." He says this with the air of Father Christmas pulling an enormous toy out of his sack. "You can teach me hockey, and I'll teach you chess."

He acts like it's a foregone conclusion that we'll be hanging out together. I give him a solid week before he starts avoiding me. "Yeah, sure. Whatever."

"Cool." He smiles at me, before carefully tucking the chess pieces away and adding the set to his backpack. He casts an appraising eye around his room, hands on hips. "Well, I think that's everything I need."

"I can always bring you back if you forgot something." I stand, pushing the desk chair back into place. He has the skinniest arms I've ever seen on an adult, so I reach over and sling his backpack over my shoulder. When I reach for the handle of the suitcase, he stops me.

"I can get it."

I knock his hand out of the way and grab the suitcase, pulling it off the bed. It's heavy. If he picked this up he'd probably topple over. Without waiting for him to lead the way, I fling open his bedroom door and head down the hallway. He mutters something incoherent behind me, before calling out for his grandma. I step outside, meaning to load the car and then wait for him there. I've barely got his stuff in the back, however, before Zeke and his grandma step out behind me. Cursing under my breath, I make sure my sleeves are pulled down over my tattoos and go over to them.

"I'll call you tomorrow, okay?" Zeke says, leaning down to hug her. "Love you."

Embarrassed, I take a step back and clear my throat, trying to give them the semblance of privacy.

"Love you more," she tells him, before turning to me. I take another automatic step back, but she smiles at me. "Next time we have family dinner you can come along, Carter. You can tell me how you got all these muscles."

Zeke grins manically as she steps up to me and pats my bicep, chuckling at her own joke. I offer my own weak laugh in return and jolt when she wraps an arm around my waist in a half hug. She's got a surprisingly strong grip. I flounder, trying to decide how to reciprocate; eventually, I settle for gentle pats on her upper back. Judging by Zeke's face, this looks as awkward as it feels.

"Drive safe now." We're waved off—literally—by Zeke's grandma, who stands outside her door waving until I can no longer see her in the rearview. Zeke, in the passenger seat, bends over to adjust the plastic shopping bag at his feet.

"What's that?"

"Food," he says, smiling at me. "Nobody ever leaves Grandma's house empty-handed. It's pretty much a rule."

"Right." I wouldn't know. Both of my grandmas were as cold and distant as my parents. They would have looked down at Zeke's grandma's house with disdain and not bothered to hide their sneers.

"Thank you for driving me and carrying my stuff," Zeke says, and I grunt, hoping he'll stop talking. He doesn't. "You really should come to dinner with us sometime. She's a great cook."

"You're welcome," I mutter, uncomfortable. Usually, people get the hint and stop talking, but Zeke seems to take my short answers as impetus to fill the silence.

"So, I know you're a hockey player. What are you studying? Maybe we'll have some of the same classes this semester."

"Business." I glance over at him. He's turned sideways in his seat facing me, with one leg bent up at an angle. There is a politely questioning look on his face; his mouth is pulled up in a small smile, and he looks like he'd love nothing more than to hear what I have to say. Turning away, I scowl at the road, unsure what to make of him.

"That's cool. What sort of thing are you hoping to do with it? That's such an open-ended degree, you'll have so many possibilities."

He sounds so sincere, like he's congratulating me on making a smart choice for my future when the opposite is true. I never had a choice at all. "My dad wants me to work for him."

"Wow. What sort of company does your dad own?"

"Listen, can we talk about something else?" I say sharply. My fingers are clenched around the steering wheel and out of the corner of my eye I see Zeke startle at the volume of my voice. "Tell me what you're going to school for."

I don't much give a shit what he's going to school for, but I don't want to talk about myself. I glance at him again. The tops of his ears are red with an embarrassed flush and his eyes are wide. Probably, not many people have ever yelled at him before. I make a mental note to try and not do that again in the future.

"Uhm, well, I'm working toward a dual degree in physics and mathematics. And I'm also going to be applying for the Master's program."

Jesus Christ. Physics and mathematics and I can't even pass a basic English class without help. "Oh. That sounds like a lot."

"It is. But it also means I'll save money, because I'm working toward two diplomas at the same time, you know? Instead of doing two separate Bachelor's degrees. And I like it, it's fun!"

Shifting in my seat, I resist the urge to look over at him

again. Now I'm the one embarrassed. He's obviously a lot smarter than I am.

"I bet you're good at math, too," he says, so confidently that I do end up peeking at him again.

"No, I'm not."

"Isn't being a goalie all about angles and velocity, though? I bet you're using math all the time and never even realized it."

I feel strangely pleased by this, like he's just bestowed a grand compliment on me. *Congratulations, Carter, you are good at math and never realized it.* It's ridiculous. Scowling, I tap my fingers against the steering wheel. Somehow, he's worked the conversation so we're talking about me again, and not him.

"That's not me doing math, that's just..." *Intuition? Spidey senses?* "It's just practice and being able to read the opposing forward. It's not like I'm sitting there working through sine and cosine."

Zeke laughs, a snorting sort of laugh that is exactly the kind of laugh I would have expected him to have. "I know *that*. Math isn't just equations on a piece of paper. There are practical applications too. Your brain might be performing mathematical gymnastics during a hockey match, and you don't even notice because it's second nature. Ergo, you're good at math!"

"Hockey game," I correct. "And okay, you win. I'm a mathematical genius. I can't imagine why it's taken somebody this long to notice."

I say this sarcastically, and probably a little bit mean. He doesn't seem to mind, though, because he laughs again. I'm relieved when we pull up to the house, the confines of the car had started to feel stifling. Just me, Zeke, and all his questions. I grab his bags for him again and don't bother waiting for him before I walk inside and up the stairs. Depositing his stuff on the floor of his room, I come downstairs just as he's putting the food from his grandma into the refrigerator.

"Your shit's upstairs," I tell him. "I'm going to go back downstairs and work out a little more."

He opens his mouth and for a second, I think he's going to ask if he can join me. "Sounds good. I guess I'll go unpack."

Turning, I head downstairs. I hadn't actually planned on doing another workout today, I just didn't want to do the whole awkwardly-trying-to-figure-out-how-to-live-together thing with Zeke. I don't even have my damn earbuds. Annoyed with myself and, unfairly, with my new roommate, I jump on the bike and prop my phone up. I'll just watch YouTube videos instead of listen to music.

LATER, I walk silently up the stairs and listen for Zeke. The main living area and the kitchen are both empty, but I can't hear anything from his room, either. His door is shut, so I'm able to sneak past and into my own room without drawing him out. I don't bother closing my own door, but strip down and head into my bathroom to shower. Later, when I come out with a towel wrapped around my waist, I can hear vague movements down the hall that alert me to Zeke's presence.

"Carter?" he calls.

"What?" I call back, grabbing boxers from my dresser.

"Can I come in? Are you decent?"

"Morally?" I ask, and he pauses. "Door's open."

After so many years of playing hockey, being naked in front of other people is a complete nonissue for me. The same cannot be said for Zeke, who inches around my doorframe with his eyes squinted like he's ready to close them at a moment's notice. I raise my eyebrows at him. He looks at the boxers clutched in my hand and the towel around my waist.

"I'll let you get dressed."

"Jesus, it's fine. What do you want?" Bending, I step into the boxers and pull them up underneath the towel so as not to offend his delicate sensibilities. Pulling the towel off, I quickly tug on a pair of sweatpants and a long-sleeved shirt. Zeke is hovering awkwardly at my door; he's watching me, but there is nothing sexual in his gaze. It's a clinical look, not an interested one. I suppose that answers one question about my new roommate.

"I wanted to see if you'd like to watch a movie," he says. He's changed into ratty pajama pants, strings fraying from the ends of the too-long cuffs. The shirt he's wearing is at least two sizes too big, and gives the impression of a kid wearing his dad's clothing.

"Sure." He probably wants to watch a documentary or some equally boring shit.

"Great! I like your tattoos." He points at my now covered arms, like I might have forgotten where my tattoos are located.

"Thanks."

He waits, and I wait, but neither of us can seem to think of anything else to say. Less than a day with my new roommate and I've already exhausted my conversational bank. Sighing, I sit down on the end of my bed.

"Listen, you don't have to hang out with me just because you're living here. If you want to do your own thing, that's fine," I tell him. I know exactly how desirous my company is.

"Oh." His face falls. "I mean...we don't have to. I just

figured it would be nice to get to know one another. Since we're, you know, living together."

Scooting back on my bed until my back hits the wall, I stretch my legs out and cross my arms. "Okay, let's get to know one another. Twenty questions."

Zeke's eyebrows rise, and half of his mouth pulls up into a smile. He still hasn't moved more than a foot into my room. "Okay."

"Have a seat." I nod toward the bed, and after a moment's hesitation he crawls onto the end and sits cross-legged. "Hit me."

"What's your favorite color?" he asks immediately.

The quick question nearly startles a laugh out of me. I try to think of a color to give him. *Do I even have a favorite color?*

"Hard question?" Zeke asks lightly, noting my hesitation. I scowl at him and he smiles. "I'll go first. Green."

"Fine. Black."

He rolls his eyes, like my favorite color has disappointed him. The neck of his shirt is stretched out and hanging low enough that I can see the prominent line of his collarbone. Every part of him seems comprised of sharp angles; he's sort of cute, in a mousy, scrawny sort of way. I like his eyes: silvery blue and so large on his narrow face that he looks like a character from an anime cartoon. He looks like a man who's been stranded in adolescence, held hostage by his small frame and boyish face.

3

Zeke

CARTER IS STARING AT ME. Like, *really* staring at me. Of course, because it's paired with a scowl, it might better be described as *glaring*.

"It's your turn to ask a question," I remind him. I'd started by giving him an easy one, but something tells me he probably won't be so accommodating.

"What do you do for fun?" he asks, catching me by surprise. I'd expected him to go right for the jugular—ask why I live with my grandmother and not my parents.

"Oh. Well, I like to read. Play chess." I cast about, trying to come up with something that doesn't sound hopelessly nerdy. "Uhm, go to movies. Oh! And sometimes I go to the zoo."

"The zoo?" he says, eyebrows rising. He's still got his arms crossed over his chest, but I don't think he's as defensive as the posture might suggest. I sort of wish he wasn't wearing a shirt with sleeves—I'd like to get a closer look at those tattoos.

"Yeah. I like the tree frogs."

Carter is staring at me as though I told him I like to make furniture out of human skin. I give him a moment to work through his thoughts.

"You like the *tree frogs?*" he says, and I nod. "That's like...I don't know, the weirdest part of the zoo. Who even goes into the Amphibian House?"

"Let me guess, your favorite part of the zoo is the Big Cats?"

"Ha! Nope. Lemurs." He looks smug; satisfied with himself that he was able to fool me with his favorite zoo exhibit.

"That's a good one." I grin at him, and his scowl loosens enough that I count it as a smile. I tap my fingers together, idly, trying to come up with another question to ask him. I'm no longer interested in putting a movie on—this is a far more enjoyable pastime. "Okay...how about this: what's your favorite tattoo?"

Sitting up, he moves over the bed toward me. Turning, he grasps the neck of his shirt and pulls it up so that his back is bared. It takes him a second to get his right arm out of the sleeve, but when he does, he points to a large piece high up on his shoulder. "This one."

I lean forward to look closer. It's a stylized black-and-white tattoo of a mask. Because I'm above average intelligence, I'm able to infer that this is some sort of goalie mask. There is a number on the temple of the mask; I point to it. "77. Is that your number?"

"Yeah." Before I can look at the rest of the tattoos, he's putting his shirt back on.

"It's beautiful. The tattoo, that is." He shrugs, moving back to sit against the wall once more. It *is* beautiful, though, the way many tattoos are little works of art. "I don't have any tattoos."

"Shocker." He's not scowling, anymore, so I take this as good-natured ribbing, and not him being nasty. "Are you seeing anyone?"

I'm not surprised this question is in the line-up, even though I hate having to explain my answer to people. I suppose it's fair of him to ask, though, since we'll be living together. He's probably wondering if I'll be regularly sharing my room with another person, like most people my age. Like him, most likely.

"No. I don't date, really. You don't have to worry about me bringing people home," I tell him. And then, because I am a little bit curious: "What about you?"

"No."

We stare at each other. I don't know him well, but I get the impression that he's got more to say on this subject. I wait him out, running my fingers over his bedspread gently. It's ridiculously soft, like it was made from angel wings. Flattening my hand, I stroke it with my palm. I wonder how much it cost.

"I don't mind if you bring people here," Carter tells me as his face hardens into something obstinate and suspicious. "I don't do it all the time, but sometimes I'll bring girls over. Or guys."

He glares at me as he says this, like he's picking a fight and expecting me to rise to the occasion. I try not to let my facial expression betray my feelings, but I've never been very good at subterfuge. I'm surprised, and a little ashamed of being so. I had expected him to be cut from the same jock cloth as the rest of the athletes on campus: hell bent on sleeping their way through the female population.

"Okay," I say, and then add, because I feel like I need to show him mine now that he's shown me his: "I'm demi. Essentially, I don't feel attracted to people sexually. Not unless we've—"

"I know what it means," Carter interrupts, glowering at me.

"Okay." I run my hand over the bedspread again, nervously. "So, anyway. To answer your question: no, not dating anyone, and probably won't be."

It's my turn to ask a question, but I'm drawing a blank. I don't usually bring up being demisexual on the first day I meet someone, and it's not as though Carter inspires a lot of confidence. It's hard not to judge this particular book by the cover. He seems to be as equally unsettled as I am—arms crossed tight over his chest and a glint of violence in his blue eyes. If he's looking for a fight, he'll have to look elsewhere.

"So—"

"I think I'm going to crash," Carter interrupts.

"Oh, sure. Right. Sorry." I climb off the end of his bed and hover there uncertainly. He hasn't moved, but is reclined back with arms still crossed, watching me. "Sleep tight."

There is a very small twitch at the corner of his mouth, like I've almost teased a smile from him.

"Sleep tight," he murmurs toward my back, as I make my way to my own room.

"I can't believe you're living with Carter Morgan. The third." Jefferson, my best friend, adopts a queenly British accent when he adds that last part. "Is he awful? He looks like he'd be awful. There's probably a reason he's letting you live there for free."

Sighing, I adjust the strap of my backpack. It's heavy, and I can feel sweat forming on my back where it rests against me. There is little difference between early September and summer in South Carolina; it's just as hot and muggy today as it was in July. Reaching up to brush my hair out of my eyes, I glance at Jefferson.

"He's not awful."

I've been living with Carter for two weeks, and he's been anything but awful. In fact, other than his propensity to treat doors roughly, he's been remarkably quiet. Even when he's downstairs working out, he does so with his headphones on and not a loudspeaker. There have been several times where I hadn't even realized he was home until I almost physically ran into him in the hallway. He's not half as unpleasant as his sour expression might indicate.

"He's actually really nice," I tell my friend, and he snorts.

"I'll have to take your word for it. He doesn't seem to have a lot of friends," Jefferson notes, as he holds the door of the science building open for me, both of us blasted by a wave of air-conditioned air. It's an old building; high-tech labs tucked into brick classrooms that are too hot in the summer, and frigid in the winter. There always seems to be a vague smell of burning, depending on which corridor you're walking down.

"No," I say slowly. "I don't think he does have a lot of friends, actually."

Unlike the rest of the student athletes, who only seem to traverse the campus in large packs, Carter is a loner. In two weeks, he's not had anybody come over to his house to hang out. The few times I've seen him on campus he's been alone —glowering and striding across campus purposefully—like he was on the way to settle some scores. I wonder if he feels a little bit lonely and out of place, but hides it behind a mask of indifference and bravado. I wonder why someone who has enough money to not charge rent would want a roommate at all.

"Are you going to go to any of his games?" Jefferson asks, as we climb the stairs.

"Yeah, I think I will. You should come with me." *Please god do not make me go to a hockey game alone.*

"Sure. Maybe I'll see if Tessa wants to join."

Tessa was Jefferson's high school girlfriend and will probably one day be his wife. They unofficially lived together with Tessa spending most nights at Jefferson's shared apartment, and are the kind of couple that make other people vaguely uncomfortable. They are always touching each other— hugging, kissing, sitting on each other's lap—in a way that makes me feel a little ill. I cannot imagine liking another person so much that I would do any of those things in public. I have to bite back a sigh. Not even a crowded hockey game will be enough to keep the PDA at bay. Still better than going alone, though.

It's Friday which means that I've got an early end to the day today. This is my last lecture before I head over to the library to get some independent study in, and that's it for my plans for the weekend. Jefferson, who is the extroverted friend of our pair, has plans to go to a party tonight and tomorrow. Me, being the introverted and, frankly, antisocial one, declined. I'd rather stay home and read my astronomy textbook.

We sit down in the lecture hall, early as usual, and

Jefferson pulls out his phone to text Tessa. Tapping my finger against the edge of my desk, I think about Carter. *Does he have any plans for the weekend?* We're still trying to get a read on one another, figure out each other's schedules. So far, from what I can tell, he leaves the house only for class and practice. Before I can change my mind, I bring up Carter's text message thread on my phone.

> Hi! What are you up to tonight? Got any plans?

> Practice.

> After that?

> Why are you asking?

Sighing, I look over at Jefferson, who's grinning down at his phone and completely enamored with whatever his girlfriend just typed. I go back to my own conversation with a brick wall.

> I was going to see if you wanted to hang out? I don't have any plans.

Three dots appear as he types, but then disappear. This happens twice more before a pair of text messages come through.

> Why?

> Sure. What do you want to do?

I decide to ignore the *Why?* and focus on the other. I hadn't actually thought far enough ahead to come up with any ideas. Would Carter want to go see a movie? Grab dinner? What do hockey boys do on a Friday night?

> Whatever you want.

I have afternoon practice. Meet at the rink at 4?

> Sounds great! :)

There is no answer after that, and no bubbles to indicate that I should expect one. I wonder if the smiley face emoji was too much. Beside me, Jefferson finally comes up for air and looks over at my phone in surprise. He's usually the only person I text regularly.

"Who are you talking to?"

"Carter. We're going to...well, do something tonight. What do you think he does for fun?"

He laughs, shaking his head. "Aren't you living with him? You'd know better than I would. What does he do at home? Video games?"

"I don't know, work out? He works out a lot. His muscles all have muscles." I cut off as the professor walks in. Jefferson sends me a look that says *good luck with that* before turning to face the front of the classroom. I try to focus on class, then, and push thoughts of Carter out of my mind. It's a problem for four o'clock.

Unfortunately, four o'clock seems to come around a lot quicker than expected; with a campus map pulled up on my phone, I head over toward the rink to meet Carter, still unsure of what we might do. I haven't spent much time on this side of the campus—hence the map—but the rink is hard to miss once you're in the right spot. Also hard to miss is Carter, standing near the building talking to another man.

His blonde hair is bright gold in the late afternoon sun, and his inked arms are on full display in his short-sleeved shirt.

Slowing, I hesitate to approach him. He hasn't noticed I'm there yet, and seems to be deep in conversation with the other guy. I don't want to interrupt. Luckily, before I have to decide what to do, he turns his head and notices me. I wave my hand awkwardly and he jerks his head in a come-hither motion.

"Hi," I say, once I get within hearing distance. I have to look up to see Carter and his companion's faces. *Why are all sporty guys so tall?*

"Hey. Vas, this is my roommate, Zeke." Carter waves a hand at me and his tall friend nods his head in a way that looks oddly like a bow.

"Hello. It is nice to meet you." He's got a hint of an accent. Something Eastern European, if I had to guess. "My name is Henri Vasel, but you may call me by my last name if you'd like. Everyone does."

He smiles and I return it easily. Carter scowls. "Nice to meet you."

"Likewise." He turns back to Carter, still smiling. "See you tomorrow, then. Enjoy your evening."

Carter grunts in a *'you too'* sort of way and glances at his friend's retreating back before looking down at me.

"He's nice," I tell him, and get a grunt of my own.

"Yeah, he's cool."

I nod. This is probably high praise, coming from him. I take a second to adjust the straps of my backpack where it's digging into my shoulders. "So, what do you want to do?"

"This was your idea," he reminds me, and lifts his arms to adjust where his hair is tied back in a small bun.

"Right..." Casting about for something—*anything*—I look

around for inspiration. There is a group of posters pinned to a board not far down the sidewalk and I squint at it. "Mini golf!"

Carter's eyebrows rise in response. He looks in the direction of the notice board and then back at me. I might be projecting, but I think I can detect a hint of amusement in his eyes.

"Mini golf?" he asks.

"Yep. Mini golf." I'm feeling pretty confident about this choice. It'll keep us outside, and it's just enough of a physical activity to hopefully keep him interested. We'll be able to talk, but won't have to maintain a conversation the way we would over a table at a restaurant.

"Okay. Do we have to change?" He waves a hand at his basketball shorts and t-shirt, and my jeans. We're both wearing sneakers.

"Uhm, no?" *What the hell does he think mini golf consists of?* "Haven't you played putt-putt before?"

"No."

"We could do something else," I offer, but Carter shakes his head and steps around me with a mumbled *it's fine*. I follow him to the parking lot and stow my backpack in the backseat before climbing into the front.

It turns out that the mini golf course isn't far from campus, and is also remarkably busy on a Friday night. Small children run amok, screaming and bumping into stranger's legs as we wait in line to pick up our clubs and balls. Carter is silent beside me, eyes scanning the crowd and mouth tight in its usual severe line. Slowly, we make our way to the front of the line and I have a momentary surge of panic as I look at the high-school kid behind the desk. *How expensive is mini golf?*

Frantically, I look at the board where prices are listed by number of holes completed and participants. Stomach sinking, I realize I should have suggested we do something at home instead of going out. Something free. Carter's watching a handful of teenagers on a group date, and is supremely unconcerned. We're called forward and the young girl behind the counter eyes Carter with a mix of interest and intimidation. She's probably wondering if he's here to rob the place.

"How many holes?" she asks, eyes flicking between us.

Carter pulls his wallet from his back pocket, slides a credit card out and hands it to the girl. He looks at me. "How many holes?"

"All of them?" I suggest weakly, eyes on the credit card. He didn't even ask if we should split the cost. "Whatever you want."

"All of them," he tells the girl, and waits while she hands us our scorecard, clubs, and a bucket to grab a ball from. I pluck out a green one while Carter shoves his hand in and chooses one at random. It's a lurid, magenta pink. "Thank you."

Feeling a little embarrassed, I trail after him as he takes long-legged strides toward the first hole. We have to wait for the couple in front of us to finish. I sidle closer to him and clear my throat.

"Thanks."

"What?" He looks down at me.

"For paying."

He looks surprised; a slight widening of the eyes and parting of the lips. "Sure. No problem."

Looking away, Carter idly tosses his pink ball in the air, occasionally letting it bounce on the ground before snatching it back out of the air. My embarrassment takes a slight detour to sympathy as I watch the motion of his hand. I wonder if Carter, who's family is obviously loaded, just assumes that he'll be footing the bill whenever people invite him somewhere. A small, mean, part of me wonders if that's the *only* reason some people invite him places.

When it's our turn to go, I wave him forward. He settles into what is unmistakably a golfer's stance, checks his positioning, and gets a hole-in-one. *Oh boy, this is going to be quick.*

"Are you kidding me?" I ask, while he plucks his pink ball out of the hole and steps back to watch me go. "Must be beginner's luck."

He twirls his stick and says, in what can only be described as a jaunty tone: "I'm an *athlete*."

I laugh. That is the closest I've ever heard Carter Morgan come to making a joke and it feels better than a hole-in-one ever could.

4

Carter

Zeke sucks at mini golf. We are seven holes in and he is losing spectacularly. He doesn't seem too put out by it though, which is refreshing. I'm so used to being surrounded by competitive athletes, it's a relief to meet someone whose mood won't plummet if they lose. I'm watching him as he takes his third shot and the ball rims around the hole but doesn't drop in. He bites the tip of his tongue in concentration as he leans over to tap it in. Triumphantly, he looks up at me.

"Four! I'm getting better." Grabbing his ball, he grins and steps so close to me his arm brushes mine.

"You are," I tell him, writing a four under his last score which was a seven.

"This is fun," he says and I take a moment to look at him while he surveys the next hole.

He's pretty pale, but the heat of the evening has given him a nice flush and his eyes are bright. He's got a nice smile, and hands it out freely—smiling at the kids we pass and greeting the people working at the course. I actually am enjoying myself, but I don't think this would be half as fun if I were with someone else. There is something charming about Zeke's enthusiasm and complete unconcern with the score.

"Yeah, it is," I agree. His head whips around and his wide eyes meet mine.

"You're having fun?" he asks excitedly.

"Yeah."

"I'm glad. Next time you have to pick the activity."

Stepping around him, I tee up my next shot. There is a dramatic groan from behind me when I get another hole-in-one, and I have to fight a smile. Turning, I see Zeke with hands on hips and a scowl on his face. It's cute. Like a puppy learning how to growl.

"You're freakishly good at this," he grumbles, and sets about trying to get a better score than four.

"My dad owns golf courses so I grew up playing," I admit. "You're holding your club wrong."

Zeke glances at me and then back down to his hands, nonplussed. "This is how everyone is holding it."

Stepping up to him, I lean over and adjust his hands. If I were hitting on him, I would have done this from behind: wrapped my arms around his smaller frame and physically showed him how to do it. I would have lingered, fingers on his, and maybe pressed my back against his a little more than would be necessary. But I'm not hitting on him, so I do none of those things. I show him how to hold the club and back up, trying not to notice the way his hair catches on his eyelashes when he blinks, or how he smells like rain.

This time, when his ball goes in, he inhales sharply and

looks at me, disbelieving. "Why didn't you show me that eight holes ago?"

"Because I want to win, obviously. I'm not going to help the enemy."

He laughs at this, shaking his head and motioning for me to hand him the scorecard. "Oh yes," he says dryly, "there does seem to be a high probability of me beating you."

He hands the card back and I tuck it into my pocket. There is a little bit of a bottleneck on this hole, which features a massive windmill. Zeke, standing next to me, watches the lazy rotation of the blades for a moment before turning to face me. His arm brushes mine again, but he doesn't seem to notice.

"Did you know Holland has over 1,200 windmills? It's known as the Land of Windmills."

I stare at him. "Why do you know that?"

"Why not?" He shrugs. "I did a report on Holland once, back in elementary school. Did you know that the Dutch are considered the world's tallest people? Oh! And Holland has the world's longest ice-skating race."

I can't remember something I learned in class last week, let alone some random facts from an assignment I did in elementary school. "That's cool."

"It is! You'd fit right in, in Holland."

He nudges me with an elbow, to let me know this is a joke. When he smiles again, his eyes are big and blue, and take up half of his face. He's nothing like the sort of guy I'd usually go for. When I pick up guys on a dating app, they're typically bigger, muscle-y dudes. Guys that look a little bit like me, and are only interested in a quick fuck. Zeke looks nothing like these men—he looks like someone whose hand you hold while you make plans for the future. He's not my type, and I don't even have to ask to know I'm not his.

We play the next few holes in comfortable silence; the crowds slowly disperse around us and the sun slowly sinks. We're meandering, not trying to race through the course, but going slow and enjoying ourselves. This is, without a doubt, the most fun I've ever had outside of hockey. It's fucking embarrassing how much I don't want today to end.

"Are you hungry?" I ask Zeke, distracting him enough that he hits his ball wrong and it hops over the lip of the course and bounces down the sidewalk. "Sorry."

"Damn." He half-jogs to retrieve his ball, while I wait. When he returns, he has to brush his hair out of his eyes again as he lines up his shot. "Yeah, I could eat."

"We're almost done." I look around, noting that there is a concession stand near the last few holes. I point to it. "Want to eat before we go home?"

I watch him bite his lip and look toward where I pointed. "Uhm, yeah. That sounds fine."

He looks put out. It's the same expression that was on his face earlier, when I caught him eyeballing the mini golf prices. I had already been planning to pay, and wouldn't have suggested grabbing food unless I was going to cover that too. He is obviously under the impression he'll be buying his own.

We finish the game; I go to return our clubs and balls while Zeke peruses our scorecard. He holds it up when I step back up beside him, one eyebrow raised in question.

"I feel like you fudged these."

"Whatever helps you sleep at night." I snatch the card back and shove it into my pocket. "What are you hungry for?"

"I'm going to have some...," his eyes flick rapidly over the menu, "french fries."

Sighing, I step forward to order. "Hi. Can we get a large order of french fries, two loaded nachos, two hot dogs...and a funnel cake. Please. Oh, and two large drinks."

Zeke's already large eyes are wide and I feel him nudge my arm as he holds out a credit card. I pluck it from between his fingers and hand mine over instead. The kid behind the counter, unconcerned, scans it and hands it back. I shuffle Zeke out of the way, stepping to the side so we can wait for our food.

"Why did you—I can pay you back for the fries."

"No."

He doesn't respond, but ducks his head and puts his card back into his wallet. I don't want to argue about money. I want to keep enjoying the day and not have him worry about how he's going to afford it. I want to be invited to more days like this, and if I have to buy that privilege, so be it. Our food comes—two heavily loaded trays—and we each take one over to a vacant picnic table. Zeke pulls his french fries off one of the trays and nudges the rest over to me. Amused, I push it back toward him.

"I'm not going to eat all of this, Zeke. That's for you. Except for the funnel cake." I point to it, sitting on the corner of his tray. "I want some of that."

Bending, I reach for the nachos and pop one into my mouth. Zeke is sitting in silence, not eating. I can feel his eyes on the top of my head and ignore him. I want him to eat; something tells me his manners will prevail and he won't let the food go to waste, even if he's not happy with where it came from.

"You didn't have to buy me dinner." He sounds puzzled, and a little bit sad.

"I'm the one who suggested it," I point out, glaring at him.

"Well, by that logic I should have paid for the putt-putt since I'm the one who suggested that."

Damn. Good point. "Listen, just forget about it, okay? It doesn't matter. I don't mind."

He looks like he has more to say, but he also looks like he doesn't want to argue. Breaking eye contact, I shovel a few more nachos into my mouth before grabbing the hot dog. Coach Mackenzie would shit himself if he saw what I was eating right now. There is a soft crunch as Zeke bites into a chip, and I glance up at him. I hope he eats that whole tray of food. He looks like he might need the calories.

"Thanks," he says.

"Don't mention it." Really, though, I hope he does stop mentioning it.

A cheer goes up from the course and we both look over. There are a group of teenagers celebrating a hole-in-one. They're all smiling, several of them wrapped up together like they're couples. It's a happy group, and I feel a familiar pang of jealousy as I watch them. I've never quite figured out how to negotiate social situations appropriately, always unsure of myself and what people were thinking about me. It's easier to just remain aloof and on the outside, so that's what I do. Turning forward on the bench seat, I face Zeke. His face is tipped upward, eyes on the sky. Mimicking him, I try to figure out what he's staring at.

"What the hell are you looking at?" I shove the rest of my hotdog in my mouth and wait for Zeke to look at me. He points a finger skyward.

"Betelgeuse." I stare at him, blankly, until he continues. "Orion's left shoulder. The constellation?"

"Okay." I look up again. All the stars look the same to me.

"Here." He moves around the table and slides in next to me. Leaning against my shoulder, slightly, he points up. "See those three stars all in a row? That's Orion's belt. His left shoulder—the star Betelgeuse—is the red star. It's 10 million years old. And get this, it's like 700 light years away, which means that it takes the light from that star 700 years to reach Earth. So *right now* we are seeing a star from 700 years ago."

He looks at me, then, smiling broadly and eyes shining with happiness. I'm a little intimidated by his ability to spout random facts at me. It sets me off balance and makes me feel like an idiot, which is stupid because he clearly isn't doing it with malice. Clearing my throat, I look away from his eyes and back up at the star.

"That's cool."

"Right? Astronomy is fascinating. Sometime, if you'd like, we could go to the planetarium."

I nod, feeling like it's easier to agree than argue. I'm not smart; if we go to the planetarium, I'll only end up embarrassing myself. Zeke looks placated, though, and has turned his attention away from the sky and back to his food. Eventually, he points a fry at me.

"What are you doing next weekend?" he asks.

"Games on Friday and Saturday. Nothing else planned."

"All right. Want to do something again next weekend? We could make this a regular thing." He grins like he'd love nothing more than to spend every weekend hanging out with me.

"Okay," I tell him, a little uncomfortable with how nice he is. "That sounds good."

"I chose mini golf which means next weekend is all you."

"Okay," I say again, because apparently, I don't have anything more concrete to add to the conversation. Zeke doesn't seem to mind, happy enough that I've agreed to his plan. I make a mental note to Google ideas of things we could do for fun.

Vas and I made plans to stay behind after practice tonight, so we're hovering by the boards and waiting for the rest of the team to clear out. Coach Mackenzie is gathering stray pucks, skating slowly around the rink and tapping them toward the bench. When he nears, I call out to him.

"Hey, Coach Mackenzie?"

He looks up at me, squinting. "Carter. What can I do for you?"

"You mind if Vas and I stay a little late? Work on some shooting drills?" Beside me, Vas looks nervous. Three years in and he's still uncomfortable asking the coaches for anything. Luckily, he's got me to do it for him.

"Of course. Would you like me to stay as well?"

Yes. I bite my tongue, before I can blurt the word out. Coach Mackenzie works hard for this team; he can be tough, but he's always fair. I like him. And I really like his partner, Tony Lawson. I struggle to remember the NHL schedule—does South Carolina play tonight or would Tony be home? I want Coach Mackenzie to stay, but I don't want to be a drain on his time. I want him to like me, and not consider me a nuisance.

"Uhm...no, that's okay. Vas and I will be fine. We can

clean up, too. Everything will be perfect when we leave." Vas nods, smiling in a conciliatory manner.

"All right. Call me if you need anything." Coach gives us a curt nod and steps carefully off of the ice. He looks tired; I'm glad I told him to leave.

"Have a nice evening," Vas calls to him, and Coach raises a hand in acknowledgment.

"Kiss ass." I whack him in the shins with my stick.

"Manners," Vas corrects, whacking me back.

I skate back to the crease and wait for Vas to gather some pucks at center ice. We work through some of the single shooter drills we do at practice, the rink mostly silent other than the sound of our skates. It's not until someone comes to Zamboni the ice that we realize we've been here far later than we had meant to be. Vas, looking guilty, apologizes to the man as I snatch up our pucks as quickly as I can. We help him pull the goals and then vacate, trudging to the locker room in silence.

"How is your roommate?" Vas asks, as we start stripping out of our practice gear.

"Good."

"He is nice. It will be good for you, to have friend at home."

Rolling my eyes, I scoff. "You sound like Coach Mackenzie."

"Coach Mackenzie is always right."

True. We continue stripping in silence, exhaustion settling over our shoulders like a blanket. It was a long day of classes, followed by a longer practice. I'm excited to go home, and though I'd never admit it out loud, part of that has to do with Zeke. Back when Dad had first bought me the house, Coach had recommended I get a roommate. I'd tried; I had an ad posted for a week of my freshman year and though several people answered it, nobody ever moved in. Frankly, I'd given up on the idea and hadn't expected Zeke to pan out either. Yet here we are, almost three full weeks into living together, and it's been fine. *Good*, in fact. He's already become more than a roommate—he's my friend.

When I pull up in front of the house later, there is light spilling from the living room window and illuminating the front lawn. Parking in the garage, I pause at the door and listen. I can hear noise coming from inside—low music and talking. *Is Zeke talking to himself?* I push inside, letting the door slam behind me. Immediately, Zeke calls out to me.

"Carter!"

"Hey." I drop my pads by the door and head into the kitchen. I'm fucking starving.

The counter is covered with the evidence of cooking. A cutting board is laid out with a knife resting on top, and dishes are stacked in the sink. I raise an eyebrow at the mess, just as Zeke steps into the kitchen behind me.

"Hi, sorry, don't worry I'll clean that up. Are you hungry? We made lasagna." He doesn't wait for me to answer, but walks over to the oven and pulls out a half-full pan of lasagna. "I was keeping it warm for you. Have a seat."

My legs are exhausted, so I do. Pushing some of the cooking shit away, I make room for the plate Zeke eventually sets in front of me. It looks like he gave me the rest of it. Reading my mind, he laughs and hands me a fork.

"Figured you'd be hungry. That's three pieces, but I can leave the rest in the oven if you think you'll need more."

"This is good, thanks." Uncomfortable, I glance behind me. "Who's we?"

"Oh, my friend Jefferson. He came over to study and we got hungry."

"So, you made lasagna?" The competency of this man is astounding and a little bit intimidating. "I would have just made a frozen pizza or something."

"Well, we had a craving." He laughs. "Do you want to eat in here? Or you could join us? You could meet Jefferson."

"Uhm." I put a bite of lasagna in my mouth to give myself a second before answering the question. I don't really want to meet his friend and pretend to be nice. I want to eat, shower, and listen to Zeke talk about nerdy shit—preferably in that order. "Yeah, I guess I can."

He beams at me. Resigned, I pick up my plate and follow him to the living room. There is a guy stretched out on the couch, textbook on his stomach and flashcards scattered on the floor. He sits up when we walk in the room, sliding off of the couch and standing. He's taller than Zeke, but still a couple inches shorter than me. His blue eyes are lighter than Zeke's, and half as pretty.

"Carter Morgan, nice to meet you. I'm Jefferson." He shakes my hand and lets go quickly. I can't bring myself to return the smile. I wish he wasn't here.

"Hey."

They both stare at me, waiting for more. Letting Jefferson and Zeke keep the couch, I sit down on the floor and put my back against the wall. Ducking my head, I start stuffing my face. The lasagna is delicious—I'm glad he gave me three large pieces. I could probably eat more, given how hungry I am.

"How was practice?" Zeke asks, and I glance up at him and shrug, mouth full. "Seemed like you were there kind of late."

Swallowing with difficulty, I cough. "Stayed late with Vas. Did some single man shooting drills."

"That's impressive—that you can practice so much and still get all your classwork done," Jefferson puts in, and I turn toward him, narrowing my eyes. It sounded sincere, but I don't know him well enough to know when he's being a dick. "I can barely get all my homework done and I *don't* play a sport."

He's relaxed back against the couch, legs outstretched in front of him. Beside him, Zeke is sitting crisscross-applesauce and watching me. When he catches my eye, he smiles.

"Uhm, yeah, it can be a lot, I guess." If I was going to be honest with him, I'd tell him it's really fucking hard. I'd probably be a decent student without the added stress of a sport, but with hockey I'm barely staying afloat. I've never been great at school, and now I'm damn near terrible. It's hard to make myself care about anything but hockey.

"Zeke said you're studying business. That sounds interesting."

"Not really." Jefferson laughs at this, nodding as though to say *fair enough*. Maybe he's not so bad. "What about you?"

"Chemistry."

"Sounds hard," I say honestly.

"Oh, but it's fun." He sits forward, balancing his elbows on his knees but still using his hands to gesture.

Pulling my knees up and balancing my plate on top, I listen in silence while I eat. Zeke is watching his friend wax poetic about chemistry with an amused look on his face; every now and then he glances over at me. Every time he catches my eye he smiles.

5

Zeke

CARTER WALKS into the kitchen looking like he's fresh off of a wild night. Pieces of his hair have fallen out of its bun and there is a little drool crusted on his cheek. I bite my lip to keep from smiling. When he notices me sitting at the counter with my homework spread out in front of me, he squints and scratches at his chest. The shirt he's wearing has a stain on the stomach, leading me to believe he snatched it up off the floor instead of grabbing a clean one.

"Good morning," I say cheerfully, after checking the clock on the oven to ensure it is, in fact, still morning. Carter grunts, moving over toward the coffee pot. "How was your game?"

"We won," he says, back toward me and voice scratchy with disuse.

I already knew this. In honor of my new roommate, I'd put the game's livestream up on my laptop last night and watched as I studied. I had no idea what was happening half the time, but even a hockey-illiterate like myself could tell that Carter played well. The other team only scored twice on forty-three shots on goal. The announcer guys spent a lot of time talking about Carter's draft prospects, whatever the hell that means. Apparently, they think they'll be good.

"I saw. You played well." He turns to look at me then, leaning back against the counter and wincing as he takes a drink of too hot coffee. Reaching a hand to his face, he discovers the dried drool and rubs at it, scowling.

"You watched?" he asks, with no small amount of incredulity.

"Of course. I tried to pay attention to the game, and not only you, but I had no clue what was happening half of the time. No offense to hockey or anything, but my interest in the sport starts and ends with you."

Carter doesn't look offended by this. If anything, he looks pleased—there is a small twist to his mouth, like he's trying to remember how to smile. I lift the corners of my own lips, trying to coax one out of him.

"Ohio State is good," he tells me, and I nod as though I had known this. "It's a pretty big deal for us to beat them."

"That's great. You earned it." Though I might not understand the specifics of the game, *that* much was clear. It was a fast-paced game, and at one point Carter saved a shot that was clocked at 78 mph. I felt inordinately proud, after he saved that, like I was the one who'd done it and deserved to be cheered. I wanted to text all my friends and tell them what my roommate did.

He grunts again, and covers his embarrassment by taking another gulp of coffee. "What are you working on?"

"Ah." I look down at the textbook and notebook in front of me. "Differential geometry."

"Fun," he says skeptically.

"Probably not as much fun as your hockey game. But, safer." Carter snorts, straightening and turning around to refill his coffee mug. I continue talking to his back. "What are you doing today?"

He stiffens, shoulders tightening visibly. He doesn't turn around before answering. "Did you want to hang out, still? If not, that's cool."

His voice and posture are defensive—already braced to be let down. I hadn't asked because I don't want to hang out anymore, I'd asked in case he was too tired after the game last night to do anything.

"Of course, I do. I was just going to say we could do something here, if you were too tired to go out and *do* something. That hockey stuff looked hard."

The shoulders don't loosen, and he's frowning when he turns back around. He doesn't laugh at my joke. "Whatever you want."

Closing my textbook, I rest my forearms on the counter. "I want to hang out."

Carter nods, but doesn't look convinced. I wonder what it would take to earn his trust. He glances at the clock on the oven, sipping his coffee. "You good to leave in an hour? I made a reservation."

I raise an eyebrow at this. "Sure. What are we doing?"

Shrugging, he walks out of the kitchen. Raising his voice, he calls back to me: "Wouldn't you like to know?"

"Are you serious?" I ask, staring down at the liability waiver I was just handed. "Axe throwing?"

"Dead serious." Carter signs his own waiver without reading it, a quick flick of the wrist, and slides it back over the counter to the girl on the other side. She looks like Christmas came early, eyes skating over his muscled arms and tattoos, an unmistakable *yes please* in her eyes. He doesn't seem to notice. "It'll be fun."

Sighing, I sign my own and hand it back to the girl. She doesn't even look at me. "Maybe for you, super athlete. I'm going to be terrible at this."

"I've never done it before, either. You won't be any worse than I am."

I wonder if I should point out the presence of all those muscles in his arms, and the absence of them in mine. I feel very strongly that this activity will not be my forte. Determined to at least try, I follow behind Carter until he glances over his shoulder at me and waves me up beside him, impatiently. The hallway isn't quite wide enough for us to walk abreast without brushing against one another, but he doesn't seem to mind. We're taken to a sort of alley with a large wooden bullseye on the far end, caged in by netting on the sides.

The axes they give us are smaller than I would have expected; hefting one, I test the weight. It's not nearly as heavy as I thought it would be. Maybe I'll be better at this than I thought. Beside me, Carter picks one up as well, flipping it in the air and catching it. *Show-off.*

"You first?" he asks, sweeping a hand toward the target.

"Oh no, no way. This was your idea, you go first."

He steps forward, turning the axe in his hand a couple of times. Setting his feet, he starts to lift his arms above his head but stops and turns back around. He eyes me for a moment, before waving a hand at me.

"Back up a little bit, I don't want to hit you."

I retreat until my back hits the wall. I'm pretty sure the only way he could have hit me was if he accidentally let go of the axe on the backswing, but I appreciate his concern nonetheless. We had to sign a waiver to do this—clearly someone was hit with an axe at some point. Satisfied that I'm in the safe zone, Carter turns back around, sets his feet and raises his arms. He throws the axe and it hits the target with a resounding crack before dropping to the ground.

"Damn," he says, jogging up and snatching up the axe. He joins me on the wall, putting a hand on the center of my upper back and giving me a gentle push forward. "Your turn."

Sighing, I step to the line and try to mimic his stance from before. Lifting the axe above my head in a two-handed grip, I take a step forward and throw. It bounces off the same way Carter's did. Before I can collect the fallen axe, Carter is next to me and holding out his own.

"Try again, you almost got it."

I bite my lip in concentration, facing the target once more. This time, when I throw it, the axe sticks in the wood with a satisfying thunk. My jaw drops and I whirl to face Carter.

"Did you see that?" I ask excitedly.

"I did." He smiles.

It's little more than a faint curl of his lips, the corners of his mouth depressing slightly. On anyone else, it wouldn't count as a smile. But this is Carter, whose mouth only seems to turn downward. I smile back at him, wide and without restraint.

We trade turns, more axes hitting the floor than sticking in the target. Neither of us hit the bullseye, but it hardly matters. I'm having a blast; this is far more fun than I'd thought it would be. Carter too, seems to be enjoying himself.

The scowl has been chased away, and though I wouldn't call his expression happy, it's close.

I'm a little bit sweaty and my arms are sore by the time we head toward the exit. I'm not one who's comfortable going to the gym, so physical fitness often falls by the wayside for me. Perhaps, if working out was this much fun, I'd do it more often. Of course, Carter doesn't appear to have sweated a drop. I try not to hold it against him.

"That was fun," I tell him, as we climb into his car. "And thank you, for paying."

I hadn't realized this morning, that when Carter had said he'd made a reservation it also meant that he had paid in advance. I'd asked him if I could pay him my half and he'd looked so mad about it, I immediately dropped the subject.

"It's fine," he says harshly, without looking at me.

I want to ask about Carter's family, and his seemingly bottomless well of funds. I want to tell him that he doesn't have to pay my way to get me to hang out with him—I'd do that no matter what. But that's hardly a conversation I can start without admitting my own problems with money; essentially, that I have none. I table it for the moment, but it's a conversation we're going to have to have at some point. He's already letting me live with him practically for free, so I need to pay my way somehow.

"How about we do the zoo next weekend?" I turn slightly in my seat so I can look at him. He doesn't glance over at me, but keeps his eyes on the road.

"You want to hang out, again?"

"Sure do." I keep my voice chipper to combat the disbelief in his. "So, the zoo? We've already established it's something we both like."

"As long as we don't spend the entire time in the tree frog room."

Pleased that he remembered, I turn to face forward in my seat. I smell faintly of sweat, and my arms really are starting to hurt. I suppose I shouldn't be surprised that Carter chose an activity that had a more physical aspect to it. He probably expects me to choose more cerebral ones—I'll have to think outside the box and keep him on his toes.

"Can I ask you something?" he asks suddenly, bringing me out of my reverie.

"Sure." I turn back toward him. He's got both hands on the steering wheel and is resolutely avoiding my gaze.

"Why do you live with your grandma?" He glances over then, a quick, furtive look. Before I can answer, he gives a firm shake of his head and continues speaking. "No, never mind. Sorry. None of my business."

He sounds mad, like he's annoyed at himself for asking an intrusive question. "It's all right, I don't mind. We're friends," I remind him, and his fingers relax a degree on the steering wheel. "My parents died in a car accident when I was young. I don't really remember them. It's been Grandma and I for as long as I can remember."

"Fuck," Carter breathes, flexing his hands. "Sorry."

"It's okay." I shrug. "Like I said, I can hardly remember them. It'll be worse when Grandma goes—she's all I've got."

Carter's mouth twists into a grimace, and I wonder if I've overshared. But then, he reaches a hand across the center console and rests it on my knee, squeezing gently. His hand is big enough to cover a lot of surface area, the warmth from his palm seeping through my pants. It's quick, his hand there and gone in the next second, but the phantom touch remains long after. It's the first time he's touched me like that.

"You're still invited to Sunday dinner, by the way," I remind him, very gently. I've picked up a ride share to my grandma's house every Sunday since moving in with him, not wanting to impose and ask him for a ride; not wanting to make him feel obligated to come with me.

"Maybe I can come next weekend," he says, as we pull into the driveway and he waits for the garage door to open. He sounds a touch worried when he continues. "You don't think she minds that I…"

Carter waves a hand at his face and down one of his arms, encompassing the half-shaved head, nose ring, and tattoos.

"Do I think she minds that you look like a hoodlum?" I fill in helpfully. Parking the car, he shoots me a wry look.

"Yeah. That."

"Nope. She's a cool grandma." Following him inside, I eye the long line of his back. I've become pretty adept at reading the many emotions of Carter's back muscles. "Seriously, she liked you. You're a lovely boy, remember? She doesn't care what you look like, Carter, she cares that you're kind. Which, by the way, you are. Even if you pretend not to be."

This earns me a rather frightening scowl, thrown over his shoulder. I smile back, because I can also see that he's faking it.

"All right. Next weekend, then. After the zoo." This last part is added under his breath, the tone hopeful and a little bit sad.

"That's right," I agree, watching him walk up the stairs toward his room. "After the zoo."

6

Carter

> Good luck tomorrow, kid. I'll be watching, so you'd better win.

I STARE DOWN at the text message, fighting the urge to grin like a lunatic. I don't grin. If I were to start, it might scare people. But it's not every day that people get text messages from their heroes. I decide to add a smiley face emoji to the text as a compromise.

> Thanks, Tony :). If I win, it'll be for you.

I decide against adding a kissy-face emoji as well. Probably overkill. I slide my phone back into my pocket just as the professor walks into the room. He scans the rows of seated students, and I don't think I'm imagining the way his eyes linger on me. I'm sure he remembers me. Not many people fail English Lit II and have to retake it. I tell myself I'm also imagining the look of smugness on his face.

He starts class almost the exact same way he did last year: a speech meant to awe and frighten us. It's a little less impressive hearing it the second time around. Not like I'd been mesmerized the first, either, but now it's just embarrassing. Unfortunately, this is a required course to graduate, so I've nothing to do but pay attention. I *have* to pass this class.

He goes through the syllabus, gleefully outlining the books we'll be studying this semester. Stomach sinking, I read through the list twice to make sure I'm understanding it right. It's nearly double the reading list from last year. And I *failed* last year. Cold pricks of sweat break out on the back of my neck as I look at some of the titles on this list. Even someone like me—who never reads unless they're forced to—knows that most of these books are hundreds of pages. I'll be lucky to finish a third of these.

By the time class ends and I head off to practice, I'm in a terrible mood. I'm glad I, at least, have hockey to look forward to. Sometimes I regret my decision to play net, and wish I was one of the forwards or D-men, if only because they get to *hit* people. Maybe Coach Mackenzie will let me try my hand at it one of these practices. He is, after all, always encouraging us to try new things. Feeling marginally better than before, I yank open the door to the practice rink and step inside my favorite place in the entire world.

I CAN HEAR the music all the way in the garage when I get home. It sounds like a mariachi band is in my living room. Shouldering my bag, I shove through the door and am immediately assaulted by the unmistakable smell of Mexican food. It smells like cilantro and refried beans and a thousand other things I can't name. My stomach growls loud enough to be heard over the music. Dropping everything unceremoniously on the floor by the door, I follow my nose toward the kitchen.

Stopping in the doorway, I take a second to enjoy the view while my presence is yet unknown. Zeke has his back toward me, standing at the counter and chopping something on a cutting board. He's got Spanish music blaring from his phone on the island and he's swaying his hips in time to the beat. He's trying to sing along, but can only muster one of every handful of words. It's ridiculous, and unbearably cute. I watch the motion of his hips and decide that cute might not be the best description.

Zeke turns, sees me standing there and stops dead. He blushes a fierce red that travels all the way down his neck to the collar of his shirt. Even his ears are red. *Jesus Christ, even that's cute.* I raise an eyebrow and lean nonchalantly against the wall, speaking to be heard over the music.

"Shakira, huh?"

He reaches over to the phone and taps it off. The sudden silence is deafening. Scratching at the back of his neck, Zeke shoots me a chagrined smile. "I lost track of time. Didn't think you'd be home quite this early."

"I decided to shower here, instead of in the locker room. Glad I did. I can't believe I almost missed the show."

The smile grows less embarrassed and more playful. "Nobody can resist the power of Shakira. You *must* dance."

"I seemed to be resisting just fine," I point out.

"Yes, well, just because I haven't found any bodies doesn't mean they aren't there. I haven't ruled out the possibility of you being a psychopath."

Snorting, I lean over the counter and inhale. I'm hungry enough to eat Zeke at this point and it smells fucking amazing in here. Unfortunately, I do not smell amazing. Wrinkling my nose at my own stench, I step back so as not to asphyxiate Zeke.

"I better go shower."

"All right. Dinner will be served when you return, sir." He sketches a mock bow, speaking in an English affectation. He's weird, and nerdy; I really wish I didn't find it as adorable as I did. He's my roommate and roommates are off-limits. Turning, I head upstairs to shower, lips twitching up into a smile as I think about Zeke dancing around the kitchen.

He's as good as his word—when I walk back downstairs, hair wet and shirt clinging to my still damp skin, there are two plates of enchiladas sitting on the island. Assuming the plate with twice the amount of food on it is mine, I sit down and pull it toward me.

"This smells so fucking good," I tell him, snatching up the fork. "I should probably tell you that you don't have to cook for me, but I'm afraid you'll stop if I do."

He laughs, and a little flutter of happiness kicks around my stomach at the sound. When he sits down next to me, our elbows touch and his knee bumps mine beneath the table. I have to continually remind myself that Zeke isn't doing this as a sly come-on; in fact, he'd probably be embarrassed if I explained that touching people like that can sometimes be a hint that you're interested in them.

Carefully moving my arm out of reach, I shove a forkful of enchilada into my mouth and groan. Not bothering to wait until I swallow, I speak around a mouthful of hot food.

"Holy shit, this is good."

Laughing, Zeke puts a much more manageable bite into

his mouth. Employing his manners, he waits until he swallows to talk. "Mexican is my specialty. And by that, I mean that enchiladas are the only thing I can make."

"Why bother making anything else, when this is perfect?" I ask, and he beams at me.

"That's nice of you. But I could hear your stomach growling from across the room. Something tells me you'd be impressed with anything, right now."

"Lies," I mumble around a mouthful. I'm halfway through my plate already, and still starving. "Is there more? Or is this it?"

"There's another pan in the oven," he tells me, laughing at my panic. "You eat like a baby dinosaur."

This startles a laugh from me, and I choke on enchilada. Turning away so that I don't hack up a lung onto our plates, I feel Zeke's hand patting my upper back ineffectually. Catching my breath, I turn back around and point my fork at him.

"Nothing more from you when I've got food in my mouth."

Biting his lip in amusement, he gives me a silent salute. By the time we've finished dinner, I've eaten nearly an entire pan by myself. I feel pleasantly full, and am dreaming of crawling into bed and sleeping for ten hours. Unfortunately, the thought of bed only serves as a reminder of the reading I need to get a head start on tonight. It's not going to take much for me to fall behind. Good mood evaporating like smoke, I help Zeke clean up and trudge upstairs to my room like a man sentenced to death row.

Flopping onto my bed, I pull *Lady Audley's Secret* from my backpack. It's thick, and I already hate it. Glaring at it and hating my life, I hardly notice Zeke's soft knock on my open bedroom door.

"The door is open, Zeke, that means you can *come in without knocking*." The rebuke comes out sharper than I'd intended and I flinch at myself. It's not *his* fault I have to read this stupid book.

"What are you reading?" he asks, coming into the room but hovering by the door. I hold up the book for him to see.

"Oh, that's a good one."

Of course he's read it, and obviously understood it well enough to enjoy it. Because he's smart, and not a fucking idiot like me. "Great."

Clocking my tone, he moves closer to the bed and holds out a hand. I hand him the book, silently. Aimlessly flipping through the pages, he glances at me and away again, back at the book. When he hands it back to me, I slide over until there is enough room on the bed for him to sit down next to me.

"You don't like to read?" he asks. I close my eyes, sighing.

"I don't know. I'd probably like it more if I was better at it." I'm not sure this is true, but I hope it is. I've always equated reading with intelligence, so the harder reading became for me, the less I liked doing it. Of course, this only made it harder still. Now, reading anything feels far too much like a chore to be any sort of enjoyable.

"What do you mean, better at it?" Zeke asks curiously.

I think about that for a second. My normal response would be to tell whomever asked that to fuck right off, but this is Zeke. I don't think he'd laugh at me, even if I told him I was illiterate. "I don't know, it's just fucking hard. I can't concentrate. And the books we have to read for school suck ass."

"Mm. Some are better than others." He runs a palm over my bedspread, eyes on his fingers. "Have you tried audiobooks, instead?"

"No." The idea hadn't even occurred to me. "Should I?"

"Might help." He looks at me, still trailing an idle hand over my comforter. "Want me to read some to you?"

"What, right now?" I ask, lifting my head and propping myself up on an elbow to look at him better. "Are you serious?"

"Sure." He holds out a hand and waits for me to put the book into his palm. Sliding back until his back is more comfortable against the wall, he crosses his legs and flips to the first page. Laying back down, I rest my hands on my abdomen.

"This is so weird," I tell him, and he chuckles.

"Feel like your mom is reading you a bedtime story?" he jokes, and I snort.

"My mom never read me a bedtime story. Also, don't talk about my mom when *we're* in bed. Gross."

His chuckle turns into a full-on laugh at that. It takes him a second to compose himself; once he does, he starts reading in a steady, soothing voice. Closing my eyes, I listen hard to the words and try not to think about the way his slight weight is compressing my mattress. Soon enough, the irritation melts away and I find myself almost enjoying the experience. Zeke's voice is musical; he reads each sentence with a smooth confidence that I envy. If I'd been asked to read this book out loud, I'd be tripping over every other word.

By the time he stops reading, I've been lulled into a kind of trance. It takes a hand on my shoulder to jar me back to alertness, and I blink open my eyes to look up at him sheepishly. He leaves his hand on my shoulder, the long, fine-boned fingers curling over lightly on my skin. I'd like to ask him to keep reading; I have the sudden, nearly irresistible urge to ask him to stay.

"Did you fall asleep?" Zeke asks, smirking.

"Surprisingly, no. I was just listening. You..." Pausing, I try to decide what I want to say. I don't want to make him uncomfortable. "You have a nice voice. And you were right—that worked. I feel like I actually retained some of that."

He smiles. "That's good. Want me to keep going?"

Boy do I. I hesitate, unsure whether this is the sort of thing platonic roommates would be doing and whether or not I care about the distinction. "If you don't mind."

Apparently, he doesn't. He shifts beside me, settling in. The motion brings him closer to me and his hip nudges my shoulder where I'm sprawled out on the bed. He doesn't shift away, so I don't either. Closing my eyes once more, I enjoy the contact and the calming sound of his voice as he reads to me.

He stays—long past the time the pair of us should have gone to bed—and reads until his voice becomes scratchy with overuse. I sit up when he stops and swings his legs over the side of the bed, setting the book on my nightstand. Feeling suddenly awkward, like he's a one-night stand I'm sending on their way, I cast about for something to say. Since what I really want to do is invite him to spend the night, I end up opting for silence.

"You better get some sleep," Zeke says, turning to look at me. "Game tomorrow, right?"

"Right." I clear my throat. "Thanks. For, you know, this."

I wave toward the bed between us, like a fucking idiot. It sounds like I'm thanking him for a good lay. Apparently, Zeke's mind is firmly outside of the gutter, though, because he doesn't comment. He just smiles and stands up.

"You're welcome. We can do more another time, maybe."

I nod, watching as he walks out the door. He's so small—bony shoulder blades and no hips. He always looks like he's wearing clothes a size too large for him. Trying to remind myself that he's *not my type*, I get up to strip and get ready for bed. When I come back to the bedroom, my eyes immediately track to the impression Zeke left on my bed. *Off limits*, I remind myself, sternly, as I shut off the light and crawl into bed.

Immediately, as though a projector was flipped on in my mind, my thoughts turn to Zeke and other things that might be done in this bed. I wonder how he kisses. Probably gentle, and a little unsure. I can practically feel the phantom touch of soft fingertips on my skin, as I think about it. He'd probably be shy, uncertain where to touch and when. I wouldn't mind teaching him.

But all this is just a fantasy. An enjoyable one, but an indulgence that borders on delusion. Zeke and I haven't known each other long, and even if we were to form a close bond there is no guarantee that he would ever be sexually attracted to me. It's not impossible, but it's also not something I'd place money on. Someone like him doesn't fall for someone like me. I'm a one-night stand, and that will never be something he is into.

Shutting down all thoughts of kissing and what Zeke looks like beneath those loose shirts, I tug the blanket over myself and roll over. I've got a game tomorrow—a game Tony is going to be watching—and the last thing I need is to be distracted by adorable nerds.

LIFTING MY HELMET, I turn and grab the water bottle off of the back of the net and squirt a stream into my mouth. The fans behind my net are cheering; it's some sort of goalie chant, which features heavily on telling me how much I suck. I raise a hand and curl my fingers in a *let's hear it* motion. Let them chant and heckle all they want—I'm about to end this game on a fucking shutout. Pulling my mask into place, I wait at the top of my crease for play to resume.

Penn State is good, but they're also young. Their team is comprised of mainly freshman and sophomore students, whereas we have a pretty even spread of upper and lower class athletes. The division between team structures is showing tonight. Penn State came out of the gate playing hard in the first period but have quickly become sloppy with every goal we score and every shot I save.

Five minutes left in the third period and the puck is in our zone. I'm hugging the right post, staring at the puck so hard that my eyes are dry from not blinking. One of the Penn State forwards—fuck if I can tell who it is—fires a shot that I barely deflect with my shoulder. The puck wings over the net and I push to the other side in case any forwards are lurking outside my line of sight. Sweat trickles down my brow, stinging my eyes.

The crowd is still cheering but it's a dull, wordless roar to me. The only thing I'm listening for is the call of my teammates. Penn State fires a bullet toward me and I glove it down but don't hold it. Vas is off of my right shoulder, where I knew he'd be, and ready when I tip it to him. He takes off down the ice toward the opposing goal, but I stay vigilant. Too many times in the past I've let in goals I should have saved because I wasn't expecting my team to turn it over. *But not today, bitches. Today, I'm getting a shutout.*

And I do. When the final buzzer sounds, SCU wins the game 5-0; even Coach Mackenzie is wearing a begrudging smile. The team lines up, knocking their helmets against mine and occasionally giving me the odd hug. This is my favorite part about being the goalie, though I'd never say it out loud. I've never made good friends with any of my teammates beyond Vas, but after a win any animosity is gone—they all treat me like we're brothers no matter how little I've done to earn that.

As always, Vas waits until last and gives me the biggest hug of all, nearly knocking me off my feet. When he talks, he sounds so excited that the German accent is heavier than I've heard it.

"A shutout! Well done, my friend."

We skate toward the bench. "You, too. Nice goal."

He waves a gloved hand through the air as if to chase the compliment away. I give one last obnoxious wave to the crowd before we head down the chute. Coach Mackenzie pats my shoulder as I walk by, and my chest burns with pride. He looks proud, the way I've always wanted my father to look after watching one of my games. Of course, for my dad to be proud of me he'd actually have to *watch* one of my games.

Chasing away thoughts of my parents, I begin the process of removing my pads. Vas is beside me, both of us silent in the jubilant locker room. Every time one of my teammates passes by, they thump me on the chest or the arm. I fucking love winning. Coach isn't big on speeches, but he gives one tonight. All of us listen, rapt. Coach Mackenzie is something of a god to us—universally loved and respected by every member of the team.

When we get to the team bus, Vas sits next to me like usual. Immediately, he pulls out a textbook and a reading light. Leaning over, I take a peek at the cover. It's a math book, which naturally makes me think of Zeke. Pulling out my phone for the first time since the game ended, I see there isn't a single text from my parents. *Didn't watch the game, then.* Frowning, I pull out earbuds and am just about to put on some music when a message from Zeke comes through.

> Great game! You got a shootout!

I snort a laugh, and Vas looks over in surprise. I hold up my phone in answer.

> Shutout.

> Whatever, same thing. You were very skilled at defending the crease. No puck breached your five-hole. Nobody was going to score a backdoor tonight, not in your kitchen.

> Okay, that's enough, get off of the internet.

> Hockey terms are fucking WEIRD.

> Seriously, though. Good game. That was fun to watch. The people in the crowd were kind of wild, though.

> You mean the goalie chant?

> Yes! So mean! They should have been ejected for unsportsmanlike conduct.

> And yes, I googled that too.

> It's all good. The goalie always gets heckled. Just part of the game. We don't get home until late tonight.

> I'll wait up for you. Make sure you make it okay.

I stare down at my phone, warmth pooling in my stomach and diffusing through my body. I should respond with something flippant—make a joke or some snide comment. I'm not sure Zeke even realizes he sometimes acts like we're in a relationship, and I wonder if I should enlighten him. Roommates don't cook dinner for each other, or read to one another, or stay up until the early hours of the morning to make sure the other gets home okay. But I don't want him to stop, and I'm selfish. If I tell him he acts like we're boyfriends, he won't do it anymore.

> Sounds good. See you soon.

> Fly safe!

Looking up, I lock eyes with Vas. He's watching me with a small smile on his face. Scowling at him, I queue up some music on my phone and lean back in my seat, closing my eyes.

7

Zeke

THE SOUND of the garage door startles me awake. I jolt, sitting up and causing the book on my chest to slide to the floor with a thump. Disoriented, I scrub a hand over my eyes and try to locate my phone. It's dark in the living room but for the single lamp I'd left on to read by. Finally, just as the garage door leading into the house opens, I find my phone in between the couch cushions. Tapping the screen, I check the time—3:52 a.m.

Carter walks into the room just as I stand up, and we eye each other across the dim room. He's wearing sweats and an SCU hoodie; there is a heavy look to his eyes, as though he's having trouble keeping them open. Stepping closer, he smiles the barest hint of a smile. It's little more than a faint indentation of his cheeks at the corner of his mouth, but it does more to brighten the room than the lamp.

"You waited," he says, surprised.

"I said I would." I have to clear my throat to dispel the

gravel. I must have been asleep longer than I thought. "Was the flight okay? And the drive? You look tired."

"Both were fine. You do, too."

I *am* tired. It feels ridiculous to complain, though, since all I did was homework. Carter is the one who did the traveling and played a hockey game. "Are you hungry? I could heat you up—"

"Zeke."

"Yeah?"

"Let's just go to bed. We've got the zoo tomorrow, right?" He voice tilts upward at the end, like a little hopeful question mark.

"Right," I confirm, stepping around the couch to stand beside him. He nods, happy with my validation. Whenever we make plans, he always assumes I'll cancel. He hasn't said it, but I can tell by the look in his eyes that he's continually expecting me to find something better to do. Or someone better, perhaps.

Carter turns off the lamp, plunging the room into blackness. I'm just about to ask him to turn on the stairwell light when I feel a light touch at my elbow. He leads me upstairs, only turning on a light when we reach his bedroom. Up close, I can see the strain of the night around his eyes and he's leaned up against the doorframe like it's the only thing keeping him standing. His hair glows gold in the light from his room and his eyes are the darkest blue I've ever seen. He is really quite handsome.

"See you tomorrow, then," he says, and I nod.

"Yes, tomorrow. Sleep tight." This has become something of an inside joke with us, and I can see the glint of amusement in Carter's eyes as he says it back to me.

The next morning, I'm awake before him and decide to

make pancakes. I'd bought the pre-made mix but have yet to use it, and a zoo day seems like a good day to break into it. I've got the coffee percolating and the first batch of pancakes on the stove when Carter strolls in without a shirt on. He's got the kind of muscles that suggest he's never eaten a pancake in his life.

"Good morning." I push a coffee mug toward him. He grunts, which is his usual form of morning greeting. Turning back to the stove, I give him time to introduce caffeine into his bloodstream and focus on turning the pancakes.

"Hey."

Carter's voice pulls my gaze to where his blue eyes are surveying me over the rim of his mug. "Yeah?"

"You know you aren't required to cook me food, right? Or to have dinner ready for me when I get home. I don't..." He takes a sip of coffee, clearly trying to find the correct words. "Just—don't feel like you *have* to do that, okay?"

The funny thing is, I don't feel like that at all; I like making him dinner. It's oddly satisfying, watching the way Carter's eyes light up when he sees me cooking for him. He's letting me live here practically for free, so really, catering to him a little bit is the least I can do.

"I don't mind doing it, every now and again. Besides, if I'm going to make something for myself, I might as well make enough for you."

This seems to mollify him, and he nods as he drains the mug and goes to pour more coffee. I plate the first three pancakes and hold them out to him, wordlessly. He takes it, holding it up to his face and inhaling. When he looks at me over the pancakes, his eyes are serious.

"I think I might love you," he says, and I give a bark of

startled laughter. Whacking him on the leg with the spatula, I shake my head.

"Go eat and get dressed. I want to see some tree frogs today."

THE ZOO IS, of course, ridiculously fun. I'd made the mistake in the car of telling Carter that I'd been an aspiring zoologist growing up, and that I knew all sorts of random facts about the animals in the zoo. Naturally, as soon as we got to the first exhibit, Carter took it upon himself to test this boast. He slapped a hand down over the writing on the sign, angling his body so I couldn't see around him, and pointed at the exhibit. It was the camels.

"Okay, go."

"Go where?"

"Camel facts. I want to hear them, Einstein."

Pursing my lips to keep from laughing, I scrunch up my face in a semblance of hard thinking. Clearing my throat, I step close to the exhibit and swing my arm wide like a presenter on a game show. Carter's lips twitch. "Here we have two types of camels. The Bactrian and the Dromedary. Do you know how to tell them apart, sir?"

"No," he says, in a strangled voice. He's trying not to smile, and doing an admirable job.

"Bactrian camels have two humps—easy to remember because their back looks like an uppercase B, see?" I mime a B in the air and wait for Carter to nod. "Dromedary only have one hump. They're also known as the Arabian camel and are the most common. In fact, about 90% of the world's camels are Arabian camels."

"Wow—"

"That's not all!" I interrupt, and see Carter bite his lip. I *will* make him crack a smile today, if it's the last thing I do. "Did you know that camels store fat in their humps, which can be converted into energy and allows them to travel long distances without food or water? They can go without water for *weeks*, Carter. Weeks!"

"That's pretty interesting," he says, and looks down at the sign. I step closer to him and we look up at the camels.

"They've got super long eyelashes, see?" I point to the nearest one.

"Is that to keep the sand out?" Carter asks, pointing at the photograph of the sand dunes featured on the sign. I smile at him.

"Exactly! Come on, let's see what's next."

We walk abreast, meandering down the path and dodging running children. We're both wearing short sleeved shirts, and every now and then our arms brush. Carter, with his tattoos and nose ring, has gotten several raised eyebrows and quite a few double-takes as he walks by. Hardly seeming to notice the people around us, he gives all his attention to me and the animals. For all his talk about occasionally bringing men and women home, he doesn't seem to care much about dating. There are at least a dozen people, in this section of the zoo alone, who would happily go out with him if I asked for volunteers.

"What are you looking at?" Carter asks, frowning at me. I've been staring at him.

"You. Haven't you noticed all the attention you're getting?" I nod my head toward a group of young women, openly ogling him. When he looks in their direction, one of them waves at him, bravely. He scowls at her, and turns back to me.

"So?"

"Well, I don't know. I guess I just don't understand you, is all. You said you sometimes bring people home, but you haven't. And evidently, it's not for lack of options."

There is an unrecognizable look on his face; the line between his eyebrows deepens as he frowns and looks down at his feet. I can tell he's doing some quick thinking, and that I've made him uncomfortable.

"Never mind, I shouldn't have—"

"I've met up with people a few times after practice. From dating apps," he tells me, and then clarifies when I look at him in confusion. "For hook-ups. But no, you're right, I haven't brought any of them home."

"Oh." I feel strange, hearing this—a sort of uncomfortable, prickly sensation over my skin as I think about Carter going out and finding random people to sleep with. It makes me feel sad and a little bit lonely, which makes no sense. "Well...all right then."

"Does that bother you?" he asks sharply. His eyes are narrowed and his shoulders are thrown back, like he's looking out for a fight.

"No. Well, yeah, I guess a little bit. You're such a great guy; you deserve to be happy. You're too good for random one-night stands." I flinch, not liking the words even as I say them. I'm not trying to shame him for having casual sex, I just don't *understand* it. I've never been able to wrap my mind around people's ability to be intimate with someone they just met.

Carter makes a disgruntled noise and scowls at the polar bears. I wish I'd never started this conversation. I've ruined what had, thus far, been a perfect day. An apology is right on the tip of my tongue until he starts to speak. "One-night stands are *all* I'm good for, Zeke. I don't know if you've noticed, but people don't particularly like me."

I'm not sure if this is true. People avoid him because he radiates unfriendliness, not because they don't like him. It's probably more accurate to say people are intimidated by him. If anyone made an effort to know him, they'd see that he's actually selfless, kind, and has a sharp sense of humor.

"I like you," I tell him. He looks at me, and if I had to guess I'd say his expression was unhappy. *But that can't be right, can it?* His scowl is fixed back in place a second later, and I wonder if I'd imagined the pain.

"I like you, too," he says gruffly, before gesturing at the polar bears. "Now, hit me with some knowledge."

Grinning, I inch close enough to him that our arms brush. "Polar bears are the only member of the bear species to be considered a marine mammal."

Carter raises an eyebrow at me. He hasn't moved his arm away, and his skin is sun-warmed against my own. "Really?"

"Really. They're also the largest species of bear *and* the largest land carnivore."

"Huh...what about water? What's the largest...aquatic carnivore?" he asks, looking down at me.

I squint, biting my lip and thinking hard. "Uhm, sperm whale, maybe? Yeah, I think that's right."

He shakes his head and makes a tsking noise with his tongue, adopting an exaggerated look of disappointment. "Really, Zeke? Guessing?"

Smiling, I bump him with my shoulder; he doesn't budge. "Okay, okay, come on then. It's time to look at the frogs—I'm about to blow your mind with all of these facts." Linking my arm through his elbow, I pull him toward the Amphibian

House. When I go to remove my arm, he tightens his and locks me in place.

"I cannot fathom how I've managed to survive this long without frog facts," Carter says, so dryly that someone who didn't know him would think he was being serious.

When we get to the Amphibian House, he lets go of my arm in favor of opening the door for me. We step inside the dark, humid room and pause to let our vision adjust to the low light. Someone walks in behind us and I feel Carter place a gentle hand on my upper back to steer me away from the door. When he drops his hand I feel a momentary pang of loss, and consider tucking my arm through his once more. Before I can, he sets off toward the first exhibit and I have nothing to do but follow.

We move slowly through the exhibits, Carter giving me ample time to expound on all the frogs that we see. He listens intently whenever I talk, and it's a heady feeling. I know I get a little *too* excited about things, and people's attention spans start to wander while I'm talking. This doesn't seem to happen with Carter, though. His eyes crinkle and his mouth turns down in a frown when he's listening hard, and he'll sometimes ask follow-up questions. Right now, he's bent over with his face nearly pressed into the glass, peering intently at a red-eyed tree frog.

"It's kind of cute," he says, frowning.

"And, not poisonous!" I raise my eyebrows at him and he snorts, shaking his head. Straightening, he beckons for me to lead the way to the next exhibit. I feel like a zookeeper, taking him on a private tour. It's ridiculously fun.

By the time we get through the entire zoo, it's late in the day—we don't have time to go home and change before going to my grandma's house for dinner. Carter, settling into the driver's seat and starting the car, looks relaxed. His shoulders are dropped away from his ears and there is an almost tranquil expression on his face. I wonder if he's forgotten that he agreed to come to dinner.

"Do you still want to come to dinner, tonight?" I ask him, keeping my voice light even though I'm nervous to hear his answer. I'm desperate for his continued company. I want to keep this day going for as long as possible.

"Yeah. If you want me to." When he puts the car in reverse and uses a hand on the back of my seat to turn around, I get a good look at his face. The peaceful expression is gone, replaced once more by the scowl.

"I want you to," I say firmly, and he nods. I don't like the thought of him rattling around that big house all alone, while I have a cozy dinner with my grandma.

We lapse into silence, then, but for my murmured instructions on where to turn. I can tell he's nervous, the tension in the car settling over us like a blanket. By the time we pull into the trailer park, his hands are white-knuckled on the steering wheel and his jaw is clenched. Really, he looks like I've asked him to dinner with Hitler and not my grandmother.

"You ready to go in?" I ask lightly, when he makes no move to get out of the car.

"Yeah," he sighs, and pushes open his door.

I let us inside after using my special knock, calling out for Grandma and hearing her in the kitchen. Carter follows so closely behind me, I'm surprised I can't feel his breath on my neck. For some reason my own heart is racing, like his nerves are a tangible thing that he's infected me with. When I get to the kitchen and stop walking, he bumps into my back.

"Sorry," he says, when I turn around to look at him. I feel

like I should grab his hand and reassure him that Grandma doesn't bite, but I'm not certain he wouldn't smack me away. Turning back around, I hold my arms wide and meet my grandma halfway.

"Hi, Grandma. Smells amazing in here." I squeeze her as tightly as I dare, inhaling her baby shampoo smell.

"Hello, dear. And you've brought Carter with you!" She lets me go in favor of welcoming the guest. The guest who looks like he's going to puke when she hugs him, too.

"Oh," he says, returning the hug belatedly, "hi. Thanks for inviting me."

"Well, you can come anytime, of course. Sit, both of you, sit." She waves us to the table, which looks laughably small when Carter takes up an entire end of the table.

"You look like a giant," I tell him, sitting in the seat closest to him and nudging his knee with my own below the table.

"The table is small," he whispers back, scowling and hitting my knee with more force than I'd used. He's not wrong. It's a table meant for two people who live in a small mobile home, not a table meant for big hockey players. Grinning, I turn to look at my grandma.

"We went to the zoo today, Grandma."

"Did you, now? You love the zoo," she tells me fondly, and brings over two glasses of green Kool-Aid before turning back to the oven. I almost laugh at the look of surprise on Carter's face. Leaning over, I press my knee back against his and bring his gaze to mine.

"We always have green Kool-Aid with dinner—ever since I was a kid. You can have something else though, if you'd prefer."

"No." He says it fast, the word cracking through the small

space like a shout. "No, this is fine. I don't need anything special."

To prove his point, he takes a pointed sip of his drink. I press my lips together to keep from laughing at the effort it takes him not to wince at the sweetness. Beneath the table, our legs are still pressed together; I make no effort to move away, though, and neither does he. Something tells me he needs the silent support.

Over at the counter, Grandma has her back to us and is rambling on about people neither of us have met. From what I can gather, the story is about the school friend of the daughter of one of her neighbor's brothers. Carter's brow is furrowed in concentration as he tries to hold on to the salient points. It's no use—the best you can do when she starts telling these stories is to nod along and smile like you know exactly who she's talking about.

"Can you believe that?" she finishes, turning around and looking at us.

"That's crazy," I say, and Carter nods in solidarity.

"You know, if I'd tried that in school, I would have been smacked!" she says, and chuckles. "Okay, boys, here we are."

She sets down a casserole dish on the table and dishes some onto Carter's plate. It's probably a third of the portion size he usually eats. Once we've all been served, she sits down. I watch her carefully, noting with dismay the careful way she lowers into the chair. I know her knees have been bothering her and that she's supposed to see her primary care doctor about it. I make a mental note to remind her before we leave.

"So, tell me about the zoo!" she says, and looks at Carter. He swallows a half-chewed mouthful of casserole and coughs into his hand.

"It was fun." He looks at me and I nod: *yes, it was fun.* "Did you know that polar bears are considered an aquatic mammal?"

I nearly choke. Lifting my shirt, I cover my mouth while I hack until I'm able to swallow down a gulp of Kool-Aid. Grandma reaches over and pats my arm.

"Chew your food, honey," she reminds me, before turning back to Carter. "That's quite interesting! I had no idea. My boy here was always watching those nature programs and reading books, but I can't seem to hold onto information like that."

She waves a hand to indicate how the information might fly out of her ear. I don't bother reminding her that she knows and remembers every bit of information about every single person she's ever met.

We chat pointlessly through dinner, covering any topic that pops into our heads. I watch as Carter's muscles slowly unclench through dinner, whatever tension he was holding onto slowly seeping away as he becomes more comfortable. One day, I'll ask him why a simple family dinner is so fraught with anxiety for him.

The pair of us handle the clean-up, as Grandma sits at the table and regales us with more tales from the neighborhood. She even gets Carter to laugh, when she goes on a vitriolic rant about people who walk through the park but don't pick up after their dogs. She's wearied of cleaning her shoes when she comes back from her daily walk, she tells us, and Carter nods solemnly while biting his cheek. When we are sent on our way—we need to be home before it gets too dark, or it won't be safe to drive—the pair of us are clutching Tupperware containers of homemade cookies and given a firm hug.

She watches until we're out of sight of her house, waving at the retreating form of Carter's car.

I look at him when I can't see her any longer. There is an air of melancholy around him, and his downturned mouth speaks more of sadness than anger. I realize that I've really only seen two easily identifiable expressions on his face: anger and sorrow.

"I wish I had a grandma like yours," he says.

Oh. "She's pretty great," I say lightly, and wish we were still in a position where I could press my knee to his in silent support. "What are your grandparents like?"

He blows out a hard breath, not looking at me. "They're just older versions of my parents. Whenever we went over to their house for Sunday brunch, we had to dress up. I spilled something on the rug, once, and, I don't know, I guess it was a really fancy, expensive rug, and we weren't invited back for a while. Not until I was old enough to not spill things."

He laughs, a terse, sharp laugh that is not paired with a smile. I don't laugh with him, because it's not funny. It's not funny at all. *What kind of grandparents stop inviting their grandson over because he accidentally spilled something?*

"But that's all right. Wasn't missing much, by not going over there." He shrugs. "My whole family is kind of like that, though. Rich and snobby. Except for my Aunt Franky, though. She's badass. She lives in Rome, in this tiny little flat, and works as an English tutor. How cool is that?"

"Very cool." I try to sound enthusiastic in my response, even though this entire story has made me feel awful. "Does she come visit?"

"Oh, yeah, sometimes. She's my dad's sister, and they don't get along. But I love when she's here. She flew in for one of my games once!"

His voice rises in excitement, suddenly, and he looks over at me. I smile, even though my stomach curdles at the implication of who *doesn't* make an effort to go to his games. I'd bet good money that his "rich and snobby" parents don't travel to watch him play, even though they live in the States.

"I introduced her to Coach Mackenzie and everything. It was pretty cool." He shakes his head, clearly still astounded that someone put in so much effort for him. "My parents haven't ever watched me play. They *hate* that I play hockey."

And there it is. "That's awful."

He looks at me, startled. "It's fine. I mean, I can't complain, obviously. We have a lot of money—I've never gone without anything in my life."

Except, apparently, love and attention. "Have you visited your aunt in Rome?"

"Yeah, once. Have you ever been?"

"No, I've never even left the state before," I admit. "But I've got a list a mile long of places I'd like to visit, one day."

"Next time I go see Franky, you can come. We'll charge two first class seats to Dad's credit card and send him a selfie from the plane."

I can't help but laugh at the smirk on his face as he imagines it. Something tells me this isn't an empty gesture, either. He probably would buy us plane tickets to Italy if I agreed to go.

"Maybe she'd like a visitor this weekend?" I ask, and he glances at me and smiles an eighth of a smile. I feel like a fucking hero, earning that smile. Sighing, I sit back in my seat although I keep my face turned to keep Carter in profile. "What's the plan for the evening?"

"Homework, I guess," he says, sounding less than thrilled. "I have to read more of that stupid book."

"Want me to do the reading?" His eyes flick to me and away again so fast I might have imagined it.

"Yeah?"

"Sure. I did all my homework yesterday, in preparation for the zoo today."

"You did all your own work, so now you're offering to help with mine?" he asks, incredulously.

"What can I say? I'm a giver."

Carter huffs a soft laugh, shaking his head. I could easily get used to hearing those spurts of laughter and catching those rare smiles. It's heady, getting to peek behind the curtain of Carter's façade and see the real man underneath.

8

Carter

I LEAN FORWARD, wincing, and clench my fingers into the bedspread. Behind me, Jackson pushes my legs further apart and shoves his fingers inside me so roughly, it feels like he didn't even use lube. He's not aiming for pleasure, but for getting the prep done as quickly as possible. Biting my lip, I try to relax, knowing that it'll hurt less if I do. He's pumping his fingers in and out, too fast to be anything but jarring. *God, I fucking hate doing this.*

A ridiculously short time later, and without asking if I'm ready, I feel him line himself up behind me. I brace myself, knowing that this neanderthal is just going to push inside without giving me time to adjust. Indeed, he ignores any resistance and immediately starts jackhammering his hips like we're in a race to the finish line. Thankfully—due to sheer dumb luck rather than any sexual prowess on his part—his dick rubs against my prostate and the pleasure starts to mix with the pain.

Jackson is grunting, one hand clenched hard on my hip and the other pressed firmly against my middle back like he's trying to shove me flat on the bed. He's really going hard now, jolting me forward with every slap of his hips against my ass. He's mumbling something beneath the grunting— incoherent dirty talk that makes my skin crawl. *You take my dick so good* is not a sexy thing to hear when you're not having a good time.

I want to finish and get the fuck out of here. Since he doesn't seem inclined to do it, I take a hand off the bed and reach for my dick. Almost immediately, he presses between my shoulder blades and finally succeeds in pushing my face down onto the bed. The comforter is scratchy against my cheek, making me long for my own. Closing my eyes, I jack myself quickly. By some miraculous twist of fate, Jackson and I both come at the same time, and I feel a surge of delight when I see the mess I made of his bedspread. *Have fun washing that, fucker.*

He pulls out with the same care with which he's done everything else, and I bite my lip to keep from making a sound. The second his hand is removed, I push back onto all fours. This is always the worst part of one-night stands: the aftermath. I don't have the stomach for it tonight, though, so I don't delay in swinging my legs off the bed and reaching for my boxers.

"That was fun." Jackson leans over and grazes his teeth on my shoulder. I put a hand on his chest and shove him back.

"Don't," I warn.

Standing, I pull the rest of my clothes on hastily and check to make sure my phone and keys are still in my pants pockets. I left my wallet in the car. After checking I have everything, I turn to see Jackson leaned back on the bed, casual and sated. The used condom is laying on the floor next to the bed. *Fucking disgusting.*

"I don't suppose we have to pretend that we'll see each other again, do we?" he asks, smirking. The way he's leaning makes his shoulder muscles and biceps bulge in a way I'd normally like. Right now, the sight only makes me feel vaguely ill.

"Nope, we don't," I confirm, and fling open his bedroom door so violently, it crashes into the wall and knocks a frame off of his dresser. I don't bother stopping to apologize, but leave the apartment as quickly as I can. I feel disgusting—like I've spent the last half hour covered in maggots.

It's worse by the time I get home. Desperate for a shower, I take the stairs two at a time and slam the bathroom door behind me. I hear the faint call of Zeke's voice from downstairs, but I ignore him. The spray of hot water feels heavenly against my skin, and I do nothing but stand under the stream for several minutes. Eventually, I grab the body wash and go through the motions of cleaning another person off of my body. When I reach between my legs, I flinch as the soap touches the raw skin.

I stay in the shower until the water runs cold and my skin prunes. I'm not sure what's wrong with me. This isn't my first Grindr hook-up, nor the worst one. Ignoring the churning in my stomach and the lingering pain in my pelvis, I tell myself to suck it up as I leave the bathroom. Zeke is seated on my bed, waiting for me, and I'm grateful for the caution that had me wrapping a towel around my waist before opening the door.

"Hey!" he says, smiling at me.

"Hi," I mumble, turning my back to him and moving toward my dresser to grab some clothes.

"How was your night?"

"Fine." I tug boxers and sweatpants on before discarding the towel. When I reach for a hoodie, I've yet to turn around and look at him. "How was yours?"

"Nothing special. Hey, Carter?" Something in his voice has me peeking at him. He's not smiling, but watching me closely. Our eyes meet and continues. "What's wrong?"

"Nothing's wrong." My voice is harsh. I want him to drop this line of questioning.

He's sitting on my bed in an almost identical pose to the way Jackson was sprawled earlier: hands placed behind him on the mattress, holding him up in a casual recline. In Zeke's case, however, there is no evidence of muscles and the sharp angle of his shoulders make his collarbone protrude. His dirty blonde hair is messy on one side, like he was sleeping on it. I want to comb it with my fingers so badly, I have to clench my hand into a fist to hold myself back.

"Something's wrong," he presses. It's maddening. How the fuck does he know something is wrong? Because it's my usual reaction to unwanted situations, I don't fight the anger back when it rises to the surface.

"Well, if you must know, my ass fucking hurts because I just got railed by a dude I met on Grindr." I stare at him aggressively, but he remains infuriatingly impassive. He just stares at me with those huge fucking eyes. I blow out a hard breath, trying to dispel some of the anger. It's not Zeke's fault, and yelling at him will only make me feel worse. "I usually don't like to bottom, that's all."

I'm still standing awkwardly by my closet, while Zeke sits on the end of my bed and faces me. He sits forward, resting his hands in his lap and twisting his fingers together.

"Did he force you?" he asks, voice steady and eyes unwavering on mine. There is no hint of a smile on his usually happy face.

"No, Jesus, of course not."

"Why were you...bottoming," he stumbles slightly, over the verbiage, "if you don't like it, then?"

"It's not that I don't like...I don't fucking know. Because the guys who want to hook up with me are always toppy, and it's not like I can say *oh hey, never mind, I'm just going to get dressed and go unless I can be on top.*"

"Can't you?"

"Can't I what?"

"You said it's not like you can change your mind and leave. But...you can, right?" He squints at me, hands clenched together tightly in his lap. "You *can*. You can always say stop if you don't want to do something."

"Yeah, I know, that isn't—listen, let's just forget about this, okay?" I walk around to the side of the bed, conscious of Zeke's eyes following me as he turns to keep me in sight. The mattress shifts as I climb up and put my back against the wall; I run my palm over the comforter. Adjusting my hips, I try to find a comfortable position. Apparently, I do a poor job of hiding my wince at the twinge of pain because Zeke rises and whirls to face me.

"Are you *hurt*?" he asks indignantly. The tips of his ears are red, from embarrassment or anger, I can't tell.

"No, just a little sore." More than a little, but I'm not going to tell him that. "Not enough prep, that's all."

"Do you need me to take you to the doctor?"

I close my eyes, rubbing my hand over the bedspread once more. *What I wouldn't give to be able to turn the lights off and go to bed right now—end this miserable day.* When I open them, Zeke is still there, fuming like a pint-sized thundercloud.

"No, I don't need to go to the doctor. That's ridiculous."

"Were you bleeding? Just now, in the shower, was there any blood? Having anal sex without proper care can cause fissures which can then lead to infection. They're also severely painful, and—"

"*Stop.*" I hold a hand up and he snaps his jaw shut. I'm not sure how we got here, having an argument, but I don't like it. I also don't like talking about anal fissures. Patting the bed next to me, I beckon him over. I would do anything—*anything*—to stop having this conversation right now. "Just, come here. Please."

He does, crawling onto the end of the bed and sitting with his legs crossed. We're sitting exactly like we did on that first night he moved in, when he came and asked if I'd like to watch a movie. The difference between that night and tonight is glaring: neither of us are having a good time.

"I'm serious, Carter. If you're hurt, you need to tell me." He thinks about this for a second. "Or, better yet, a medical professional."

"I'm fine, okay? Please, just drop it. It was just rough sex, that's all."

"So, you had fun?" he challenges, and then adds, after seeing my face: "Don't lie."

"All right, fine, you win. I didn't have fun, but *I'm fine* and I'd really, really appreciate it if you would just let this go. *Please.*"

He looks like he wants to continue talking so badly that holding the words back is causing him physical pain. His hands are clenched on his knees, knuckles white. After holding my gaze for a moment, he looks away. This, I suppose, is the closest Zeke gets to pissed off. I feel like a dick, though I can't pinpoint precisely why.

"I'm sorry," I say, and his gaze snaps to mine.

"*You* don't have to be sorry. Whomever you were with tonight should be sorry. I just—," he holds his hands up, and closes his eyes, "—I just don't understand. I really don't understand. You met this guy to have sex, but he wanted to have the kind of sex you don't like. And now, because you did it anyway, you're in pain. I mean...are you...are you going to see him again?"

"No, of course not."

Zeke throws his hands up in exasperation. "Then what was the point? Oh my god, Carter." He scrubs both hands over his face before dropping them and looking at me, frustration clear.

"The point was just to get laid, Zeke. Simple as that." Disappointment is evident on his face, and shame curdles in my stomach. I like him—far more than I'd been expecting to —and his opinion of me matters. I've not done myself any favors with this exchange.

"Well, I guess you accomplished that. But it doesn't seem worth it, to me."

No, it wasn't. Crossing my arms over my chest, I look away from him. I'm going to delete that fucking app off of my phone. No hook-up is worth a conversation about anal fissures with Zeke. The mattress shifts, drawing my attention to where Zeke is still perched on the end of the bed. He scoots up until he's seated next to me, back against the wall and shoulder pressed against mine. We sit there, not speaking, each waiting for the other to talk first. It's Zeke, who's never met a silence he didn't want to fill with words, who breaks first.

"Sorry, I know what you do, or who you do it with, is none of my business. I didn't mean to get carried away. I just wanted to make sure you're all right, that's all."

Inhaling, I lean my head back against the wall. Zeke's narrow shoulder is pressed against my own, his slight weight leaned against me. I want to put that arm around him so badly. The strength of my sudden attraction to him worries me; it doesn't make sense and it's unlikely to go anywhere. I need to get myself under control before I end up making a mess of our friendship and hurting my own feelings in the process.

"I know," I tell him. "I...I appreciate it. You don't have to worry about me, though, I can take care of myself."

"Right," he mumbles, twisting his fingers together in his lap.

Feeling like the lowest scum of the Earth, I lean a little of my weight against him. I don't know how to redeem this conversation without digging myself further into a hole. The truth is, I've never had a relationship that lasted longer than a few weeks. The sum total of my adult relationship history begins and ends with Grindr. Zeke won't be able to relate to any of it, and I'd only embarrass myself further by bringing it up.

"You free this weekend?" I ask quietly. He shrugs, arm jostling my own. Neither of us have moved away from the other, our sides warm with shared body heat. We turn to look at each other at the same time, our faces close in the shared space of the bed.

"Yeah," Zeke says. The smile makes a reappearance, and I breathe a sigh of relief to see it. "Did you have something in mind?"

Slightly embarrassed to bring this up, but too committed

to turn back now, I clear my throat. "Actually, I was wondering if you'd want to come to the game? It's a home game on Saturday. I could get you tickets. Only if you want to go, though. No pressure."

Zeke sits up, turning toward me. Disappointed that he moved, and we're no longer touching, I frown at him. He retaliates with a smile.

"I'd love to come! Can I bring Jefferson? How cold is it in there?"

"Sure, I can get you two tickets. You can bring anyone you want. And yeah, you might want to wear a hoodie or something." I eye his skinny arms. "Or maybe a jacket. You might get cold, just sitting there."

"Okay! This will be so fun." He smiles wide, as though our earlier disagreement never happened. Perhaps it's just that easy for Zeke: never holding onto grudges, or giving grievances more time than they're worth. "I need to get a jersey."

"A jersey?"

"Yeah, to support you!" Zeke's eyes are wide and bright with excitement. Something warm and fuzzy curls up in my chest at the words. The thought of seeing him wearing my jersey is dizzying.

"Uhm...yeah, you could wear my jersey, if you want." My voice sounds husky, and I hasten to clear it. "But just so you know, that's kind of a thing that people do when they're together."

"Oh. That makes sense." He laughs, shaking his head at himself.

"But we could get you a shirt," I say quickly. "A SCU Hockey one. Or you could borrow one of my hoodies—I have dozens."

I'm obsessed with the thought of him wearing my clothes. It'll be huge on him, and nobody but the two of us will know it's mine. Maybe it'll smell like him when he gives it back.

"That's perfect. Thanks! I'm excited. I'll have to get a book from the library ahead of time. *Hockey for Simpletons*, or something."

I laugh, climbing off the bed to go to my closet. I make sure to keep my face turned away from Zeke so he can't see the flinch from the twinge of pain. Rifling through the hangers, I pull out the smallest hoodie I have. It's from my freshman year, when I was two inches shorter and thirty pounds lighter. It's soft and faded from use, but the logo is still clearly visible on the front. I hand it to Zeke, wordlessly. He lifts it to his face and inhales, causing my stomach to clench painfully. He needs to stop doing things like that—I don't do unrequited crushes, and this is fast becoming one.

"Smells good, like you." He eyes me, grinning. "Well, when you're not sweaty, that is."

"Wait until you smell me after a game. I'll make sure not to shower in the locker room this weekend; give you the full experience."

He wrinkles nose adorably. "Please don't. I think I'll be okay without the full experience."

Flopping back on the bed next to him, I stretch out and pillow my head on my arms. He's looking down at me, hoodie still clutched in his hands. There is a pensive look on his face that has me narrowing my eyes.

"Zeke. We're not talking about anal fissures any longer. Never again."

He raises his eyebrows and looks away with a huff. "Okay! Okay. I won't bring it up again, I promise."

I'm staring at his face so I see the way his eyes bounce to

me and away again. He sighs, chest rising and falling dramatically. Reaching a hand up, I pat him on his back, lightly.

"Thanks, though. For being my friend." I can feel my face burn, slightly, as I say this—embarrassed, even though I mean it. I've not had a lot of solid friendships in my life, so I know a good one when I see it.

Another sigh, as Zeke reaches over to my bedside table and grabs the book. Regretfully, I drop my arm back down and rest it on my stomach. It would be weird, to keep touching him when there isn't any reason. He opens up the book and pauses to reorient himself with our location. When he starts reading, I close my eyes and let myself enjoy it. It's the only thing from the evening that doesn't hurt.

9

Zeke

JEFFERSON'S EYES are wide as he looks around us. I can see his lips move as he says something to me, but I can't hear his words over the music in the arena. I lean closer to him.

"What?" I shout.

"Is the whole game like this." He waves his hands to encompass the flashing lights and blaring music. It feels like we're at a rave.

"No, this is just the intro," I assure him. I wish I had thought to bring a water bottle. I have a feeling I'm going to need it after tonight.

The music stops and the light returns to normal. The rink doesn't get any quieter, though. If anything, the volume rises as the game begins; the people around us are all sporting SCU hockey gear and are screaming with the bloodthirstiness of Vikings as one of the opposing players is hit into the wall in front of us.

"Good lord," Jefferson says, as the glass sways dangerously.

Leaning forward in my seat, I scoot all the way to the edge and point to the goal on the left side. "That's Carter."

"Yes, thank you, I was able to figure out which goalie was ours," he says dryly.

I keep my eyes on Carter while simultaneously stabbing an elbow into Jefferson's ribs. He looks ridiculously large in his goalie pads, all puffed up like a Pillsbury dough boy. He's also, I notice, remarkably flexible; a great deal of his goalie moves seem to involve doing the splits. I'd been impressed with his ability to do this when I'd watched his games online, but now I'm *really* impressed. It's impossible to keep track of the puck, and I've got the benefit of a raised seat—I can't imagine how hard Carter has to work to stay focused on that little rubber disc.

I clench my fingers on my knees as Carter somehow catches a shot from midair and slaps it down to the ice. The fans around us cheer, but I can hear a few boos speckled in as well. Jefferson turns around in his seat, affronted.

"Are people booing?" he asks.

"Yeah, probably the other team's fans."

"Well, that doesn't seem very sportsmanlike." He turns back around, and shakes his head in disappointment. Carter told me the heckling and booing was all part of the game, but I'm with Jefferson. I want our team to win, obviously, but I'm not going to verbally abuse the other side to get there. They're working just as hard as our players.

"Good lord," Jefferson mumbles again, as we watch Carter try to defend his net while the opposing team fires shots and skates too close to him for comfort. "This is rather nerve wracking, isn't it? I realize they have pads, but Jesus. Did you hear that announcer? Fifty-seven miles per hour!"

"I know," I agree. My heart has been pounding since we got here and my fingers ache from clenching them too tightly.

It seems to me that everyone is getting far too close to Carter. I'd thought that the blue area painted by the goal was off-limits for anyone but the netminder, but apparently, I was wrong. The opposing team has skated through it multiple times, and during their last attempt on goal one guy was directly behind Carter—practically inside the net. I'd done enough research to know that the goalie wasn't supposed to be interfered with, but my definition of that must be different than everyone else's. If you ask me, there is a great deal of interfering going on.

When the period ends with the score tied at zero, the team skates toward a hallway that I assume takes them to the locker room. Carter is the last to get to the bench, where he joins Vasel, who's waiting for him. Before he steps off the ice, he turns and looks in our direction. I raise a hand even though he can't possibly see me from that far away. He turns away and follows his teammates to the locker room. Beside me, Jefferson chuckles. I look over at him and find him watching me with an amused expression on his face.

"What?" I ask, a little defensively.

"Nothing. I'm just surprised, is all. That you and Carter Morgan seem to get along so well."

Immediately, I have an urge to protect Carter. "Why? Because Carter isn't as friendly as everyone else? I've already told you, he's really nice and a good guy."

Jefferson's eyebrows rise at my waspish tone. "Actually, no.

I'm surprised that *you* have gotten friendly with him in such a short amount of time."

I stare at my best friend in silence, confused and a little bit hurt. "What do you mean?"

"Zeke!" he says, turning toward me. "We met freshman year, first day of move-in, remember? I spent months—*months*—trying to get you to come out with me to a movie, or a party, or dinner, and you never would. And yet here you are, going on grand day-dates with Carter Morgan every weekend and then coming to watch him play a sport you have zero interest in. I've never seen you warm to somebody so fast, and I'm not just saying that because he looks like an ex-con. I'm saying that as your best friend who had to work very hard to earn that title."

I look out at the ice, noting that there are still a few minutes left in the intermission. I hadn't realized it before, but everything he's saying is true. I'm usually a little more discerning with whom I spend my time with. I like to take things slow, get to know people bit by bit before I commit to more. It's not that I want people to *earn* my friendship necessarily, but that I want to make sure they're someone who's going to stick around if I get attached. Too often, people give up and move on, preferring fast relationships to meaningful ones. With Carter, all of that seems to have gone out of the window.

"I don't know, I just...he felt right, is all." I blush as I say this, the tips of my ears burning. There's no better way to explain it, though. Carter was inevitable.

"Do you even have anything in common? What do you talk about?"

The teams retake the ice, and I watch as Carter goes through some quick warm-ups. I twist my fingers together to keep from waving at him again. I *really* want him to know I'm here. He'd bought the tickets and left them at will-call, texting me to let me know it was okay if I didn't make it, but there were tickets waiting if I did. He was giving me an out if I'd decided that I didn't want to spend my Saturday evening at a hockey game. My stomach had twisted unpleasantly, and I'd hurried to text him back and confirm that I would be at the game no matter what. I hope he saw the message before he took to the ice.

The game has restarted and SCU has the puck. Carter is bent over, resting his forearms on his massive leg pads as he watches the action on the other side of the ice. I think about Jefferson's question; *do* we have anything in common? No. The truth is we don't have anything in common except living quarters. And yet, we never seem to run out of things to talk about.

"I guess we don't, really. But we talk about a lot of stuff—everything. When we went to the zoo, I told him all sorts of animal facts."

He smiles at that, knowing how much I love watching documentaries and learning about animals. "Sounds like fun."

"It *was* fun. He's a good listener." I tuck my hands into the sleeves of Carter's hoodie. I had to roll them back in order to use my hands. "I really like him."

"Well, I'm glad. I'm happy it worked out for you."

We're interrupted, then, by someone from our team scoring. We climb to our feet and cheer with everyone else; the crowd barely has time to sit down before SCU scores again. This time, I cheer a little louder as Vasel skates down the bench, tapping the gloves of his teammates. Carter, on the other end of the ice, skates out of his goal and back again as though he's stretching his legs.

The game gets a little more violent after that—the opposing team trying to fight their way back from a 0-2 deficit. I flinch every time someone is slammed into the wall; the glass shakes dangerously, like it's one good hit away from shattering. I'm eternally grateful that nobody can hit Carter. I'm not sure my nerves could take it.

When the game ends with an SCU win, I stand up and cheer as loud as I can for Carter. He let in one goal, but as far as I'm concerned, he played perfectly. The rest of the team lines up and take turns congratulating him by his net—tapping their helmets against his, or giving him a hug. Once the entire team skates by him, he's the last to head off toward the bench.

"Well, that's oddly precious," Jefferson notes, watching the procession of teammates hugging Carter. I nod, keeping my eyes on him until he's out of sight and in the locker room. We join the queue of people walking up the stairs to exit the arena. I stick close to my friend, not wanting to be separated in the sea of bodies. Before he can head toward the nearest exit, I tug on the back of his shirt to get his attention.

"Do you think we could meet Carter?"

He stops abruptly and I bump into his back. People walk around us, shooting us disgruntled looks. He pulls me to the side to stand against a wall where we won't be disrupting the flow of traffic.

"Sure, do you know where to go?" he asks, and both of us look around as though expecting Carter to coalesce from thin air.

"Uhm...maybe we should ask someone." I eye an usher. Jefferson waves me forward. Sighing, I approach the man. He was the same usher who'd helped us find our seats earlier. Catching his eye, I smile in what I hope is a trustworthy way. "Hi. Uhm, I'm—well, we—are with one of the players? Carter Morgan?"

I try to sound confident, like I know what I'm doing, but each sentence comes out as a question. The man eyes me and smiles, kindly. I must look nonthreatening, because he places a hand on my shoulder and bends down to speak to me so he doesn't have to shout. "Are you needing to know how to get to the locker rooms?"

"Yes," I respond in relief.

Motioning for Jefferson to join us, the usher sets off at a fast pace. I'm practically jogging, trying to keep up with the man, and by the time we reach the locker rooms I'm out of breath. Before I can stop him, he bangs a fist on the door and sticks his head inside to call for Carter. Blushing furiously, I tuck my hands into the front pocket of his hoodie and wish I could will myself into invisibility. Beside me, Jefferson has an amused expression on his face.

"All right, son, he's on his way over." The usher looks at me and smiles kindly. I nod, managing a small squeak of thanks.

As promised, Carter flings open the door a moment later. It bangs against the opposite wall and I hear a few voices call out a complaint from inside. He's scowling until he sees us standing in the hallway; his eyes widen and his lips part slightly, surprised.

"Zeke," he says, stepping out and letting the door close behind himself. He doesn't sound displeased.

I take a good look at him, my own eyes widening for a different reason. He's half undressed, sporting padded shorts that are held up by a pair of suspenders over his shoulders.

He's wearing the sort of skin-tight shirt that leaves absolutely nothing to the imagination; it's short sleeved, showing off the flow of ink down his arms. He's so sweaty, the hallway lights reflect off his damp neck and face. I swallow, audibly. I believe I understand why hockey players are considered sexy.

Probably noticing that I've lost the ability to form coherent sentences, Jefferson speaks up. "Good game!"

"Thanks," Carter grunts, glancing at him and then back to me. His eyes skate over my face, uncertainly. I've been staring at him blankly, but quickly put a smile on. He relaxes, visibly. "Did you have fun?"

"We had a blast," I tell him. Before I can second guess myself, I step forward and wrap my arms around his middle.

He jolts, and I have a moment of panic when I think he won't return the hug before his arms come around me. It's a gentle hug—one of his hands cups my shoulder and the other rests safely on my mid back. I can feel him inhale, his chest expanding against my cheek before he lets it out slow. He is disgustingly sweaty and very large.

"You stink," I tell him, loosening my arms. He drops his own so quickly, it makes me wonder if he's uncomfortable. I step back far enough to see his face and grin up at him. He scowls.

"Yeah, sorry, I just played sixty minutes of hockey so I might have sweated a little bit." He nudges me to let me know he's playing around. I want to hug him again. "Glad you came."

He clears his throat when he says this, voice gruff with embarrassment. "Me too."

"Me too," Jefferson says, making me jump. I'd forgotten he was still standing there. Judging by Carter's expression, so had he. Jefferson notices, and eyes us with a sardonic twist to his mouth. "I'll head out, leave you guys to it."

"Oh, you don't have to go—" My ears burn in embarrassment. *Did you really just forget your best friend was standing right there?* "I can..."

I trail off, looking at Carter. Jefferson laughs softly, and shakes his head. "I've got some homework I need to get done. Will you be okay to get a ride home?"

He looks between Carter and I. I open my mouth to answer but Carter cuts me off, running a hand over his sweaty head.

"Give me fifteen minutes to shower and change, okay? I'll meet you back out here. We can head home together."

This had obviously been what Jefferson had been trying to engineer, based on the glint in his eye and the smirk on his face. He reaches out a hand to me, placing it on my shoulder and squeezing gently. Looking at Carter, he says: "Thank you for the tickets. It was a good time."

We watch him stroll off down the hall the way we came. Carter, pawing again at his hair, looks at me when he reaches his other hand back for the door handle.

"Fifteen minutes," he promises, swinging the door wide so it bounces of the wall. He kicks a foot back to catch it before it can hit him in the back on the rebound. "I'll be right back, okay?"

Nodding, I walk a little way down the hallway and press myself back against the wall. It's only minutes later that the first of his teammates comes out of the locker room; a pair of guys make their way loudly down the hall, laughing and jostling together, and still obviously enjoying their win. They ignore me completely, as though I were simply a part of the wall. This happens several more times, until a very tall man in a suit stops abruptly and turns to me.

He's got a severe looking face, which isn't helped by the addition of a few small scars on his forehead. He looks *pissed*—an angry furrow indenting his brows and his eyes narrowed in a scowl. I have to crane my neck to look him in the eyes.

"May I help you with something?" he asks, evidently suspicious of a stranger lurking in this hallway.

"Oh, no, thank you," I mumble, "I'm waiting for Carter. Morgan? I'm waiting for Carter Morgan. The third."

I tack the last part on obliquely, unsure what the hell his hockey friends use to identify him. The man's eyebrows shoot up his forehead in surprise and he stops scowling at me quite so fiercely. There is an appraising look to his eyes now, like he's measuring me.

"I'm Nico Mackenzie, Carter's coach." He holds out a hand to me, and I shake it. His fingers are long and thin, and completely engulf my much smaller hand.

"Oh, hi!" I suddenly remember Carter's story about his aunt meeting his coach, and the excitement with which he told it. "Zeke Cassidy, Carter's roommate."

"Are you," he says, in a way that is less a question and more of a musing. "I'm glad to hear he found someone. How are things working out?"

"Great," I say, and smile at him. He has his hands tucked casually into the pockets of his dress pants and is listening to me so intently, I can't help but keep talking. "We always hang out on Sundays. We did mini golf one weekend, and then axe throwing the next. We've also gone to the zoo, which was really fun. I'm not sure what the plan is for this weekend, since it's Carter's turn to decide. Probably something crazy, like archery from horseback, or something."

Coach Mackenzie listens to this word vomit without once changing his expression until I mention that last part—his lips pull up in a small smile, and his face looks only half as frightening as before. Before he can reply, the locker room door opens and Carter steps into the hallway. He looks both ways, searching for me. When he sees me standing with his coach, his face breaks open into what I can only describe as happiness: a softening of his mouth and brow, and a widening of his eyes. He walks toward us, quickly.

"I've just been chatting with your friend," Coach Mackenzie says, when he stops next to me. His eyes travel between the two of us, consideringly. "Sounds as though the pair of you have been enjoying yourselves."

"Yeah. I know all sorts of shit about animals now, so if you ever have a need..." Carter trails off, tapping his temple and winking. The effect is slightly threatening, since he's back to his usual sour expression—like being winked at by an executioner.

"Mm. Well, you boys better get on your way home. Not going out tonight, I presume?" Coach Mackenzie looks at Carter as he talks, narrowing his eyes. This is voiced as a question, but is clearly a strong suggestion to *not* go out.

"Nope. We're going home. Right, Zeke?"

"Right," I scramble to assure Coach Mackenzie, who turns that piercing gaze back to me. This man is wasted as a hockey coach, he needs to be interviewing murder suspects for the FBI.

"Drive safe." He steps to the side to let us pass.

"See you, Coach. Say hi to Tony for me," Carter calls back

to him, as we walk down the hallway. We're still close enough to hear the massive sigh that is heaved behind us at these words. Carter smirks, and nudges me with his elbow. "Want to grab something to eat? I'm fucking starving."

10

Carter

"So, that's Coach Mackenzie? The one from your story?" Zeke asks, and I nod, mouth currently stuffed full of burrito. "Wow, he is *scary*."

Swallowing quickly so that I don't choke, I hack out a laugh. Coach Mackenzie is absolutely scary. I kind of love the guy. "Yeah, he is. But he's great. Like, a really great coach. And he's got a ton of NHL and AHL connections, so we're always having professional hockey players come by to practice. Here, look at this."

Dropping my burrito onto the little plastic tray and scattering rice over the table, I wipe my fingers clean and pull out my phone. It takes me barely a second to find the photo since I'd favorited it. Turning it around, I slide the phone over to Zeke.

"Wow!" he exclaims, staring intently down at the picture before looking back up at me with a sheepish expression. "I have no idea who those people are."

I laugh, shaking my head. How can you *not* know who Troy Nichols and Corwin Sanhover are? *God he's fucking cute.*

"The guy on the left, with the black hair? That's Troy Nichols. This," I point to Sanhover, "is Corwin Sanhover. They play for South Carolina's NHL team. They're, like, a really big fucking deal. And get this."

I lean toward Zeke, pressing my chest into the edge of the table. He mirrors the movement. If the pair of us were to move a little closer, we could kiss over the top of the table.

"Troy Nichols is gay." I wait for this to have an effect on him, but Zeke just stares at me. "He's a professional hockey player, Zeke! Literally the first gay player to come out in the league. He's pretty much a national hero."

"Oh, wow," he breathes, looking back down at the photo.

"That's not all." I reach over and swipe across the picture, changing it to one of Tony and I. "*This* is Tony. Well, Anthony Lawson, but I call him Tony. He's the goalie for South Carolina—he plays with those other two guys I showed you. And guess what? He's dating Coach Mackenzie."

I sit back and cross my arms, satisfied by the shocked look on Zeke's face. He looks back down at my phone, using his fingers to enlarge the photo and zoom in on our faces.

"This guy?" he asks incredulously. In the picture, Tony is smiling wide and has his arm flung over my shoulders. He's scruffy, and his hair is a little bit wild. Nobody would ever pair him with Coach Mackenzie, who could easily be mistaken for an undertaker.

"That guy," I confirm. Zeke zooms in on the picture again, but this time centers it over my face. He studies it for several long moments before he looks up at me over the table.

"You're smiling," he points out.

Frowning, I look at the picture. I cross my arms a little

tighter over my chest and shrug. "I guess so. What does that matter?"

"You never smile." Setting the picture back to rights, he taps lightly on Tony's face. "So, I'm guessing that's a pretty big deal, judging by your tone—two queer hockey players?"

"Oh, there's more than two. That's what's so cool. Troy Nichols came out and then there was just this," I roll my hands over one another in midair, "snowball effect. Other players started coming out, or just stopped hiding. Grayson Brody, who plays for Calgary, and two guys who play for Colorado. It's like...I don't know. It's just cool, that's all."

Self-conscious, I sit back against the seat again. I never talk this much. It's probably part of the reason Zeke and I get along so well—he can chatter away while I listen and only contribute to the conversation when needed. But talking about hockey always gets me going, and I want him to understand why this is a big deal.

"That sounds brave," Zeke says, and gratitude bubbles up inside me. I *knew* he'd get it. "I can't imagine it was easy for... Troy Nichols, to be the first one."

"God, right?" I shake my head. My eyes catch on my half-eaten burrito, reminding me that I need to eat. My stomach also chooses this moment to put in a reminder of its own. Snatching it up, I take a big bite and chew thoughtfully. "And he's good, Zeke. Like...probably the best player in the league, right now."

Zeke slides my phone back to me; I leave it on the table in favor of eating my burrito. Across from me, Zeke now has his own phone out and is tapping his thumbs rapidly across the screen like he's texting someone. I stare at him while he's distracted, my stomach clenching painfully. *He looks good in my hoodie.* When he looks back up at me, I glance away, ashamed to have been caught gawking at him.

"Did you know that he's married?" Zeke asks, bringing my attention back to his face. "Troy Nichols?"

"Oh, yeah, Coach Mackenzie went to the wedding with Tony." I screw up my face, thinking hard. "I don't actually know who Nichols is married to. Just a regular dude, I guess."

"Sam Jameson," he informs me, holding up his phone and showing me a photograph of a handsome blonde man standing next to Troy Nichols. I lean forward for a closer look. He's got friendly brown eyes and an adorable spray of freckles across his nose and cheeks. Standing next to his husband, he looks like the happiest man on planet earth. "It says he played hockey for Harvard and he was a goalie, like you."

I feel ridiculously pleased to find another point of similarity between me and Troy Nichols. I've begun thinking of Coach Mackenzie's connection with Tony and the rest of the guys as my own; every time I hear their names in the media, or watch their games, it feels like I'm hearing about my friends. A therapist would probably have a few things to say about me creating imaginary friendships, I suppose, but it's nobody else's business what happens in my own head.

Clearing my throat, I lean back and Zeke puts his phone back down. "Yeah, like me," I agree.

"They look so happy," he notes, glancing once more at the photograph before closing down the web browser. I'd just thought the same thing.

"Yeah." I feel sad, all of a sudden. Troy and Sam's happiness holding a mirror up to my own and making me realize that the only time I really, truly feel joyful is when I'm on the ice or with Zeke. "Thanks again, for coming to the game tonight. I uh...it was... Jesus, never mind. Thanks—that's all I'm trying to say."

What I'm trying to say is that I can count on one hand the number of people who have come to a game with the express purpose of watching *me* play. I'm trying to tell him that I thought about him the entire game, and felt like a better player because of it. It's different, winning for someone other than yourself. I want him to know a lot of things that I'm incapable of putting into words.

"Of course, Carter. I'll be at all of the home games," he plucks at the front of my hoodie, "as long as I can keep this for a little bit longer."

"You can keep it," I tell him, practically salivating over the thought. I really need to tone it down with the crushing-on-Zeke thing.

"Yeah?" He brightens, eyes glinting silver in the artificial light of the restaurant.

"It's all yours," I respond. He grins, shaking out the sleeves so that his hands are free to pick up his burrito and take a bite. It's the smallest piece of clothing I own, yet still far too big on him. I like that fact far, far more than I should.

We finish eating and make our way out of the restaurant. True to the promise we made to Coach Mackenzie, we head straight home. It's dark, and by the time we get there I've lost any remaining adrenaline from the game. I'm exhausted, and ready for bed. Unfortunately, I have yet another stupid ass book to read for class, and if I don't start it tonight, I'll never finish it in time. I want to ask Zeke if he'd mind reading a little bit to me, but am afraid he'll say no.

When we get upstairs, I peel off toward my room and immediately start changing into something comfortable. I hear a throat clear, from the doorway, and glance over to see

Zeke standing there. Unbuttoning my shirt, I maintain firm eye contact with him; I do *not* check him out. Not that there is much of him to check out, with his body swimming in my hoodie.

"What are we reading, tonight?" he asks, with a nod to the book face down on my bed.

Groaning, I pull my undershirt over my head and toss it to the floor. Grabbing a hoodie and sweatpants from the closet, I step into the bathroom to change since Zeke is in my room. I shout so he can still hear me from the bathroom. "I don't know, 1748 or some shit."

"Uhm," he pauses, and I can tell he's moved farther into the room by the way his voice is louder, "do you mean *1984*? By George Orwell?"

"That sounds right." I pull my pants up and shove open the bathroom door. Zeke is seated on the edge of my bed with the book in his lap. When I enter the room, he smiles and moves back to the head of the bed, stopping when his back hits the wall.

"Well, come on then," he coaxes, patting the bed.

I heave a sigh of relief, and climb up next to him. I lay down close enough that my arm touches his leg, and hold my breath, hoping he won't move away. When he starts reading without moving, I bite my lip to keep from smiling in triumph. I have to keep my eyes open as he goes, or this time I really am liable to fall asleep. I'm just so fucking *tired*.

He reads for a solid fifteen minutes before he takes a break. Keeping his place with his thumb, he slides down until he's lying next to me. He's no longer pressed against me, but this change of position is a definite improvement. I have to take several deep breaths through my nose, trying to keep from getting a hard-on. My body can only focus on the simple fact of Zeke lying next to me in bed, no matter how platonic the gesture really is.

He holds the book above his face and continues reading. I want to turn on my side and face him, watch his mouth as he speaks. I want to inch close enough to smell him, maybe drape an arm over his middle so I can feel the rise and fall of his stomach. Instead, I remain flat on my back, miserable with my thoughts of all the things I know I can't have.

I WAKE up and blink into the bright light. Lying on my side, I spend a few fraught moments trying to figure out where I am before I recognize I'm in my bedroom. Realizing I must have fallen asleep while Zeke was reading, I roll over to the other side and just barely stop myself from bumping into the sleeping form next to me.

Zeke is flat on his back, head turned toward me and mouth parted slightly. *1984* is resting on his stomach, as though he put it down with the intent to rest his eyes for a second. His dirty blonde hair is fanned out across the pillow, eyelashes fluttering against his cheek as he sleeps. Propped up on my elbow, I gaze down at him. White hot desire floods my system; the wanting is so strong, I can hardly breathe around it. Deciding that the best course of action will be to sneak out and let him sleep in my bed, I inch toward the edge of the mattress.

I'm almost off the bed when Zeke's eyes open and he makes a soft, sleepy sound. It takes him a second to focus on my face, and I tense, waiting for the moment when he realizes he fell asleep in my bed. He doesn't sit up in shock, but rubs a hand across his eyes and rolls onto his side to face me.

"I fell asleep," he says.

"We both did," I whisper back, and he smiles. "You can stay here, though. Go back to sleep."

I climb all the way off of the bed and pad softly over to the door, meaning to hit the lights on my way out of the room. Zeke's voice calls me back. I turn to find him pushed up on his elbow, watching me. He's replaced the book onto the nightstand.

"Where are you going?" he asks blearily.

"I'll go downstairs and sleep on the couch." He blinks at me, owlishly. "You can stay here, go back to sleep."

Before I can move, he brings me back again. "Carter. This is your room, I'm not kicking you out of your own room. You come back to bed and I'll go to my room, don't be ridiculous."

He grumbles something about sleeping on the couch, and sits up fully. Watching from my vantage point at the door, my stomach sinks. I don't want him to go back to his own room. He slides out of the bed, stretching his arms above his head and yawning. Leaning forward, he pulls back the covers for me. My throat tightens painfully, and I'm grateful that I can't speak around it or I might beg him to stay. He passes me on the way out the door, not looking the least bit embarrassed to have fallen asleep in my bed. Probably because, to him, we are nothing more than friends.

"G'night, Carter." He smiles up at me, soft and sleepy and tempting.

"Goodnight." I try to smile back, but can't seem to get my facial muscles to work.

Watching until he's across the hall and his door is closed behind him, I lean back and thunk my head against the door-frame. I think it might be time to admit I might be more than a little bit interested in Zeke. I wish I knew what the hell to do about it.

The next morning, I'm awake and out the door before Zeke. I have early classes today, followed by a late practice, which means I won't have to see him until later. Unfortunately, as it often does when you are wanting to avoid something—time seems to speed up, and soon enough I'm walking out of practice and dreading going home. I need to figure out how to act normally around Zeke, and today was not enough time to do so. I'm so in my head I barely even register somebody calling my name.

"What?" I snap, turning around and taking a quick step backward to stop Vasel from running into me. "Oh, sorry Vas. I didn't hear you."

He eyes me, frowning slightly. "Are you all right? You have seemed off all of today and you did not pay attention in class. Are you ill, perhaps?"

Yes, Vas, I have developed a crush on a skinny little nerd and it is making me physically ill. Thank you for noticing. "Uhm, no, I'm fine. Just distracted."

"I shall give you my notes, so that you do not fall behind in economics." He smiles at me and nods, as though the matter is settled.

"That would be great. Thanks."

He stares at me, not appearing to be mollified by this. He's cleverer than most people give him credit for. He's quiet, which people assume means that he's stupid and doesn't understand English well enough to join conversations. Really, it just means he's a good listener, and is a skilled observer.

"Are things well with your roommate? Zeke?" he asks.

"Things are well," I confirm. Vas waits, and I sigh, looking around the parking lot in agitation. He's a patient bastard, which means that if I don't come out with it, he'll only keep pestering me until I do. "If you must know, I've got a bit of a thing for him and I don't know what to do about it."

"Oh." Vasel's expression clears, eyes brightening. "This is simple. Ask him out on a date, yes?"

"Not yes. I can't just ask him out, he's not...he wouldn't..." I huff, frowning impatiently at my feet as I scuff a rock against the asphalt. How the hell do I explain this to him? "He's demi, so he's not attracted to me like that."

Vas cocks his head, puzzled. "Maybe I am not understanding. Why does this mean he is not attracted to you?"

"Because he's not going to form a sexual attraction to anyone unless he's already emotionally attached to them. I've only known him a few months, Vas. It's too quick." I think about the way Zeke was completely unaffected when he woke up in my bed last night. Unlike me, who was so worked up afterward that I couldn't fall back asleep until hours later.

"I think perhaps you are wrong, in this," Vas says kindly. "There is no timeframe for emotional attachment, yes? You are assuming it must take a long time, but this is not true. It is different, I think, for all."

Scowling, I think through what he said. He's right—I had been correlating emotional attachment with a long period of time. "So...what? You think I should just ask him out?"

"Well, yes. This is what one does."

"I don't," I say baldly. Vas sighs expansively.

"You prefer picking people up on dating apps because then you do not have to worry about being rejected," he tells me, and then shrugs when I raise my eyebrows at him.

"Jesus, whatever you say, Doctor."

One of our teammates calls out for Vas from across the

parking lot and he raises a friendly hand in greeting. There is a nervous anticipation churning in my gut. Could it really be so easy as to just go home and ask Zeke out? I'm not familiar with this sort of dating, much preferring, as Vas pointed out, the shadowy and altogether safer world of internet hook-ups. There is a lot less on the line when you're dealing with a random stranger.

"So," Vas turns back to me and we start walking toward where our cars are parked side-by-side, "what have we decided? Are we going to do it?"

"I guess...so, what? I just ask him to go on a date with me?"

"Yes." He nods encouragingly and declares: "New experiences are good for us."

Snorting, I toss my bag into the back of my car and slam the trunk shut. My heart is beating a staccato rhythm in my chest and my fingers are tingling with eagerness. I'm going to do it. I'm going to go home and ask Zeke out on a date.

11

Zeke

The door slams so loudly, the walls shake. In dismay, I look down at the math homework I've just mutilated when I startled. Sighing, I set about trying to fix it with an eraser when I hear my name being shouted from down below.

"Zeke!" Carter calls, evidently trying to ascertain whether or not I am home.

"Up here!" I shout back, dropping the eraser onto my desk and sliding the chair back. I'm just standing up and stretching my arms over my head when Carter steps into the room. He got here so fast he must have jogged up the stairs.

"Hey," he says.

"Hello, there," I respond cheerfully. He looks a little flushed and he's rocking back and forth on the balls of his feet as though he's got pent up energy. *Didn't he just come from practice?* "How's it going?"

"Fine." He bites the word out, staring at me and chewing

on his lip. He's acting decidedly strange. Before I can open my mouth to ask if he has a fever or something, he continues. "So, hey, I was wondering, if you're not doing anything Friday night, would you want to go to dinner? With me. Dinner, with me?"

I stare at him, quizzically. What a completely normal but oddly peculiar request. "Sure, dinner on Friday sounds great. But don't you have games every Friday?"

"Not this Friday," he says quickly, almost before I can finish my question. "This Friday we are free, and Coach actually gave us the night off of practice. And I get out early from classes, too, so..."

Carter trails off, scowling and looking vaguely around my bedroom. He seems a little worked up about something, but it can't possibly be the prospect of dinner. We eat together all the time. Was he worried I'd say no?

"Oh, well great. Dinner it is then." I smile at him and watch as he physically deflates. He lets out a whoosh of air and his shoulders relax. There is even something of a smile playing around his mouth.

"Great," he echoes. "It's a date, then."

He nods decisively, and opens his mouth as though he wants to say something else. Deciding against it, he casts his eyes around my room until they land on my desk. Seeing my homework spread across the surface, he backs slowly toward the door.

"I'll leave you alone."

"Oh, you're fine, you can stay—" But he's already gone.

Scratching a hand across my chest, I shake my head in amusement. I wonder what *that* was all about. Unfortunately, I don't have time to wonder long, because this homework won't do itself. Casting another glance at the doorway in case

Carter comes back, I sit down in my desk chair and get back to work.

JEFFERSON SLIDES into the seat next to mine in the lecture hall and drops his bag onto the floor with a thump. We're early, as we usually are, so few seats are filled besides ours. He drops his head back against the seat and groans dramatically. The sound echoes through the open space and draws the eyes of the scattered students in the room. I jab him with my elbow.

"Shush," I admonish.

"This isn't a library," he tells me, but lifts his head and turns to face me in his seat. "I need you."

"Uh-oh."

"You know how Tessa is part of the drama club? Well, we agreed to go to this party at one of their houses tonight but Tess isn't feeling well and she can't go. So, one would think I don't have to go, right? Wrong. Apparently, I am still obligated to attend which means I am coming to you on bended knee and asking that you *please* do not make me go to this party alone." He widens his eyes and leans toward me. "Do not leave me alone with the drama people."

"I can't tonight. Carter and I are going to dinner, remember?" I remind him, laughing at his hangdog expression.

"Fuck!" One of the students in the first row turns around and glares at us. "I completely forgot about that. Bring Carter! Bring the whole hockey team, I don't care."

"Well, I don't know...I could ask, but—"

"Come on, Zeke, you never come out to parties. It'll be fun! Seriously, bring Carter. Please come."

Sighing, I bite my lip and watch a few more students

trickle into the hall. It *has* been a long time since I've gone to one of Jefferson's parties with him—I'm long overdue on my best friend duties. And maybe Carter won't mind a slight change of plan; we'd still be hanging out, which was the whole point of grabbing dinner together on his free night. It'll be a win-win situation, with both Jefferson and Carter happy with the outcome.

"Okay, I'll ask him when I get home from class. He's already done for the day since he finishes early on Friday."

Jefferson throws his arms up in the air and lets out a whoop. This time, the girl in the front row tells him to be quiet but my friend ignores her. He beams at me.

"Fantastic. Thank you, thank you, *thank you*. You have saved me from the unimaginable boredom of an evening spent talking about Shakespeare. You, my friend, are a hero."

Amused, I turn to an empty page in my notebook. "I didn't say we'd be going for sure, I said I'd *ask*."

I walk home after class, backpack over my shoulders and Carter's hoodie looped through the straps. It's definitely getting colder, but still not quite winter in South Carolina. It is, without a doubt, the best time to live here—when the oppressive heat gives way to a semblance of autumn and you have to dress in layers. I'm in a ridiculously good mood when I step through the front door and drop my bag.

"Hey, Carter!" I call out as I head up the stairs toward my room. I'd taken a little longer walking home today to enjoy the nice weather, so it's already past five in the evening.

At the top of the stairs, I pause and poke my head into Carter's room. He emerges from the bathroom with a towel slung across his hips, arms raised as he uses another to vigorously dry his hair. When he sees me standing in the doorway, the corners of his mouth curve up the tiniest bit. I try not to stare at his naked torso, but it's not easy. The play of muscle beneath skin is fascinating; I want to walk over and press my hand to him to see how it feels.

"Hi, Zeke." There is a strange undercurrent of nervousness to his tone, like he's fighting back tension. I lean against the doorway and smile at him, trying to put him at ease. He's been acting strange all week, looking away swiftly when I catch him watching me and forgetting to scowl. It's starting to make me nervous. "I'm just going to change and then I'll be ready, okay?"

"Okay." I stand up straight. "I'll go shower and change, and then meet you downstairs."

Leaving him to it, I go to my room and toss Carter's hoodie onto the bed. I probably don't need to shower since I've done nothing but sit in class all day, but I might as well. I linger in the shower, too, cranking the heat and steaming up the bathroom. I'm actually looking forward to this party—it's been a long time since I've gone to one, and it'll be fun having Carter tag along.

Putting on a clean pair of jeans and a faded black t-shirt, I head downstairs. It took me a lot longer than expected to get ready; Carter is standing at the kitchen island, waiting for me. I stop dead in the doorway and stare at him. Unlike me, he's obviously gone to some lengths with his appearance tonight: fitted dark wash jeans and a long-sleeve Henley in a dark olive-green color. His hair looks freshly cut and is shining gold in the kitchen light. Even from across the room I can smell something masculine and earthy, like he put on cologne or aftershave. Probably feeling the weight of my eyes on him, he looks over and smiles. It's the same smile I saw in the picture he showed me with Anthony Lawson, but the first time I've seen it in real life. It makes me want to wrap my arms around him and *squeeze*.

Realizing that I've done nothing but stand here and stare at him, I clear my throat. "Hey, so question for you. Do you think we could adjust our plan for the night a bit? There's a party Jefferson wants me to go to, and I thought we could check it out. It might be fun. Something different than what we usually do, anyway."

The smile fades slowly. There is a deep indent between his brows where they are scrunched together in confusion. "Oh. Well, yeah, that's...is that what you want to do?"

He looks away from me and glances down at something he's got pulled up on his phone. I can't place his tone, but it sounds too close to *hurt* for comfort. Butterflies erupt in my stomach, and my scalp itches uncomfortably.

"We don't have to stay long. We could just stop by after dinner, maybe? Or..."

I trail off, wanting him to fill in the blanks for me. When his eyes meet mine again, they are carefully blank. His voice is wary, like he's working hard to modulate his tone. "If you want to go, then we'll go. What time were you going to meet your friend?"

"He said around eight, but we could get there whenever. After dinner. We can do both." I am desperately trying to figure out where I went wrong here. Carter's smile is gone, and I'm afraid I won't be able to get it back.

"Yeah." He looks down at his phone again, which is lying flat on the island and has a webpage up. "I just need to make a quick call, and then we can go."

He snatches up his phone and steps carefully around me, not meeting my eyes. I want to grab his arm and apologize. I'm unsure exactly what went wrong, but sometime between my arrival home and now, I've clearly fucked up. But his back is rigid and I'm not brave enough to touch him without permission. I let him pass, watching as he steps out into the backyard and brings his phone to his ear. It's quick, and barely a minute passes before he's coming back inside.

"All right," he says. "Ready to go?"

"Sure. Yeah. And hey, we don't have to go to the party, okay? Let's just do whatever you had planned. Let's just do dinner."

I'm trailing behind him as we walk toward the garage. He holds the door open for me—gently, which sends another bout of nerves scurrying down my spine—and then steps around me to open the car door for me as well. He doesn't answer until we're inside the vehicle.

"It's okay, Zeke. We'll go grab something to eat and then go hang out with your friends." He doesn't look at me when he says this, as he's concentrating on backing down the driveway, but he doesn't sound angry. My nerves calm, slightly.

"All right." I clench my hands together on my lap and look unseeing out the windshield. Thank god Jefferson will be at this party. I need to talk to someone who understands social cues better than I do.

He takes us to one of our favorite Mexican restaurants. It's a little hole in the wall joint, where the floor is sticky and the silverware is tarnished, but the food is phenomenal. The old woman who leads us to a table fawns over Carter. Usually, when we come here, he's just come from practice and is dressed accordingly. Today, he looks like an Abercrombie model.

"Oh, Mr. Carter you look so nice! So handsome." She's holding his hand, tugging him along to one of the many empty tables. "You are such good boy. I introduce you to my granddaughter."

I bite my lip to keep from laughing at the look on Carter's face. She pulls out our chairs for us and pats his shoulder as he sits down, mumbling something in rapid Spanish.

"Thank you," I tell her, as she pats my hand on her way to the kitchen.

"I bring you something good to eat," she calls back, not bothering to take our order. Turning and grinning at Carter, I nudge his foot beneath the table to get his attention. He's got his Carter-mask in place, frowning at me over the table.

"You do look nice," I tell him. The V at the neck of the shirt keeps drawing my eyes. I can see part of his collarbone.

"Thanks," he mumbles, looking uncomfortable.

"How was class, today?" I ask, and he shrugs. Carter hates class.

"Fine. You?"

"Good!" Leaning forward, I launch into an in-depth description of one of my lectures. Carter also hates talking about himself—the best way to get him to relax is to fill the silence for him, so that's exactly what I'm going to do. I can't get over the feeling that I've done something wrong.

"I don't understand a single word you just said," he tells me, when I come up for air. I laugh.

Our food arrives and we lapse into silence as we eat. I sneak glances up at him every now and then, trying to gauge his facial expression. Maybe I should just ask him what was wrong, back in the kitchen. I'll never be able to figure it out on my own. Opening my mouth to do just that, I'm interrupted by Carter's phone ringing. He glances at the caller ID before declining the call.

"Who was that?" I ask, curious.

"No one. Just the restaurant calling me back, I guess." I watch as he switches his phone to silent and slides it into his pocket.

"The restaurant?"

He glances up at me and back down to his plate. Scowling, he pops a bite of food in his mouth and chews slowly. "Yeah. I had reservations at a place on the coast, so I'm sure they were calling back to try and reschedule."

Setting my fork down, I press my hands against the table. "You had reservations somewhere? For tonight?"

"Yeah. It's not a big deal."

"Oh, Carter. I'm sorry, I didn't realize." No wonder he looked put out, earlier, he might have had to pay to reserve a table. "We should have just gone, instead of doing this stupid party. I'm really sorry."

"It's *fine*, Zeke, seriously. I just want to do whatever you want to do tonight, okay? You tell me."

I frown, looking down at my hands and scratching a fingernail against the plastic top of the table. "Let's not stay long at the party. We'll go, say hi to Jefferson, and leave."

"Sure," he agrees, and reaches a hand out to the young girl who just walked up with our bill. He glances at it, jots down the amount he wants added for a tip, and then hands it back to her with his credit card. I wait until she's out of earshot.

"What do I owe you?" I ask. He looks at me, incredulous.

"I'm paying."

"We always split," I remind him. I'd finally talked him into letting me pay my half of the bill whenever we went out to eat, and I wasn't about to lose that ground now.

"Not tonight," he says firmly. When his receipt is handed to him, he shoves it roughly into his pocket and stands up. I want to ask to see it, so I can Venmo him my half, but he looks...strange, again. There is a barely discernible air of melancholy around him tonight, the downward tilt to his mouth lacking its usual anger as it leans toward sadness.

"Is something wrong?" I cannot take it any longer. Guessing what is happening inside his head is getting me nowhere, and obviously I can't do anything right tonight.

"No."

He holds open the car door for me again, waiting until I'm seated before closing it gently. I wait until his own seatbelt is clicked into place before turning as much as I'm able and facing him.

"*Something* is wrong." For a split second I think he's going to tell me. He glances at me and back to the road, fingers clenching around the steering wheel.

"Do you have an address for this party?" he asks. I pull it up on my phone and wordlessly hold it out to him. I've never been comfortable with confrontation or silence, so I keep up a cheerful stream of chatter all the way to the party and hope that whatever is bothering Carter will be forgotten. By the time we've pulled up in front of the house, I've teased a couple of laughs out of him and the set of his mouth is less severe.

Unfortunately, all of that goes out the window when we arrive. Carter walks a step behind me as we enter the party, scowl firmly in place and unfriendliness radiating off of him like heat waves. It's later than I had expected to get here, so the front room is full of people milling about and lounging on the furniture. It looks more like a book club meeting than a party.

"Zeke! Carter! You guys made it," Jefferson's voice calls out and he threads his way over to us. Carter is standing so closely to me, I can feel his chest brushing my shoulder blades when he breathes.

"Hey, yeah, we made it." I smile at my friend and hear Carter mumble a greeting of his own.

"Do you guys want something to drink? Have a seat."

I look around. There are no places left to sit down, unless one wanted to sit on the floor. Instead, I lead Carter over to a group of people standing by the far wall; luckily, I know all of them. The moment we join the group and I introduce Carter, I'm pulled into a conversation about a recent article that was published in National Geographic Magazine about astrophysics.

Carter is silent as a statue beside me; he's very obviously being left out of the conversation, and a part of me wonders if they're doing it on purpose. Jefferson, who's thinking the same thing, judging by his furtive glances toward us, makes a wildly transparent effort to change the subject.

"So, anybody going to the hockey game tomorrow? Zeke, Tessa, and I have tickets."

Everyone looks at him like he's just asked them if they'd be up for a bout of freedom running. Gemma, whom I know from chess club, shakes her head. "No. Do you play hockey, Carter?"

"Yeah," he replies, and they all stare at him as they wait for him to say something more. He doesn't, so I rush to fill the dead space.

"He's the goalie. The team has only had two losses, this season. Everyone keeps talking about how this is the best hockey team SCU has had since the club was formed."

I can't hide the note of pride that threads its way through my words. I want them all to understand how hard he works, and what an accomplishment it is to play as well as he is.

"You guys should come to a game, sometime," Jefferson adds. "Seriously, it's a lot of fun. The fans are wild, the game is wild. Everything is *wild*."

Carter huffs a laugh, so softly that I doubt anybody heard it but me. I turn my head to smile at him.

"Well, maybe I'll come with you, sometime," Gemma says, clearly trying to sound enthusiastic but failing. She looks from me to Carter, who is standing behind me and well within my personal bubble. "I didn't realize that you were seeing one of the hockey players, Zeke. You've never struck me as a sports fan."

"Oh, we're just roommates," I correct. "And I wouldn't say I'm much of a sports fan, per se. More of a Carter fan. But I'm getting there."

Jefferson makes a choked noise, drawing my attention to his face. He's not looking at me, however, but over my shoulder to where Carter is looming above me. I turn to look as well, locking eyes with him.

"I'm going to get something to drink," he says quietly. "Do you want anything?"

"No, I'm good. Thank you."

I watch him until he's disappeared into the kitchen before turning back to the group. Jefferson is staring at me and frowning. Now that Carter is gone, the conversation reverts back to the physics article but I'm distracted by the look on my friend's face. He tips his head slowly to the left in a clear invitation. It takes us a few seconds to break away from the group, but the moment we do he grasps my elbow lightly and leads me out of earshot of the others.

"What's up?" I ask.

"You tell me," Jefferson counters. "What is going on with you and Carter?"

"Nothing is going on. Well," I reach up to push my hair out of my eyes, "actually, something has been off all night. All week, kind of. I think something is bothering him, but he won't tell me what it is. Also, I messed up his plan for the night by asking him to come here. He apparently had dinner reservations, so I feel kind of awful about that."

Jefferson's eyes close and he takes a deep breath like he's centering himself. "Okay, hold on. Were you going on a *date*, tonight?"

"No, we went out to dinner."

"How did he ask you if you wanted to grab dinner? The exact words."

"He just said that, *do you want to have dinner with me* or something like that. And I said yeah, because we always have dinner together when he doesn't have a game, and he said *it's a date*."

"You're on a date," he declares.

"No, you don't get it. We eat out together all the time, it's not as though—"

"Zeke!" Jefferson holds his hands out to the side in exasperation. "He used the word *date*, for fuck's sake. The man made a reservation! You cannot tell me that he usually dresses like that." He points to the kitchen, where Carter has yet to return from. He holds a hand in front of himself and starts ticking off a list on his fingers. "He asked you out to dinner and made sure to use the word date so that you would know it was meant to be different than usual. He dressed nicely. He made a reservation. And, last but not least, he looked like you punched him just now when you said *he's just my roommate*. You are on a fucking date."

I stare at him in dismay and think through what he said, trying to find holes in his argument. There aren't any. I feel itchy and uncomfortable all of a sudden, my back hot under the fabric of my shirt. I feel foolish.

"Oh no," I say.

"Oh no," Jefferson agrees. "That poor guy thought you'd agreed to go on a date with him, and then you turned around and invited the drama club along." He waves a hand at the room.

"I didn't mean to do that, I just thought we were..." I press my palms to my eye sockets, trying to block out the room. "I'm an idiot."

"Well, no, but you are a bit clueless. Oh, Zeke, I'm sorry. I shouldn't have made you come to this stupid party."

"I'd only have been on a date without realizing it was a date!" I rub a hand over my chest. My heart is beating rather painfully.

"Do you *want* it to be a date?" He drops his voice and loses the exasperated tone. "With Carter? Are you interested in him, like that?"

"Jesus, I don't know! He's not...have you seen him? He shouldn't want to date someone like me, it makes no sense."

A chorus of laughter from across the room draws our attention. I scan the room, looking for the recognizable form of Carter, but he's nowhere to be found. When we'd first arrived, he'd been standing so close to me that I could feel the warmth of him through my clothing. Now, the cold absence is an unwelcome shock to my system. *How could I have misunderstood so catastrophically?*

"That's not what I asked. I think you need to be very certain of how *you* feel about *him* before you do anything else. If you don't like him like that, you need to tell him. Either way, you owe the guy an apology. And so do I. Good lord, what a mess."

I nod, miserably. I've never been good at navigating the world of dating. Too often, the people I become interested in don't reciprocate or they move on long before I'm at the point where physical attraction occurs. It all seems too much. I'd never have considered Carter to even be an option. Carter, who uses dating apps to pick up random men and women; Carter, who possesses the type of physical beauty that could get him anyone he wanted. Someone like him could never want someone like me.

"I better go."

"Me too," Jefferson says. "You go find your hockey player, I'll tell everyone we're heading out. No more parties for you and I—we cannot be trusted."

I laugh, weakly. He brushes a hand on my shoulder as I turn around and set off to find Carter. It becomes very clear, however, after fifteen minutes of fruitless searching, that he's no longer in the house. Stepping outside with the intent to check the car in case he's sitting in there, I find him on the porch. I hadn't quite been expecting him to be there, and the sight of him hits my system like a burst of cold water.

He's sitting on the porch swing, one leg kicked out and the other bent at an angle so he can rock the swing. He's mostly in shadow, as half of the porch lights don't work; I can see enough of his face to know he's neither smiling nor scowling. He's just...sitting. The blank expression is somehow worse than the frown.

"Oh, hi." Nerves erupt along my spine, and I wrap my arms around my middle. "Sorry. I was looking for you."

"Just getting some air," he says mildly. "Figured I'd let you catch up with your friends. Are you cold? There's a jacket in my car."

Before he can get up and go get it, I step closer and stop

him. "No, that's okay. Do you want to leave? We can leave. I only wanted to stop by, anyway. We could go get some ice cream, or take a walk? Or, if you want, we could put on a movie when we get home. Something just the two of us."

I add this last part in a desperate attempt to bring this night back on track, but Carter has no reaction to the offer. He only stares at me, blank-faced and contemplative. A loud noise from inside draws his eyes away for a moment, before he turns back to me. He hooks a finger behind him, in the direction of the party.

"We don't have to go if you wanted to hang out for a bit longer. I'm okay waiting until you're ready."

A sharp prickle forms behind my eyes, and I swallow past a lump in my throat. "I'm ready. I'm ready to go."

He stands, gesturing for me to lead the way to the car. Before I can do it myself, he reaches around me and opens the passenger door the same way he's done all evening. The same way someone would do for their date. When the door is closed and Carter is walking around the front of the vehicle to the other side, I look out the window and will myself not to cry. I think I've probably fucked this up, and that feels terrible. But what feels worse is the knowledge that I've obviously hurt Carter's feelings.

I sit there quietly, stewing in my misery and too afraid to talk to Carter about it. We're nearly halfway home before he speaks, looking over at me across the dark expanse of the car. I'm glad he can't see my face in the dark and that I've still got time to get myself under control before we get home.

"Did something happen at the party? While I was outside?"

I turn my head and he catches my eye, frowning at me. I shake my head, *no*. He frowns with renewed vigor. I clear my throat to make sure there are no tears lodged there. "Nothing happened."

"You're never this quiet," he points out.

"Are you mad at me?" I ask quietly, and watch as his eyes pop wide in surprise. He's forgotten to maintain the frown.

"No, of course not. Why the hell would I be mad at you?" He sounds incredulous, like he can't think of anything more ridiculous than him being upset with me.

"Because I ruined our date." I'm watching carefully when I say this, so even in the dark car I'm able to see the way his shoulders sag. He waits to speak until the car is parked in his garage and the engine is turned off. The sudden silence feels encompassing and damning.

"You didn't ruin anything."

He doesn't look at me when he says it, and I can't pick out a lie from his face anyway. Opening my door, I get out of the car. I hate confrontation, and this is the worst sort. My hands are shaking as I trail Carter slowly through the door.

"Carter," I call to him softly, before he can disappear up the stairs. He halts, back rigid and shoulders set in discomfort. "Do you want to stay up for a little bit? I'd like to talk to you."

"Let's talk tomorrow. I'm going to crash, all right?"

He doesn't wait for me to respond before he goes upstairs. I watch him until he's out of sight, suddenly feeling too weary to follow. Taking a seat on the couch, I rest my head back and close my eyes. I need to think of what to say to him tomorrow to help him understand that I made a mistake. I need him to know that had I known we were going on a date, I never would have agreed to meet Jefferson at the party. But I also need to make sure he understands what dating me might look like. I'm not the kind of person who will just jump into bed with someone, and I'm unsure whether that will be okay with Carter.

Sitting up, I make my gloomy way upstairs. Reaching the top of the stairs, I stop dead. Carter's door—which has remained wide open since the first day I set foot in this house—is closed. I stand there, staring, for what feels like an eternity. Forcing my feet to move, I continue down the hallway to my own room. Closing the door silently behind me, I put my back to the wall and slide to a seated position on the floor.

12

Carter

I SLEPT like garbage last night, which is no big surprise. I've woken up with a headache and my stomach feels as though it's been tied in a dozen knots. Lying in bed and trying to muster up the desire to move, I think about last night. *This,* I think, *is why I don't do dating.* I'd gotten excited—far more excited than the situation warranted—when Zeke agreed to dinner. It was all I could do to make it through the week and get to Friday night; Coach Mackenzie had been on my case all week for being distracted.

I should never have let Vas talk me into asking him out. Now, all I've done is make a fool of myself and possibly ruin our friendship. I knew—I fucking *knew*—he'd never go out with me. But of course, Zeke is too nice of a person to flat-out tell me no. Instead, he'd engineered it so that we'd be surrounded by his friends. *He's just my roommate,* he'd said, and all of them had nodded because naturally he would never be with someone like me. Sitting up, I hunch over and scrub my palms over my face.

Flinging the covers away, I get up and get dressed as quietly as I can. I'd like to avoid Zeke for as long as humanly possible. I have a feeling he's going to want to talk and I'm not sure I have it in me today. I'm just so fucking *disappointed*. I should have been happy with what I had—a roommate and a friend—instead of looking for more. It's my own damn fault if I've ruined everything.

Eyeing his closed bedroom door, I tiptoe down the stairs and nearly shit myself when I run straight into Zeke. I catch his shoulders to keep him from falling back against the island, but let him go and step away the moment he's steady.

"Sorry." I clear my throat, feeling my face warm. I pick a spot on the wall over Zeke's head to stare at so I don't have to look at his eyes.

"Morning, Carter," he says, and his voice sounds so strained I can't help but look down at him. He's got eyes made for anguish: blue and so big they seem to take up half of his face. "How are you? Did you sleep okay? Are you busy or could I make you breakfast?"

He sounds breathless and he's clenching his hands together in front of himself. I have to clench my own hands into fists to remind myself *not* to reach out and touch him. When I caught his shoulders just now, I could feel the heat of his skin through the thin shirt; my hands are still tingling with the contact. I am so utterly and completely fucked.

"I slept fine," I lie, because of course I didn't sleep at all. "I don't know about breakfast, I think I might just go down and hop on the treadmill…"

"I'll join you!" Zeke says frantically. His voice cracks like he's close to tears, and my heart clenches like someone reached into my chest and squeezed.

"You want to go for a run?" I ask incredulously, because I've never seen him partake in any sort of physical activity.

"Well, *no*, but I want to talk to you so if you're going to be running, I'll just come along."

"Okay, fine, no running," I admit defeat, stepping around him and into the kitchen. Flinging open the refrigerator door, I catch it with my foot before it can slam back into me. "How about omelets?"

"Sure, yeah, omelets. Why don't you sit down? I'll make it, and I'll do all the talking, and you can just listen, okay?"

Sliding the egg carton onto the counter, I toss out some cheese and spinach as well. Peering around, I grab a jar of mushrooms and add that to the counter as well. These are going to be the most boring omelets in the history of omelets.

"I can make my own," I tell him, and then jump when I feel Zeke touch my arm. I scowl at him. He can't touch me if I'm going to have any hope of getting rid of these goddamn feelings.

"Please? Let me," he says, and punctuates it with a swipe of his thumb on my arm. I step away immediately, and his hand falls to the counter.

"Okay. I'm going to go jump in the shower." I turn my back and head toward the stairs.

"Carter," Zeke's voice stops me before I can put a foot on the bottom step, and I close my eyes. He sounds as awful as I feel. "Can we talk?"

"Do we have to?" I turn around and try to keep my tone friendly. "I don't...I'm pretty fucking embarrassed and I'd rather just forget about it and try to go back to the way things were."

"Can I just...I really think I need to explain," he says, hands flat on the island in front of him and tone placating. "You'll understand if I can just explain. And then...if you want to go back to the way things were before, we can do that. But please, just hear me out for a minute."

Fuck it. I step forward and yank out one of the barstools; it scrapes across the hardwood floor, making Zeke flinch at the sound. Throwing myself down, I gesture for him to talk. "All right. Go ahead."

He takes a deep breath, like he's getting ready to give a speech. The omelets have been forgotten. "Okay. Okay. So, first off, I didn't realize it was a date. Not, like, a *date* date."

I scoff, opening my mouth to argue, but he holds up a hand to silence me.

"I know, Carter. You said it was a date," he says wearily. "I don't have a lot of experience though, and when you said that it never crossed my mind that you would mean it the way you did. Guys like you don't ask guys like me out on dates. My grandma says 'it's a date!' when we make Sunday dinner plans; I genuinely thought you meant it that way."

I nod, the tightness in my chest lessening by a degree. *That explains wanting to go to that party, then.* "Okay. It's fine, don't worry about it."

As though he knows I'm going to push back from the counter and stand, he reaches across the island and grabs my hand. I saw him coming, this time, so I don't flinch. He's across the counter from me and not close enough to get a good grip; he grasps my fingers with his as well as he is able. Thoughtlessly—as though my body unconsciously reaches for his—I move my hand toward him so that he won't have to stretch so far across the island to reach me.

"No, it's not fine," he says earnestly. "I wouldn't have

suggested we cancel your reservation and meet up with Jefferson, if I'd known. And if I'd been paying a little more attention, I might have figured it out. So, I'm sorry. I feel terrible that I...hurt your feelings, and that you feel embarrassed."

Jesus, and now I'm more fucking embarrassed. "It's fine. You just said you didn't do it on purpose."

"Yes, well, unintentionally hurting someone is still hurting them," he says, huffing an exasperated breath. He's still holding my hand over the counter; I flip mine so that our palms are pressed together. "So...I was wondering if you could reschedule that reservation you had and maybe we could try again."

Zeke's ears turn red when he says this, and his fingers tighten incrementally on my hand. The words make me want to yank him across the island and hug him.

"Are you sure? Because you don't have—"

"I'm sure. But I do think I should explain...that is to say," he clears his throat and looks away, eyes landing on our hands. "Okay, I'm just going to tell you that dating me isn't going to be like dating anyone else. I'm not the kind of person who just hops into a sexual relationship with someone, so if that's going to, uhm, be an issue..."

He trails off, losing the thread of where he wanted that sentence to go. I decide not to let him flounder. "That's fine. I wasn't expecting you to 'hop into a sexual relationship' with me. I just thought we'd have dinner."

Zeke laughs, eyes brightening and a smile spreading across his face. It dims, slightly, after a moment. He bites his lip. "Right...but the thing is, Carter, I might not *ever* be ready for that kind of relationship, with you. Or...or it might take a long time, and that's not fair to you. I don't expect you to just wait around and—"

"Dude, chill. There isn't exactly a line of people desperate to go out with me. I'm not going to be *waiting around* for you to suck my dick."

"You have an impeccable way with words," he mumbles, and I raise my voice to talk over him.

"I don't need to get laid every night, and I wasn't expecting you to be the guy who'd rush into that anyway. Like I said, I just thought we'd go to dinner and start there."

"Start there," Zeke repeats, as though he's turning the words over in his mind. "Take things slowly and see what happens?"

"Exactly."

He lets out a great rush of air and presses his free hand to his abdomen. "Oh, *thank god*. I was up all night, nervous about talking to you about this. Obviously, I like you, but it seems so preposterous that you'd be interested in me. And then I was convincing myself that you'd lose interest if I didn't want to have sex right away. Seriously, I was up *all night*. Massive doom spiral."

My mind snags on 'obviously, I like you' and stays there. I feel ridiculously pleased with myself. "You've got to quit with that shit. Guys like me are lucky to be with guys like you."

These words—though true—have me feeling distinctly hot. I never talk like that. I'm rarely this interested in dating as a whole, either. Probably, I shouldn't be embarrassed to say shit like that, but it's going to have to be something to work up to. Especially if it has Zeke looking at me like *that*: eyes soft and mouth pinched in one corner like he's holding back a smile. It's another expression to add to my *Adorable Zeke Faces* collection.

"All right," he says, giving a single shake of his head and sliding his hand away from mine. "Omelets."

I watch as he turns around and starts making breakfast. Wracking my brain for the next free weekend, I come up empty. The whole point of going out on a date last night was because it was a rare free evening. Usually, during the regular season, we don't have Friday, Saturday, or Sundays free—those are always game days. Zeke cracks a couple of eggs into a bowl and starts whipping them together with a fork.

"How about Wednesday?"

"How about Wednesday, what?" He half turns around and smiles when he sees me watching him.

"For dinner. I have practice until seven but we could go after that," I suggest, and then add: "I'll shower, don't worry."

Snorting, he turns back to the oven, but raises his voice a little so that I can hear him over the crackle of the skillet. "Yes, please shower. Also, please wear the same thing you were wearing last night because that was…nice."

Fighting a smile, I make a mental note to wear more green. When Zeke slides an omelet in front of me, I grab his wrist in a light hold and wait until his eyes meet mine.

"It's a date," I tell him. My heart soars when he nods and repeats it back.

VASEL SITS DOWN NEXT to me in the locker room and starts to carefully remove his gear. I'm already half undressed, and full of nervous energy. I told Zeke I'd pick him up from home at eight which gives me plenty of time, but also makes me feel restless with impatience. I don't want to cut it close enough that I might risk being late.

"And so, how was it, then?" Vas asks, and I look over at him quizzically.

"What the fuck are you talking about?"

"You have said nothing about your date. All weekend I give you, and still you say nothing," he says, smiling as he carefully removes each layer of padding and puts it in his stall.

"Oh, well, Friday didn't really work out," I pause, debating how in-depth I want to go with him on this. "We're actually going to grab dinner tonight."

"This is great news!" Vas exclaims, grinning and patting my shoulder. He's far too nice to say 'I told you so'.

"Yeah." I pull off the last of my clothes and grab a towel. "Sorry, Vas, but I can't talk. I've got to go."

He says something else that I don't hear as I step into one of the shower stalls. Biting back the desire to wash quickly and be done with it, I force myself to take my time. Even so, when I'm walking back into the locker room with a towel wrapped around my waist, I'm one of the only ones already showered. Bastian, one of our freshmen, opens his mouth like he wants to give me a hard time, but thinks better of it and instead goes back to stripping down.

I dress carefully, wishing I had a mirror to check my hair. The review mirror in my car will have to do, however, because there is no way in hell I'm going to preen in front of a locker room mirror. I'm already drawing enough strange glances as it is. Throwing my bag over my shoulder, I call out a goodbye to Vas who's on his way back into the room.

"Goodnight, my friend," he replies.

"Have a good one, Morgan."

Startled, I look over at Bastian. He smiles and gives an

awkward hand gesture—something between a wave and a salute. He looks like he's regretting speaking up.

"Yeah, you too Bas."

I'm practically jogging down the hall toward the exit when my name is called. Groaning, I barely hold myself back from tipping my head back and screaming in frustration. Turning around, I try to tone down the scowl. Coach Mackenzie doesn't look fooled.

"Carter. Do you have a moment?"

Feeling a little bit frantic, I pull my phone out of my pocket and check the time. I live close to campus and there is still fifteen minutes until eight o'clock, but I don't want to push the time any closer than needed. I *need* to pick Zeke up on time, and I told him I'd be back by eight.

"Uhm." I glance up at Coach and back down at my phone. I watch the time tick to 7:46. "Sure?"

Coach Mackenzie stares at me. The silence goes on long enough that I fidget. Sometimes I wonder if he can read minds.

"You're in a hurry," he says, in a way that makes it clear he's not asking a question. "Big plans, tonight?"

"No. I mean, yeah. Kind of." *Oh my god, Carter, calm the fuck down.* "Uhm, I have a date, actually."

"Do you?" Coach's expression softens into a small smile. He sounds pleased. "Well, I won't keep you. We can talk tomorrow. Please, drive safely and have fun."

He starts to turn away, but I take a step toward him. I want him to know, suddenly, who my date is with. "With Zeke. My roommate. That's who I'm going out with. On a date. You met him, remember?"

Shut up, Jesus Christ. Cringing, I clamp my lips shut. I hope I can get control of myself before tonight. I sound like a blithering idiot. Coach Mackenzie looks at me, head cocked slightly to the side. Once more, I have the uncomfortable sensation of being X-rayed.

"Is that so? I'm glad to hear it."

I feel like I'm glowing. Coach Mackenzie's approval ranks higher than anyone else's. "Yeah, thanks. So...can I go? Or..."

"Yes, go. We'll talk tomorrow," he sounds amused as he waves a hand to send me on my way.

This time, when I head out toward the parking lot, I really do start to jog. Nerves and excitement war for dominance in my gut. I take a second to check my hair in the visor mirror; my silver nose ring glints in the overhead light of the car. Debating for a second whether I should take it out or not, I slap the visor back up against the roof. I'm being ridiculous.

13

Zeke

STARING at myself in the bathroom mirror, I sigh. Unfortunately, this is as good as it is going to get. Snapping the light off, I bemoan the fact that the length of my hair is getting quite ridiculous at this point. I desperately need a haircut. I also desperately need new clothes. Looking down, I smooth my hands over the nicest shirt I own and try not to feel badly about it. I remind myself that this is Carter I'm going out with, and he's the least materialistic person I've ever met. He probably won't even notice what I'm wearing.

Going downstairs, I settle on the couch to wait. It's about ten minutes until eight, which probably only gives me a few minutes to sit here and freak out. I've been on so few dates in my life that each one feels like a massive hurdle. I'm always wondering if I'm acting weird, talking too much or too little, or if there is food stuck in my teeth. Almost every single date I've been on has ended with me wondering why I even bother.

I hear the car seconds before headlights swing into the driveway and illuminate the living room. Standing up and wiping my sweaty palms on my thighs, I head toward the front door. I get there just as it's opened by Carter, who looks startled to see me standing on the other side. I move back a step so I can take him in. He's wearing another green shirt, but this one is plain and short-sleeved, ink trailing down his arms. Dark jeans once more, fitted well enough to have been made for him. He smells good again, although it's a scent I can't identify. Looking at him and knowing that we're about to go on a date makes me feel strange; it feels like my insides are reaching for him.

"Hi. Sorry, I'm late," Carter says, breathless and a little bit edgy.

"You're not late." I smile. He backs up a step and holds the door open so I can walk through it. I take a big breath of air through my nose as I pass— he just smells so *good*. "Right on time, actually."

"Yeah. I was hoping to be early, though." He opens the passenger door of the car as he speaks, waiting until I'm seated before closing it gently. I have to clench my fingers in my lap to keep from fidgeting. My pulse feels thready and I'm a bit lightheaded. Carter slides into the driver's seat and I remind myself that there is no reason to be nervous.

"I am *so* nervous," I admit, and then silently curse myself. Sometimes, I have no control over my own tongue.

Carter's chest expands under the tight shirt, giving me something interesting to stare at. He's silent as he backs us out of the drive, but glances over at me and smiles, carefully.

"Me too," he says, and immediately I feel like a weight has been lifted off my chest. "I couldn't get a table at the same place as before, since this was sort of short notice. But there is a nice place on the Boardwalk that shouldn't be too busy on a weekday, and then I thought...maybe we could walk around after, if it's nice. Unless you don't want to, which is fine. Whatever you want to do. You like seafood, right?"

I'm once again struck by the sensation of my body reaching for his. He's never chatty, so he really must be nervous. It's endearing and a little bit of an ego boost, knowing that I'm the reason he's nervous. It makes me want to do something bold like hold his hand, or hug him again.

"That's a good idea. And yes, I love seafood. We didn't eat it a lot growing up, so it always feels like a bit of a treat."

He lets out a relieved exhalation and adjusts his hands on the steering wheel. "Okay, good. I probably should have asked before, if you had any allergies or anything."

"Nope, not me. I'll eat anything and everything," I tell him.

The passing streetlights offer brief illumination in the car, but it's dark enough that I can't see his face well. The radio is on, very low and barely discernible; it's something acoustic and jazzy, making me wonder if Carter put on music that he thought might be romantic. Looking away from him and out the window, I smile at the thought. Scary Carter Morgan III is a closet romantic—who knew?

It's a short drive to the restaurant, though it takes several circles before we find a parking spot. He's biting his lip as he unclips his seatbelt, perhaps wondering if the restaurant will be busier than he thought it would be for a Wednesday. Before I can push open my door and climb out, he stops me.

"Wait for a second," he says, before flinging his own door open and making me fear for the vehicle parked next to us.

I stay seated and watch as he jogs around the front of the car and pops open my door. When I slide out of the seat and stand next to him, it puts us close together in the limited space between the parked cars. He closes the door gently, clicks the lock on his key fob, and places a soft hand on my mid back. It's a careful, restrained bit of contact that makes my chest ache— he's trying to be respectful of boundaries.

"It's about a block away," he tells me, dropping his hand as soon as he's guided me to the sidewalk. I wait to see if he'll try to hold my hand, but his arms hang loose by his side as we walk. "The Pearl. Have you ever been?"

"No, but I've heard of it. It's a limited menu, right? They only serve the catch of the day?"

"Exactly. I've only been here once, with Vas, but it was really good. Chill vibes."

I snort a laugh. There is something hugely entertaining about hearing Carter say 'chill vibes' while scowling as though he means to scare all those vibes away. He glances at me, nudging my arm with his elbow and rolling his eyes dramatically.

"Shut up," he says, making me laugh harder.

"Chill vibes," I mimic, making my voice sound low and threatening, like a growl.

"I do *not* sound like that," he feigns offense, stepping forward and pulling open the door to The Pearl.

When he steps in behind me, I turn and see his shoulders visibly relax. The restaurant is only half full—we'll be able to get a seat right away. A smiling woman wearing a half-apron approaches, eyes flicking between us. Carter is standing very close to me, arm pressed firmly against mine. It's likely pretty obvious that we're out on a date.

"Table for two?" she asks.

"Yes, please," I reply. She beckons us forward and Carter's hand finds my back again. Her smile grows.

"I've got just the table. Nice and private, and with a lovely view."

So, definitely obvious that we're on a date, then. I'm glad Carter doesn't seem to mind. There is nothing worse than someone being ashamed of being romantically linked to you. He keeps his hand on my back this time, as we navigate through the other diners and tables. As I knew he would, Carter pulls out my chair once we reach the table and the hostess looks delighted. She waits until we are settled to explain the menu for the evening, her eyes warm as they bounce between us. The table is small—with our chairs pushed in, mine and Carter's legs touch beneath the table. It would take nothing at all to reach out and touch his arm with my hand.

"Sound okay?" he asks, as she walks away to help the next patrons. I hadn't been listening to the menu. I was too distracted by how warm Carter's leg feels even through our jeans.

"Sounds great!" I pause as a server comes over to get our drink orders. "How was practice?"

"Good. Coach Mackenzie mentioned that Tony will be around for a few days off here soon, so he might come to practice," he says, trying to sound as though this means nothing to him but failing. There is an unmistakable aura of glee around him. "It would be cool to see him again."

"I saw that they won their last game after a shootout," I tell him, smiling when his eyes widen in surprise. "I set a Google Alert on my phone so that I could get updates on South Carolina's season."

I sit there, proud of myself and basking in the shocked expression on Carter's face. I've begun paying a little more attention to the sport now that he's in my life, wanting to be a part of something that he so obviously loves. The surprise morphs into pleasure, and he treats me to a small smile.

"You're following hockey?"

"Well, yes and no. Only your team and the South Carolina one. I don't really care about all the rest."

"Oh, but there are so many talented players worth watching." He leans forward, eyes alight as he launches into a whole lot of sports talk that makes no sense to me at all. I listen, enjoying the cadence of his voice and the movement of his face as he talks. I try to picture what it might be like to kiss him, but I can't quite wrap my mind around it. I bet he'd be good at it, though.

We're interrupted by the server coming back with our drinks and food. Apparently, the catch of the day is sea bass. It smells divine, and my stomach gurgles hungrily as I inhale. I can only imagine how hungry Carter must be, after coming from practice. Thankfully, the portion sizes here are ridiculously large.

"This smells amazing," I groan, squeezing a lemon wedge over my fish.

"Right? I'm starving."

We eat slowly, taking our time and chatting. Carter is so easy to talk to—attending closely to the conversation, his eyes intent on mine as I speak. He's an excellent listener, and asks questions or lets me know when I say something he doesn't quite understand. He doesn't seem overly concerned that I'm more book smart than he is, almost indifferent to something that sometimes ends up being a big roadblock with others. Nobody likes feeling like they're less intelligent than someone else.

I'm disappointed when we finish our meals and the server brings our check. Carter grabs it, eyeing me as he does so for any argument. I let him have this one, waiting until we are stepping out of the restaurant to thank him.

"Thank you for dinner."

"You're welcome. Do you still want to walk for a bit? Or we could go home, whatever you prefer," his voice falls as he speaks, already anticipating me wanting to end the night.

"Let's walk." This time it's me who touches Carter's back and guides him into motion.

We stroll in silence, enjoying the warm evening and the salty smell of the air. It's dark, but the Boardwalk has lights strung up and the windows of the shops are lit from within. Hallmark couldn't have done it better. Carter has his hands tucked casually into his pockets; I glance at him, clearing my throat and drawing his attention to me.

"How do you feel about holding hands?" I ask, and enjoy his sputter of surprise.

"What?"

"Well, I was thinking it might be nice to hold your hand but I didn't want to assume you'd be okay with that," I tell him, watching the way his mouth is slowly curving upward into a smile. "There are a lot of people around."

I've become a little more aware of the queer community in professional sports, thanks to Carter, so I tread lightly. I really have no idea how many people—if any—on his team know he's bi, and I don't want to be the one to out him by accident. Granted, we did just share a romantic dinner, but still better to be safe than sorry.

He huffs a laugh, pulling a hand from his pocket and holding it out to me. When I slide my palms against his, he maneuvers his fingers until they are threaded between mine. He's got rough palms, calloused from hours spent in a gym, and his skin feels ridiculously warm in the cooler evening air.

I smile. Nobody who walks past us seems to care that two guys are holding hands.

"I don't mind holding hands," he says, and his fingers give mine a small squeeze. His larger hand almost completely engulfs mine. "You don't have to ask."

"Do...do your teammates know about you being bi?"

"Oh, yeah," he says nonchalantly. "I told my parents and the team during my sophomore year. My parents didn't seem to care, although they might not have been listening. It wasn't a big deal for the team. Besides, Coach Mackenzie is literally fucking an NHL star so he primed the pump for me."

"Oh my god," I laugh, using our linked hands to shove him. "That's cool, though. I didn't realize that sexuality was such a big deal in professional sports. Silly, I guess, but I'd just never thought about it."

"It shouldn't be," Carter says firmly. "And I think it's getting better. One day, nobody will give two shits who we're with. All that will matter is how we play hockey"

We reach the end of the boardwalk and Carter steers us back around. It's late—far later than I would usually stay out on a weeknight when I have class the next day—but going home has me feeling oddly melancholy. The night hasn't felt that much different than our normal time together, other than the holding hands. It's been easy. And I already know I don't have to worry about Carter trying to kiss me when we get home, which feels like another weight has been lifted.

"We can do this again, sometime, right?" Unconsciously, my hand tightens on Carter's and he glances over at me. "Go...out, I mean. On a date. And hold hands."

He looks like he wants to smile *so* bad. "Yeah. I'd be bummed if we didn't."

"I do *not* want you to be bummed," I joke, trying to tease the smile out for real.

The drive home is mostly silent, but it's of the comfortable variety. A couple times I've glanced over and caught him looking happier than I've ever seen him. Warmth pools in my stomach; I wish we were still touching.

"It's my weekend," Carter says, as we idle on the driveway and wait for the garage door to open.

"What?" I say, distracted by thoughts of how to maneuver his hand back into mine.

"It's my weekend," he repeats, putting the car in park and unclicking his seatbelt. "For hanging out on Sunday."

"Oh right, yeah, it is," I agree, and raise my eyebrows at his smirk. He looks devious, all of a sudden. Narrowing my eyes, I open my mouth to ask him what he has planned, but he's out of the car and rounding the hood before I can find the words. He pops open my door and gestures grandly for me to exit. "Why? What are we doing on Sunday?"

"It's a surprise," he admonishes, frowning at me as we walk inside and he flicks on the lights. "You know how it works."

"Right, except when it's my weekend I surprise you with things like the zoo, or a day at the beach. When it's *your* Sunday, you surprise me with things like skydiving and nunchuck fighting."

"We have done neither of those things," he scoffs, but pauses and considers. "Although, both are valid options. Thanks for the ideas."

Dropping my head back, I groan dramatically. Beside me, Carter sniggers. His hand brushes my arm, so lightly it's barely a touch at all. Lifting my head, I look at him.

"You'll have fun, I promise. Lots of hand holding," he says, lips twitching and eyes bright. "And, uhm...thanks. For going out tonight and giving me a chance."

He steps back as he says this, voice gruff with feelings he's not used to expressing. It seems incredible that he can look at me and find something he likes. The urge to hug him is so strong, I dig my fingernails into my palms to hold myself back. I don't want to get his hopes up that I might be ready for more before I am.

"All right, I trust you," I say, but make my tone as skeptical as I can manage it. He snorts, shaking his head in amusement. "Sunday MMA lessons it is."

"It's a date," Carter says, dropping me a wink and ambling up the stairs.

14

Carter

"Absolutely freaking not," Zeke says, halting so suddenly I'm barely able to stop without plowing into him.

"It'll be fun, I promise," I say emphatically, as I place a gentle hand on his back and guide him toward the skate rental booth. "And look, no nunchucks in sight."

He sends me a withering glance over his shoulder before looking back at the empty rink. We're at a local indoor ice rink; it's early enough on a Sunday that the ice is virtually empty. It's a blessing—I know Zeke will be more comfortable learning without dozens of gawkers around. We step up to the skate rental and give them our shoe sizes. I'm able to pay without Zeke arguing, which is a testament to how nervous he must be. When we take a seat on one of the benches lining the outside of the rink, he bites his lip and stares out at the skaters.

"I am going to be really, really bad at this," he tells me.

"That's what you said about axe throwing, and you did fine."

"Okay, well something tells me that strapping blades to my feet and skating around on ice isn't going to be quite the same thing. I'm not athletic, Carter. Like, at all. Sometimes I trip over *my own feet*."

"I'll help you, though. You won't fall, I promise." I make sure to sound as confident as I feel, trying to put him at ease. I've already got my skates laced and am waiting for him to follow suit. I nudge his shoulder and nod down at his feet. Groaning, he bends over to slip off his shoes.

"You promise? I don't want to fall and bite the tip of my tongue off, or something. Or break a wrist or an ankle. I need all of my bones intact."

Biting the inside of my lip, I rest my shoulder against his and try not to laugh. "I promise you will break no bones, nor bite off your tongue. You will leave the way you arrived. Trust me."

Looking unconvinced, Zeke stands and immediately wobbles on the narrow edge of the skate blade. Reaching out a hand and catching him around the waist, I stand with him for a moment to let him get his bearings. He's frowning down at his feet as we walk toward the entrance to the rink, and he grasps the wall once we get there, holding on for dear life. I take my hand off of his hip and step onto the ice. When I flip around and coast back to where he's clutching the wall, he's no longer scowling at his feet but at me.

"Ugh," he says, "show-off."

I laugh and he immediately smiles back. It's so easy for Zeke to be happy. I wonder if, by proximity alone, some of that irreverent joy will rub off onto me. Spreading my legs and halting in front of the rink entrance, I hold out my hands, palms facing upward, and curl my fingers in a *come-hither* motion.

"Come on, then."

Zeke stares at my hands for a full minute, at least, before he reaches one hand out and grabs ahold of me. He shoots me what he must think is a menacing look, but only looks adorable on his face.

"Do not let go," he warns, and then lets go of the wall completely and grasps both of my hands. I give him one wobbly second before I beckon him onto the ice. He's biting his lip and looking down at his feet again.

"Don't look at your feet. Look up, at me. Also, stop biting your lip or you really will be missing a tongue by the end of this."

His face snaps up, light blue eyes meeting mine. I slowly skate backward until he steps fully onto the rink. Stopping, we stand there for a moment, eyes locked and hands between us. He's holding onto me so tight my fingers are starting to go numb.

"Ready? Just shuffle your feet like a penguin. I'll do most of the work," I tell him, and he looks at me incredulously. I shake his hand a bit, jostling him. "Ready?"

"Ready to go home," he mumbles.

Laughing again, I start moving backward. Predictably, his eyes fly downward to his feet. However, I don't have to remind him to look up, because it only takes him a moment to do so on his own. I hear him mutter *penguin shuffle* under his breath. Peeking over my shoulder, I ascertain where we are on the rink and that there are no children behind me. Zeke, who probably can't see around me, lets out a strangled noise and tightens his death grip on my hands.

"Carter! What are you doing?" he asks, panicked.

"Just making sure we're not going to run into anything."

"Don't let go," he reminds me, as though I might start prying his fingers off of mine and abandon him.

It doesn't require any work to keep him upright. He's light enough that there is no strain on my arms, and I'm so comfortable in skates this is second nature to me. We make it a full, laboriously slow circuit of the ice before I see a minuscule amount of tension leave Zeke's shoulders. I pick up the pace a little bit, still skating backward in front of him and tugging him along.

"All right, let's change up the penguin shuffle a little bit. Lengthen your stride just a tad. Not much," I say, in response to Zeke's wide-eyed look of fear. "Same motion as walking, but no need to lift your knees yet. Keep the blade on the ice. And no, I won't let go."

A little kid flies past us, bumping into my leg as they pass. I adjust easily and Zeke is barely jostled. He mutters under his breath about crazy people, eyes darting away from mine to watch for any more obstacles. It takes multiple laps this time, before he becomes comfortable with the change of pace. He's got a slight flush from the exertion, and I imagine he's going to be pretty sore tomorrow.

"Okay, I think I've got this," he says confidently. He doesn't loosen his grip.

"I'll go a little faster."

"Sure, yeah, going faster sounds like a fantastic idea," he agrees sarcastically.

"You're doing good," I tell him, as I pick up the pace. He's started lifting his knees without realizing it, body already adjusting to the feel of the ice skates. Eventually, we might be able to skate side-by-side, but I doubt we'll get there today. His grip hasn't slackened once.

Every now and then I glance over my shoulder as I tow him around the rink. It's gotten a tad busier since we've been here, but is still empty enough that I don't need to pay much attention. Probably most people can see that the wisest thing to do is to give us a wide berth.

"How are you doing that?" Zeke asks, eyes flicking downward to my skates before settling back on my face. After I told him to keep his head up, he has resolutely been staring at my chin.

"Skating backward? I don't know," I glance down. "I don't really have to think about it, to be honest."

"Ugh," he rolls his eyes and repeats his earlier sentiment: "Show-off."

"That's a lot of attitude for someone who is fully reliant on me to remain upright," I note, and he smiles.

I take him around another couple of times before bringing us to a slow, controlled stop by the boards. He loosens his grip on my hands, like he's going to reach for the wall instead; I don't let him go. The whole point of doing this was because I knew we'd be touching the entire time. He lets out a long sigh and smiles up at me. Those eyes are going to be the death of me.

"Okay, so that was more fun than I thought it would be," he concedes. "Also, as if I wasn't already impressed with you, now I'm *really* impressed. You make this look easy, during your games. Nobody watching would ever think ice skating is hard."

I can't help but smile, my insides practically glowing with the praise. I'm not someone who needs attention or approval from the masses, but it certainly feels good to get it from Zeke. Reluctantly, I let go of his right hand and wait for him to grab ahold of the wall. I make sure he's stable as he steps off the ice before I follow. He wobbles, a bit, when he goes to sit down.

"Geez. Now walking on solid ground feels odd," he laughs, shaking his head and bending over to unlace his skates.

"Yeah," I sit next to him, "you'll probably be pretty sore."

"My legs already hurt. I'm not all fitness-y like you are," he jokes, and presses his shoulder against mine. I lean against him, pleased that he is comfortable with this sort of contact.

We go to return our skates and the girl at the booth wishes me luck in the game tonight. I grunt in acknowledgement and trail after Zeke to the parking lot. He looks amused; I narrow my eyes at him, frowning. One corner of his mouth twitches upward into a smile.

"That girl is a student at SCU. We've had some classes together," he explains, although this doesn't really explain anything at all.

"So?"

"She's part of a sorority, and unless I'm mistaken, by this time tomorrow half of the school will know that we just had a very romantic morning together." He adopts a breathy tone. "Me the hopeless nerd, and you the big strong hockey player who has to skate backward in front of me and hold my hands. I mean...the *romance* of it all."

He puts a hand to his chest and closes his eyes, pretending to be overcome with emotion. Scowling, I give him a shove. He snorts with laughter.

"Stop it," I tell him, and he laughs harder.

"I'm serious. There is going to be a hit out on me tomorrow. I've taken one of SCU's most eligible bachelors off of the market."

I know he's only joking, but I like the words he's saying. I wonder if I need to tell him that I *am* off the market, for as long as he and I are dating, with or without sex. I'm a one person at a time kind of guy.

"I think you're overstating things a little bit. I've never been one of *SCU'S most eligible bachelors*," I tell him, as we climb into my car. He shakes his head like he doesn't believe me. "I'm serious, stop laughing."

"Carter, you really have no idea how you look, do you?" He's angled toward me in his seat, still looking amused. "Trust me. Just because you were looking too scary to approach doesn't mean people haven't wanted to."

"Okay, well, regardless," I shift, uncomfortable with the direction this conversation has taken, "I don't want to date anyone else, but you. Just to make that clear."

I'm focusing on driving, so I can't see his reaction to this. The air in the car feels weighted, all of a sudden, and I clench and unclench my fingers on the steering wheel a few times. I hate this talking about feelings shit; I wish we could rewind and go back to the easy conversations we shared at the skating rink.

"No, me either," Zeke says, and I glance over at him. "You and me, huh?"

"Yeah," I agree, "you and me."

COACH MACKENZIE LOOKS PISSED. Granted, he often looks pissed. Tonight, though, his mouth his set in a firm line and his eyes are narrowed nearly to slits. During breaks in play, I've glanced over and seen him stalking back and forth behind the bench, like a panther with a toothache. I wonder if he's mad at the team in general, or mostly just me. Looking up at the scoreboard, I adjust my mask. We're being handed our worst loss of the season, so far: 1-5 and it's only the second period. One of the referees skates up to me.

"You good, kid?" He's leaning on the crossbar of the goal, face close to my mask so I can hear him over the volume of the stadium.

"Fine," I respond, even though my knee hurts and we're fucking losing. He eyes me like he can tell I'm lying.

"Period is almost over," he says, and I nod. He's giving me a well-timed reminder that in a few minutes I'll be able to sit down and take a break. Sometimes, the refs are the unsung heroes of hockey.

"Yeah," I agree, looking over his shoulder to see Coach Mackenzie watching us. He looks like he's chewing on rocks. "I'm good, man."

The referee skates off, signaling to Coach as he does that I'm fine after that goalie interference. Tapping my stick on each of the pipes, I bend over and rest my forearms on my legs. Vasel's line is on the ice now—*thank god*—and I'm hoping we can put another point on the board before the buzzer sounds. A deficit of four points is a lot, and I'm scared Coach Mackenzie will pull me soon if we don't close the gap.

He keeps me in for the remainder of the period, but I have a sick feeling in my gut as I skate to the bench at the end of the period. Our offense is putting in the work tonight, but nothing is finding the net. Unfortunately, the same cannot be said for the opposing lines. I feel like I'm letting the team down as we trudge down the chute to the locker room for intermission. Nobody says anything to me, or looks at me weird, but I *feel* like they are. Or should. After all, I'm the one who let in those goals, not them.

In the end, Coach keeps me in for the last period. We lose 3-6, which ends up being our worst loss of the season thus far. It's also our last game of the season before Christmas break. Pissed off and ashamed of myself, I keep my head down and don't talk to anyone in the locker room. I know that it's not up to the netminder alone to win games—I *know* this—but that doesn't make losses like this any easier to handle. Vas tries to talk to me, but I cut him off.

"Not now, Vas," I snap. I'm not in the mood for platitudes. He closes his mouth and nods, eyes downcast with hurt. Fantastic. Now I have something else to feel bad about. He moves across the room to his stall, putting his back to me before I can apologize.

I take a window seat on the team bus and watch as my teammates file past me silently. Vas sits down next to me without speaking, tucking his backpack under the seat in front of him. I nudge him with my elbow and he looks at me, warily.

"Sorry about earlier. Didn't mean to yell at you," I tell him, fidgeting. Vas is my only friend, and he's a good one. I shouldn't be snapping at him when he hasn't done anything to deserve it.

"That is all right," he says, smiling. "We had a bad night, but it is not the end. Plenty of season left, yes?"

"Yeah," I agree, turning away. My phone buzzes in my pocket. Leaning against the cool window, I watch my breath fog the glass. Vas nudges me.

"Perhaps that is your Zeke," he says, about my phone. He's probably right; nobody else texts me. I slide the phone out of my pocket and check it.

> Hey, Carter.

> **Hi.**

I'm sorry about the game.

> **Thanks.**

Did you know that ostriches have the biggest eyes of any land animal?

I stare down at my phone and let out a surprised laugh. Beside me, Vas chuckles softly and leans his head back against the seat, closing his eyes. Some of my bad mood dissipates. I read Zeke's message again and shake my head in disbelief. I'm so glad he answered my ad for a roommate.

> **Bigger eyes than you?**

I refuse to take that as anything but a compliment. Have you ever heard of ostriches burying their head in the sand?

> **Yes. Everyone has heard that.**

MYTH! Ostriches don't bury their heads. They do eat rocks, though.

> **Hockey pucks are frozen before games. Helps minimize bouncing.**

Ohhhh hockey facts!! What else you got? Hit me, baby.

> **The Stanley Cup has been stolen twice. Once in the 70s and once in…2018? I think.**

What the hell is a Stanley Cup? I thought cups were something you wore to protect your…you know.

He follows that up with a series of eggplant emojis. I have

to put the phone down for a second and lean my head against the window to keep from laughing. I wish the bus ride home wasn't so long.

> It's a giant cup that's engraved with all the playoff winners. It's badass. Definitely not used to protect our junk.

> Thanks for texting me.

> Figured you needed a distraction. Want me to wait up for you?

> No. It's going to be super late and you have early classes tomorrow.

> What time do you think you'll be back? I'll set an alarm to wake up to make sure you got home okay.

I stare down at my phone in silence, an uncomfortable burn in my chest. Nobody has ever done something like that for me, and here he is offering it up like it's not the nicest thing anyone has ever said to me. My thumbs hover over the keyboard as I war with the desire to say something flippant or something sincere. I like him *so* much, it's starting to freak me out. We haven't even kissed yet, for fuck's sake.

> Probably not until 3am. Maybe later. I don't want to wake you up, though. We can just catch up in the morning.

> See you at 3am!

Doing my best to ignore the way *that* makes me feel, I lock my phone and tuck it back into my pocket. I do need to try and get some sleep, as uncomfortable as it is to do so on the bus. Beside me, Vas is already dozing mouth open, and chest rising slow and even. He has the uncanny ability to sleep anywhere, like a cat. It's unnerving and a little bit annoying.

Leaning to the side, I settle my shoulder against the window. Despite telling Zeke that I don't need him to wait up for me I'm glad to hear that he is. I know I don't have to worry about him trying to talk to me about the game and make me feel better about how I played. He'll just be there, offering silent support and distraction through random animal facts. Somehow, this is exactly what I need.

15

Zeke

"Cassidy, you dog!"

Jolting, I lift my head and look around. When I see the smiling face of Justin Brandt coming toward me, I cringe. Only Justin would call out that loudly in a library—he plays some sort of position on the football team that he feels affords him the ability to act however he pleases. I spent an entire semester last year tutoring him in math and hating every second. He walks toward me, completely unconcerned with the students he's disturbed. I wait until he reaches my table and pulls out the chair across from me before I speak.

"Hey, Justin," I greet him barely above a whisper. He grins at me, rakishly.

"So, hockey players, huh? I'm a little offended, man. We spent all that time together last year, and you never hit on me once!" He laughs at his own joke, barely able to get the words out before he starts chuckling. I give a halfhearted laugh of my own, heat climbing up the collar of my shirt and diffusing across my face.

"Oh, right," I say, nonsensically. Glancing down at my phone, I twist my fingers together in my lap to keep from reaching for it. Carter spent Christmas at his family's house and is driving back right now. I'd told him I was going to be working in the library until the late afternoon before meeting him back home to grab dinner. I wish he was here right now.

Justin grins at me, and leans forward with his elbows on the table. He's smiling like I'm the butt end of a joke that he's telling. His eyes flick over my shoulder and the smile widens. He holds both arms out like he's welcoming someone in for a hug.

"Speak of the devil," he calls, too loud.

I turn to see who he's talking to and my mouth drops open in shock. Carter is striding toward us; he's wearing grey sweatpants, a fitted black, long-sleeved shirt, and a scowl. My stomach performs a series of gymnastics when his eyes meet mine. It seems incredible that I was just wishing for him and here he is.

"Hi," he says, stopping next to me and brushing the lightest of touches across the top of my shoulder. He pulls out the chair next to me and sits down.

"Hi," I reply, staring at him.

"Hey man, how's it going?" Justin interrupts, reminding me of his presence. I look over to see him holding his fist out to Carter who waits long enough to return the gesture that I wonder if he'll do it at all. When he does repay the fist bump, he barely touches his knuckles to Justin's before pulling his hand away.

"Hey," Carter deadpans, before looking back at me. "How are you?"

Good, except I missed you and I'm so glad you're back. "Fine, how was your drive?"

Carter opens his mouth to answer, but Justin cuts across him. "So, you two are a thing, huh? You guys are taking over hockey, you know that?"

Again, he laughs, but neither Carter nor I join in. Carter's eyes leave mine and track over to Justin slowly. I can't believe he's still laughing. I sure as hell wouldn't be laughing if Carter was looking at me like that.

"You guys?" he repeats.

"Yeah, you know, the gays," Justin says, grinning. I close my eyes, briefly, at these words. Beside me, Carter is reclined back in his seat with his hands resting nonchalantly on his abdomen. Even so, the tension radiating off of him is noxious.

"The gays," he says slowly, as though he's turning the words over in his mouth to see how they taste. "What do you mean, we're taking over hockey?"

I wonder if it would be strange if I just stood up and left. This conversation has the makings of a fight written all over it, and I'm about as non-confrontational as a person can be.

"Yeah, what is it—five now, in the NHL? And two on the same team—what are the odds?" Justin shakes his head in disbelief.

"Mm," Carter hums. "So...five is too many *gays* to have in the entire league, and two on the same team defies the odds. What's the appropriate amount, I wonder? What's the appropriate number of straight people? Is there a believable number, for you?"

These questions are all asked in a steady, monotone voice that nonetheless gives the strong impression that the answer will determine whether Justin leaves with his nose on straight. Sensing this, his smile slips a bit and he looks over at me. I try to convey *you're on your own, buddy*, as best I can. He's bigger than Carter by a couple inches, but there is an unmistakable air of barely contained violence around Carter that gives him an edge. I would never bet against him, in any fight.

"Go on," Carter says, when Justin takes too long to answer. "What's the correct number of gay hockey players? I'm dying to know."

"Dude, chill," Justin says, laughing nervously. I close my eyes again. I doubt telling Carter to chill will have the desired effect. "I was just fucking around."

"Well, how about now you fuck off?" Carter suggests pleasantly. He hasn't once raised his voice or unfolded from his lazy sprawl.

Justin stands, shakes his head and looks at us disdainfully. There is a hateful look in his eyes as they dance between Carter and I, and he opens his mouth once more before snapping it closed with another shake of the head. He shoves his chair in so hard, the table slides across the carpet. I can hear him mutter something under his breath as he walks away. I unclench my fingers in case I need to grab Carter and hold him back.

He watches until Justin is out of sight before looking at me. His usual scowl lessens a few degrees when his eyes meet mine. "Hi."

A startled laugh slips out and I smile at him. My stomach, which had been clenched in a knot during that entire exchange is now clenched for a different reason. It's been less than a week since we've seen each other, but it feels like much longer. It feels like I need to touch him to make sure he's real.

"Hi. I missed you," I tell him, because I've never been able to control the words that come out of my mouth. We'd spoken on the phone during the holidays, but the version of Carter who was with his family wasn't the one I've grown used to. He inhales at these words, long and deep.

"Do you want to go home?"

Closing my books, I slide them into my bag. Standing, I go to sling it over my shoulder but Carter stops me, pulling the strap from my grip and placing it over his own arm. He holds a hand out to me and I immediately slide my fingers through his. Outside, it's not yet dusk and the air has a definite bite to it. Carter's not wearing a coat, and his shirt looks thin enough to be no help whatsoever.

"Aren't you cold?" I ask. I'm wearing a base layer *and* a sweater, and I'm still cold.

"Nah. Feels good." He runs his thumb gently over the back of mine, which gives me heart palpitations. "Was that guy bothering you? Before I got there?"

I glance over at him. He's looking straight ahead, and the half of his mouth I can see is turned down in a frown. "Justin? No. Well, yeah, a little bit. But I know him from when I used to tutor him. He's...he's all right, but not someone I'd choose to spend time with, you know?"

The frown deepens, and Carter's hand tightens on mine. "I don't like him," he declares.

"Do you know him?" I ask, amused.

"Well enough not to like him," he says haughtily, making me laugh. "Seriously though, was he giving you a hard time?"

"No." I squeeze his hand back before letting go of him to climb into the car. I think if I answered yes to that question, he'd turn back around to find Justin and beat the shit out of him.

"Good. Because otherwise I'd have to find him and break his jaw. Defend your honor," he says stoutly. I crack up laughing and he shoots me a tiny smile. There is something ridiculously funny about Carter telling jokes with no inflection or facial expression. I'll never get tired of it.

"I feel like you might have already done that. I can't believe you told him to fuck off. In the *library*."

Carter snorts, shaking his head. "What do you want to do? Grab something to bring home or go out somewhere to eat?"

"Whatever you want," I shrug, and turn slightly in my seat, so I can keep him in view. I feel strange, being this close to him after not seeing him for a week; my skin tingles with the desire to touch him. He glances over at me.

"Let's bring something home. That way it can just be the two of us." He clears his throat, flexing his fingers around the steering wheel. Saying sweet things always makes him uncomfortable. I smile wider.

"Sounds perfect to me. How do you feel about pizza?"

When we get home, we set up in the living room. Carter puts the pizza box on the coffee table and doesn't bother grabbing plates; I grab the paper towel roll and fill two glasses of water. When I get back to the living room, he's sitting on the floor with his back to the couch. I join him, sitting close enough that I can feel the warmth of his leg through our clothing. It makes me feel shaky with possibility.

"So," I say, reaching for a slice of pizza, "how was Christmas?"

"Fine," he grunts. I lean my shoulder against him.

"That's what you said when we talked on the phone. But how was it really?"

Carter sighs around a mouthful of pizza, shrugging. "My

mom throws a party every year on Christmas Eve. They always invite the investors and board members and shit, from my dad's company. Everyone is all dressed up, and the food is catered and usually pretty amazing."

"Oh," I say, mouth twisting as I chew and think about this. My grandma and I usually play board games on Christmas Eve. We spend the entire evening in pajamas, drinking hot chocolate, and eating homemade food. By comparison, Carter's Christmas sounds kind of awful, but I don't want to say so and risk hurting his feelings. "Do you like having a party?"

"Fuck no," he says, with feeling. "I have to wear a *tuxedo*. And the food is bomb but it's, like, finger food, so you have to eat a shit ton to feel full. It's rich people food."

"Huh. Do you guys do gifts on Christmas?"

"Yeah, they gave me a card with a check inside. The usual." He shrugs as he says this, as if this isn't heartbreaking. "What about you?"

"Uhm, yeah, my grandma gave me a couple books and a hat she knitted. I told her we were dating and she felt bad for not making you something. So, don't be surprised if that's in your future."

"Oh, that reminds me," he mumbles, around a mouthful of pizza. Dusting his fingers off over the box, he climbs to his feet. "Be right back."

Nonplussed, I watch as he jogs back to the garage and disappears back inside. He's back a few moments later, carrying something wrapped in a plastic bag and smirking. My stomach falls.

"Hey, that better not be what I think it is," I warn him, pointing at the bag. I'd convinced him not to do presents for

Christmas, since we've only been dating a couple of months. It was like trying to convince the sun not to shine.

"This isn't a Christmas present," he says, still smirking as he sits back down next to me and holds out the bag.

I take it from him with no small amount of trepidation. It's a book, that much is clear. The smirk has grown into a small smile; he gestures for me to open the bag. Sticking my hand in, I pull out a heavy, cardboard book. The cover has a childish drawing of two hockey players under the title: *So you think you want to play hockey?* I feel a laugh bubbling up in my stomach and bite my lip.

"Is this a children's book?" I ask, glancing at him. "About hockey?"

Carter lets out a whoop of laughter, bending forward from the force of it. I can't help but laugh with him and for a long time the room is filled with nothing else. Eventually, wiping his eyes, he takes a couple fortifying breaths and looks at me. His eyes are shining with uncontained joy and there is an actual fucking smile on his face. A wide, beautiful smile. I've never seen so many of his teeth before.

As though my body is being controlled by a puppeteer, I lean forward and put a hand on his shoulder. I barely have to pull him toward me as I lean in and kiss his cheek. Immediately, he freezes, and because I'm so close to him, I can hear his sharp inhalation. Doubts flood me, and I pull away from him. Before I can get too far, Carter stops me. The smile is gone, but there is an unmistakable heat in his eyes now.

"Oh, uhm, sorry," I say. I'm clutching the book in my lap so hard my knuckles hurt.

"Sorry?" He gives his head a single, firm shake. "Don't be sorry. I wasn't expecting that...I figured you..."

He trails off, eyes squinting into the middle distance and

mouth creeping back down into a frown. He's not looking at me, but I'm looking at him. I'm looking at him and realizing for the first time that I want him. I *want* him. And that terrifies me.

"Zeke?" he asks, and I realize I've been staring at him, mutely. He has no idea I've just had an epiphany.

"Sorry, but you know what I just realized?"

"What?"

"That I like you. I really, really like you," I tell him, unable to keep the excitement from my tone. Carter looks confused. He glances down at the book on my lap. I look down as well and laugh again, when I see the cover.

"Uhm...have you not liked me up until now?" He's teasing, but there is a guarded look in his eyes.

"Jesus, no, I mean *yes*, of course I've liked you. What I meant is that I just realized that I *like* you. Like, I want to kiss you. And we should have sex, sometime."

His eyes widen. "Not that I'm not totally on board with what you just said, but...that's a kid's book about learning the rules of hockey. It was meant to be a joke, not an aphrodisiac."

"Oh, I know. Just a happy accident." I smile at him and he carefully smiles back. Nerves flutter in my stomach when his eyes dip to my mouth. It is *so* hot in this room. "But, uhm, if we can take things slow and work up to having sex that would be preferable."

"Damn," he says, frowning and throwing his head back dramatically. "And here I was hoping that meant you were ready for ravishing."

I let out a startled laugh and hit him with the hard edge of the hockey book. "You heathen."

"There go all my hopes for some spontaneous anal on the

living room rug," he adds, and laughs as I shove him over. He catches himself and straightens, still chuckling. He looks happier than I ever thought it possible for him to look. "I'm kidding. We can go as slow or as fast as you want to go. You're calling the shots, Zeke, don't worry about me."

Buying myself some time, I reach for a slice of pizza. It's cooled considerably since we've been here. Chewing slowly, I watch as Carter does the same. We eat quietly for a couple of minutes before I break the silence.

"Also, since we're on the subject, I might as well let you know that I'm bad at it."

"Bad at what?" Carter uses his thumb to catch some sauce that's on his lip. He pops it in his mouth and sucks, which is more alluring than it has any right to be. I don't think he was even *trying* to be sexy, it just comes naturally.

"Sex. Kissing. All of it," I wave my pizza through the air to encompass all things intimate. He scowls at me.

"No, you aren't."

"I've only kissed two people in my life. And those are the same two people I've slept with. The *only* people I've slept with, Carter. So, believe me when I say, I will not be good at any of it."

"Christ. Who cares?" He takes a bite of pizza and shrugs. "It's not a skills competition. I'm not going to be critiquing your technique, Zeke, I'm just going to be happy you're, you know, kissing me."

I relax a little bit. "That's a nice thing to say."

Still, though, the thought remains in the back of my mind. What if, after all this, we kiss and he doesn't like it? Or he doesn't like how I look with my clothes off? This, I know, is a very distinct possibility. I am the farthest thing from Carter's body type as it is possible to be. He is tall and fit, where I'm so small and skinny that people often mistake me for a pre-pubescent teenager. Not exactly sexy.

"Dude, stop worrying," Carter says, catching my chin between his thumb and forefinger. Interesting things start happening with the nerve endings on my face. "Do I need to ravish you to distract you?"

I open my mouth to answer but he swipes his thumb across the line of my jaw and I forget how to form coherent sentences. Smirking, he does it again, but lets the pad of his finger drift across my bottom lip. My heart is positively racing; I'm not sure I'd actually mind if he did want to ravish me on the rug. He drops his hand and I take a deep breath. Carter stands, closing the pizza box and reaching a hand down to help me to my feet. I grasp it and he uses it to pull me up.

"I wouldn't mind if you were bad at kissing," he muses, not letting go of my hand. "That just means we get to practice more."

16

Carter

DESPITE ZEKE'S declaration a month ago at Christmas, we haven't had sex. Or kissed. Or really done anything more than hold hands. Sometimes, when we're out on one of our weekend adventures, or sitting on the couch next to each other, I'll look over and see him watching me in a way that feels like he's undressing me. But he hasn't yet done anything about it, and I can't be the one to initiate it.

The waiting only seems to be getting harder, though, because now that he's said the words, it's all I can fucking think about. I want to run my fingers through his hair, and put a hand up inside his shirt. I've never even seen him with his shirt off, which seems grossly unfair somehow. One would think—with us living together—that I'd have seen him walking around half-naked by now, but no. He's always infuriatingly clothed. *Maybe this weekend,* I think, as I pull my sweater over my head. Beside me, Vas is doing the same.

"I have question for you," he says quietly. I look over at him as I start to remove some of my padding. He's got an odd expression on his face, something between trepidation and excitement.

"Shoot."

"You are going to enter the NHL as a free agent, yes?"

I drop my elbow pad. *Where the hell did that come from?* Vas looks a little wary as he continues undressing, like he thinks I'm going to get angry at him for asking. Mostly, the question just makes me feel like crying.

"Uhm, no, I don't think so. I can't..." I shake my head to dispel the urge to throw something against the wall. I won't be allowed to play hockey after college, not when my whole life from here has already been mapped out. "No, Vas. Short answer is no, I won't be signing as a free agent. Nobody has even approached me, where did you get that idea?"

"Why not? You want to play, yes? You need to play," he says, standing up and taking a step closer to me. His voice is quiet enough to almost be drowned out by the chatter in the locker room. "My brother is an agent, you know this, right?"

"Right." I nod.

"He says you need to find agent to help you and enter NHL as a free agent. He says you could play for the NHL. He says you need to speak to Coach Mackenzie and that he will help you." Vas nods sharply, like the matter is decided. I have the sudden urge to laugh.

"Vas, I can't. There's no way."

"You can. Have you not been listening?" He looks a little cross, like I'm being slow on purpose. "Coach Mackenzie will agree and he will help. Let us ask him."

"Dude, no, we're not going to ask him," I say in exasperation. He looks confused and a little bit annoyed. Or as close to annoyed as Vasel ever gets. "Listen, my family won't let me. I get four years of hockey and that's it."

He scrunches up his face as he thinks about this, carefully removing his chest guard and placing it in his stall. He's nearly fully undressed by the time he speaks again.

"You are adult, Carter. I do not understand how your family can tell you how to...can tell you *what* to do," he corrects himself. I can tell he's exhausted after that game—he only makes English errors when he's tired.

"Because..." I stop.

How *can* they tell me what to do? I'm twenty-fucking-one years old. Of course, the obvious answer to this is because if I don't do what I'm told, I'll be cut off. Just another rich boy whose parents will no longer fund his life until he stops straining at the lead. Vas is staring at me, waiting patiently for me to explain. Beside me, Max Kuemper is silently undressing. I wonder if he's been listening in. As though he can feel my eyes on him, he looks up at me.

"Hey," he says. He's new this year, a transfer from some college in South Dakota. He's already been drafted into the NHL, the bastard.

"Hello, Max," Vas says cheerfully. Max smiles at him, but doesn't say anything back. He's quiet, but not quiet in the way I am—more like he's shy, and isn't quite sure how to belong.

"Did you have anything to add to the conversation?" I ask, and hear Vas sigh behind me. Max looks between us.

"Your stall is right next to mine," he points out. "I can't help it if you have private conversations where I can hear them."

Before I can reply, Vas cuts in. "And you are in agreement, I assume?"

"Actually, yeah," Max picks up a towel and goes to step

around us. He looks at me. "You should consider going in as a free agent. You're good enough to make it."

Vas smiles, vindicated. He nods at me again, like Max's opinion has settled the matter. The sophomore pulls his towel tighter around his hips and ducks his head, continuing toward the showers. He's new enough that none of the guys have made an effort to get to know him yet. Vas widens his eyes and tips his head to the side. I roll my eyes.

"Hey, Max," I call. He turns to look at me, fingers clutched tight on the towel covering him, like he expects someone to yank it away. "Good game tonight. I'm glad you play for us and I don't have to be on the receiving end of that slap shot."

He stares at me for so long I wonder if he's even going to respond at all. Eventually, he reaches a hand up to cup the back of his neck—a nervous tick I've seen him do during pre- and post-game interviews.

"Thank you," he says, sounding for all the world as though nobody has ever paid him a compliment before. I watch as he turns and walks into the showers. Vas beams at me like I've just completed a selfless act of community service.

"That was nice," he tells me. I scowl at him and bend to take off my skates. "So, you talk to your Zeke about being a free agent, and then talk to Coach Mackenzie."

"Vas," I say, exasperated. "Zeke won't understand anything about the draft or being a free agent. Besides, I'm not going to do it so it doesn't matter. You've got to let it go."

He turns to follow Max into the showers. "Talk to Zeke," he calls, before turning the corner.

"Jesus Christ," I mutter, and finish pulling my gear off.

I manage not to think about it until I'm in the car heading

home. Then, as though the silence of the car allows my subconscious to stretch it's legs, the thought dances across my mind. *What if I did put myself out there as a free agent? What if, what if, what if.*

I can't deny that's what I *want* to do. Of course, it is. The only thing I've ever wanted is to play hockey in the NHL. Hell, I'd play in the minors even. As long as I got to continue playing, I couldn't care less. But I'm an only child and it has never entered into my mind that I would get a choice about what my future would be. It was certainly never presented to me any other way; my dad has always told people that I'll follow in his footsteps. The family business, he calls it. I have no idea what would happen if I turned my back on that, and told him I wanted to pursue a professional hockey career. The sick feeling in my gut warns me they don't love me enough not to disown me, if that were to happen.

When I pull into the garage and kill the engine, I sit there for a few minutes and try to get my thoughts under control. Somehow, Zeke is able to read my facial expressions no matter how much I try to control them. He'll be able to tell the moment I walk inside that something isn't right. But maybe Vas is right and I should just talk to him about it. It would be nice if somebody else would just tell me what to do, and maybe that person could be Zeke.

Decided, and already feeling marginally better, I pop the door open and head inside. The door from the garage bounces off the wall and I don't bother trying to catch it before it slams. From upstairs, I hear a laugh.

"Hi, Carter!" Zeke calls. I drop my bag next to the door with a thump and jog up the stairs. He's in his room, at his desk; the chair is swiveled toward the door as though he knew I would immediately come to his room. He smiles when he sees me. Before I can second guess myself, I stride over. Placing one hand gently on the side of his neck, I bend and kiss his temple.

Backing up, I sit down on the end of his bed and enjoy, for a second, the blush creeping across his face. His already big eyes have reached Disney Princess proportion. Pleased with myself, I put my hands behind me and lean back. Zeke clears his throat.

"Well, hi," he says, as though he didn't already greet me.

"Hi. Are you busy?" I nod toward the ever-present books scattered across his desktop. He shrugs.

"Not too busy for you. What's up?" He scoots the chair closer to me. I wish he'd join me on the bed, instead.

"I was wondering if I could pick your brain about something. Hockey stuff," I add, apologetically. I'm always aware of the fact that I probably talk about hockey too much around him. He's never told me to stop, but I know he's not a big sports fan and I don't want him to get sick of me.

"Oh, of course. What's going on?" He crosses an ankle over one of his knees, and I have to bite back a laugh. He looks like a guidance counselor.

"Okay, so I didn't get drafted when I was eighteen, obviously, but college athletes can always enter the pros by becoming a free agent and signing with a team." I pause, waiting to see if he's following. He nods encouragingly. "Uhm, but you need an agent and stuff to do it, and I don't really know how that all works, so I'd need Coach Mackenzie's help, probably. I, uhm..."

I trail off, uncertain. I don't even know how to voice this question without sounding like an entitled jackass. Especially to Zeke, who grew up in a trailer park and is here on scholarship.

"You know what, never mind. It's okay, I'll figure it out."

"Carter, no, it's okay. Tell me," he says this like an offering not a command. *Fuck it, I guess.*

"All right. All right," I repeat. Leaning forward, I rub my palms over my thighs. "So, like I said, you need an agent and everything, but if I were to get one I could potentially be picked up by a team at any time. They might not need me until I graduate, but they might need a goalie now, you know? So, anyway, the thing is...I'm not supposed to play hockey. I'm supposed to join my dad at the company once I graduate and then eventually take over from him. That's always been the plan."

"Whose plan?" Zeke asks.

"My parents'." I shrug, and he frowns at me. "So, I guess my dilemma is that I'm not sure what would happen if I told my parents that I was going to go after a professional hockey career, and not work for Dad. I think they'd probably cut me off, which means I'd have to quit school because my dad pays my tuition. And if I wasn't in school, I wouldn't be playing hockey, which means I'd *have* to get picked up by a team, which isn't a guarantee, and—"

"Hey." Zeke leans forward and puts a hand on my knee. I have to remind my lungs to work. Before he can take it away, I put my fingers over his. He moves the chair even closer, so that he doesn't have to reach so far.

"So, that's the problem, I guess. And I know it sounds so fucking entitled, and it's a ridiculous problem to have. Ridiculous to even consider it a problem. But I'd really like your advice, please. Tell me what to do."

He's so close to me now, our knees are touching. I spread my legs a little wider in the hope that he'll move the chair closer still. His hand is warm on my leg, eyes intent on mine. He doesn't rush to answer, but ponders for a few moments; I appreciate but also hate this. The longer the silence continues, the more I think he's going to tell me an answer I don't want to hear.

"Okay, well, I think the most obvious place to start is Coach Mackenzie. You can have a conversation with him and not involve your parents at all, at this stage. And you said he's with an active NHL player, right? So maybe that's a thread you can tug on, as well. He's got his finger on the pulse—he can probably tell you exactly what your odds are when it comes to finding a team."

"Yeah," I breathe, already pacified by that answer. He's right, and when you lay it out that way it sounds ridiculously simple.

"But, Carter, I really think you need to decide what *you* want to do. You're concerned about what your parents want you to do and whether or not you're good enough, which are both valid. But I don't think either should be the deciding factor. Do you want to play hockey or do you want to work for your dad?"

"Hockey," I say, before he's even finished asking the question.

"Right. So, let's figure out a way to make that happen," he tells me firmly.

"Okay, but what about my parents? Like I said, I live completely off of their dime, so..."

"Mm. But you don't have to say anything at this stage, right? You can talk to your coach and put feelers out for an agent, but continue going to school and playing for the team like you already are. I don't see that anything needs to really *change* at this point, right?"

"Yeah, that's true."

"Can I ask you something, though?" he asks carefully. I nod. "Why are you so convinced that they'll cut you off? I'm sure they'll be disappointed, and maybe a little angry...but to take away your tuition? That seems a little extreme."

I laugh under my breath. I wish I could adequately explain my family in a way that would help him understand. My family isn't a safe space for me. It's guilt and the soul crushing weight of unattainable expectations. It's never fitting in, and feeling uncomfortable in a world you're expected to live in. It's the exact opposite of the love and acceptance he gets from his grandmother.

"Listen, I'm an only child, and my parents have always hated the hockey thing. They never wanted me to play in the first place. It's always been a distraction from school, for them. It would never factor into their thinking that I love it. To them, school is for getting my degree, not wasting time playing a game."

Zeke sits up straighter and looks affronted. "But you're so good! And it's not just a game, you're still learning things even if it isn't the things they teach in class. You're learning dedication and perseverance. You're learning how to work with others as a group and not as an individual. You're...why are you laughing?" He kicks me lightly with a socked foot.

"Sorry. Please continue to expand on all the things hockey is teaching me. Like teamwork."

"Stop it." He points at me with his free hand. "I'm just making the point that playing a sport in college isn't a waste of time in *any* sense, even if you're not planning on going pro. But, Carter, I think you do want to try and go pro, and you shouldn't let your family dictate whether you do that or not. Otherwise, what? You're going to spend your life working in a job you hate?"

"Isn't that what most people do?"

"Sure, but nobody *chooses* that. Nobody looks at their best and worst option and chooses the latter. If you're lucky enough to have the choice, you should choose the one that will make you happy."

"You're right," I say quietly, toying with the tips of his fingers. When I swipe my thumb across his palm, his breathing changes. I do it again, because this is the only skin I've been given access to and I want to memorize each millimeter.

"Yes, I am right," he says, nodding resolutely. "So, you should schedule a meeting with Coach Mackenzie as soon as you can. That way you don't miss out on anyone looking for a foxy goalie this year."

Closing my eyes I groan dramatically, and Zeke giggles. "Foxy? Seriously?"

"You are," he says. "Very foxy. The foxiest."

"I mean...there were so many other words to choose. How about sexy? Debonaire? Handsome?"

"Hunky!" Zeke shouts. "Delicious. A tall drink of thrice-distilled, spring fed water."

Firming my grip on his hand, I stand and pull him to his feet. He's still laughing when I tug him into a hug. I have to let go of his hand in order to hold him properly, but it's worth it when he wraps his arms around my middle. His cheek is against my chest and his hands are on my back, warm even through the fabric of my shirt. I slide my own hand up his spine until I can feel the strands of his hair teasing my fingertips.

The back of his neck is so fucking soft, I want to put my lips there.

"I like this," he mumbles from where his face is pressed against my chest, and tightens his arms. *Me too. Me fucking too.*

We stand there a long time—or not long enough, if you ask me—before Zeke's arms loosen and he steps back. He doesn't go far. Leaving his hands on my waist he stands less than an arm's distance away and looks up at me.

"You know what?" he asks.

"What?"

"You're so damn tall that if I want to kiss you, I'll have to get a step stool. Or yank your face down, I guess." His voice sounds like a smile when he says this, and he looks at where his hands are touching my hips. Almost as though wanting to see what reaction it might induce, he sneaks his fingers under the hem of my shirt and swipes his thumbs across my skin. "Or you could come down to me."

You have to breathe to talk, and it takes a moment to remind myself how that's done. Zeke's no longer watching his hands, but looking at my face. It's very hard to concentrate with his fingers moving like that.

"Is that what you want me to do?" I ask, and hope that the answer is yes. If not, I'm going to be taking a very long, very cold shower just as soon as I leave this room.

"Yes, please," he answers politely, and then rises up on his tiptoes because apparently, he hasn't killed off enough of my brain cells yet.

I catch his face in my hands and lean down. *Remember to breathe*, I remind myself, and then I kiss him. All jokes about ravishing aside, that is *not* my goal here. I want to go slowly—not ask for or take too much too fast. But if he keeps making noises like *that*, my control isn't going to last long. Zeke moans, low in the back of his throat, and slides his hands up my sides until every inch of his hands are touching me. My skin zings at the contact, and if I wasn't enjoying the way holding his face feels, I might do a little exploring of my own.

Angling my head to the right, he makes a soft sound of surprise. He's moved his hands up so far, they're now cupping my ribs; my shirt is pulled up along his forearms, the cool air on my stomach providing a direct contrast to the heat of the moment. It's laughable that Zeke was worried he'd be bad at sex. All he's going to have to do is kiss me like this and make soft, adorable noises as he does it—I've never been so worked up in my life.

He drops back down so he's no longer standing on tiptoes, which breaks our mouths apart. I'm still touching his face, but loosely enough that I'm not holding him back from pulling away. I notice for the first time how hard he's breathing; there is a flush across his cheeks and his eyes are bright. It's probably the visual I'm going to be jacking off to in the shower tonight, while I think about the way he tastes.

He drops his forehead down against my chest and inhales, long and deep. Moving one hand up into his hair, I tangle my fingers loosely in the dirty blonde strands. I hope he's just catching his breath and not thinking up ways to let me down easy. If he breaks up with me after that kiss, I'm not sure I could survive it.

"Zeke," I murmur, when I can no longer stand the silence. Funny, really, since he's the one who usually can't shut up.

He lifts his head to look at me. His hands are still underneath my shirt, though I almost wish that they weren't—I'm not sure how a man can be expected to concentrate while being touched like that.

"Well," he says, and has to pause to clear the gravel from

his throat, "two things. One: I don't think I'm going to be able to concentrate on homework any longer, so I think we should just sit on the bed and keep kissing. Two: I know I've seen you without your shirt on, but I hadn't realized how...bumpy and hard you are."

Laughter bubbles out of me so hard my body jolts. Zeke snorts, and soon we're just standing there hugging and laughing. Eventually, we do let each other go, and I sit down on the end of his bed, rubbing my chest as I try to control the laughter still trying to claw its way out. Nobody in the world makes me laugh the way Zeke does.

"Bumpy and hard, Jesus Christ," I mumble, shaking my head. He sits down next to me and pokes a finger into my thigh.

"What's your body fat percentage?"

"What's yours?" I fire back and he grins crookedly at me. I smile back and Zeke's eyes drop to my mouth. *Goddamnit, I'm going to need that cold shower sooner rather than later.*

"I really like you, Carter Morgan. I like you more than I've ever liked anybody before." His hand finds my thigh again, but this time he rests it closer to my groin than my knee. I try to think un-sexy thoughts. "And I know how emotional declarations make you uncomfortable, so I'll stop there."

He's not wrong that I'm not super comfortable *voicing* emotional things, but I damn sure like to hear them. *I like you more than I've ever liked somebody before*—couldn't have said it better myself. I like nobody as much as I like Zeke. It's a little frightening, this depth of emotion. I am very, very conscious of the fragility of our relationship—born from proximity and barely a handful of months old. There are a lot of things I could survive losing, but Zeke Cassidy isn't one of them.

"Yeah. Me too," I agree, because I'm incapable of voicing

any of the words rattling around my head right now. He pats my thigh.

"All right, no more of that. You look like you're about to puke," he tells me, and then smiles when I scowl at him. "Now, that was a pretty epic first kiss. How about we try and top it for the second?"

Unable to maintain the glare, I laugh and reach for him.

17

Zeke

JEFFERSON DROPS his books down onto the table next to me and I slam the laptop cover down, guiltily. I fight the flush I can feel burning my ears and turn to him. He's looking down at me, eyebrows raised.

"What's all that about, then?" he asks, taking a seat next to me.

"Nothing," I say unconvincingly. His eyebrows climb still higher, and he presses his lips together in amusement.

"Please tell me you weren't watching porn in the *library*, Zeke."

"I was not watching porn in the library, and keep your voice down, oh my god," I hiss at him, looking around to make sure nobody heard him say the word 'porn'. He tries to slide my laptop out from under my hand and I firm my grip. "Stop it."

"What were you doing that has you looking so guilty? Is your screensaver a naked photo of Carter?"

"All right, all right, if you *must* know." I look around again. The library is still empty, as it often is on a Saturday morning. Jefferson is smiling so widely I can count every single one of his teeth. "I was just doing some...research. Personal research."

"Personal research," he repeats, slowly enunciating each syllable. "Well, I love a good deep dive. What are we researching? Does this research require the use of a private web browser, perchance?"

"You can't make fun of me, okay?"

"I would never."

Sighing, I open up the laptop cover and Jefferson scoots his chair closer to mine. He doesn't laugh, thank god.

"Okay." I stop, gathering my thoughts. "So obviously I've been...thinking about things...and I, uhm, don't have a lot of experience. Well, *none*, actually, when it comes to this." I wave my hand at the screen, where I'd been reading about how to have anal sex.

"Hm. Well, I won't be any help with practical knowledge on this one, because Tess and I have never delved into the butt before."

Now *I'm* the one who has to hold back laughter. He grins at me, as though he said this in a deliberately funny way. I have to hold myself back from swiveling my head around to check the proximity of other people again.

"I dated a guy once in high school, but we never got this far." I nod at the screen.

"Why don't you ask Carter? I'm sure he'd love to give you a tutorial," Jefferson says evenly, though his lips twitch like he wants to smile.

"I just want to have a solid informational foundation before I jump into it, you know? But now I'm feeling a little overwhelmed, because there are, like, tons of positions, and Carter is a lot bigger than I am, so I don't know *how*—"

"He's not that much bigger than you."

"He's five inches taller and at least a hundred pounds heavier. And he's pretty much solid muscle. Trust me. I've touched his stomach."

"I'll take your word for it. But really, this isn't something to worry about. Big people have sex with small people all the time, and vice versa," he says, shrugging. "Also, and feel free to tell me to fuck off if this is none of my business, but...are we really at this point? I know you *very* well, my friend, so I'm going to go out on a limb here and assume his stomach is the only part of him you've explored so far."

"Well...that's true. But we kiss all the time now. Like, *a lot*. I'm getting chapped lips and an addiction."

This time Jefferson can't contain it and bursts out laughing. The librarian shushes him; I close the laptop in case she comes over to reprimand us. Putting his palms over his eyes, he takes a couple shaky breaths, trying to control himself.

"All right—addiction to kissing aside—I still don't see how we've gotten from point a to z. I'm glad to hear you're enjoying your make out sessions, but this is a big leap." He taps a finger on my laptop. "Carter isn't...pressuring you to do something, right?"

"*No*. Oh my god, no," I say vehemently. "Listen, are you sure you want to talk about this?"

"We're best friends, Zeke. If you can't talk about butt sex with your best friend, are we even friends?" He nudges my knee with his, below the table. "No need to be embarrassed."

"Thanks. I guess I'm just thinking about what might happen. What if we're kissing and things are going places, and this happens." I widen my eyes at the laptop.

"Yeah, I don't really think anal just *happens*," he says dryly.

"No, I know. I guess I'm just sort of confused by it all. On one hand, the thought of having sex with him makes me nervous, but on the other it's something I *want* to do. And I've been thinking about it a lot, which makes me more nervous, and more excited, and kind of makes me feel sick. Also, Carter is super-hot, which makes me anxious for other reasons."

"Well, you shouldn't be doing anything unless you're comfortable with it, and you don't have to, anyway. Also, I really shouldn't have to point out that, while yes, you and Carter have dissimilar body types, that shouldn't be something that makes you anxious. He obviously likes what he sees when he looks at you, and that's not going to change with your clothes off. He's openly invested in this relationship and you look the same now as you did at the beginning. I really don't think it matters."

He's right. Of course, he's right. I've never cared what others look like, nor have I ever felt an immediate sexual attraction to someone based on it. But Carter *does* experience that sort of attraction, and I know I'm not the body type he usually prefers. Just because it's something I shouldn't be concerned about doesn't mean I can control the worry when it arises.

"To be honest, I think this made me feel worse," I admit, fidgeting with my laptop. "The more I read, the more I feel like I'm out of my depth. Even foreplay sounds like a lot. What if I can't do any of it? What if I'm bad?"

Jefferson stares at me, looking uncharacteristically serious. He's leaned back against his chair with his arms crossed over his chest. I can see an indent in his cheek where he's chewing on it.

"I don't think it matters if somebody is bad at it," he says, and then uncrosses his arms to hold up a hand when he sees me start to interrupt. "No, seriously. Who cares? That just means you do it more often, right? And this sort of thing isn't really about what you're doing or how you're doing it. I think *who* you're with means more. Carter could be a truly terrible kisser, but how would you know? *You* enjoy kissing him, and that's all that matters."

"Okay." I nod. "You're right. Of course, you're right."

"You know what else I think?" he asks cheerfully. "You should talk to Carter about this. Pencil in an anal chat in-between hot and heavy make outs."

"I wish I'd never told you about the kissing."

"Make sure to keep enough lip balm on hand," he adds, grinning devilishly as I start packing up my things.

I'D rode in with Carter to campus this morning, but told him I'd walk home. It's nice enough out and I wasn't sure how long I'd stay at the library, or whether my timeline would coincide with his practice. When I turn down Walnut Ave, my gaze is immediately drawn to the house and the unfamiliar vehicle in the driveway. I assume this is Vasel's car, since, as far as I know, Carter has no one else he's particularly close with. Opening the front door, I hesitate to call out, not wanting to interrupt him when he's with his friend.

"Zeke?" Carter yells, and I hear the slam of a cupboard door. "Is that you?"

Smiling at how pleased he sounds, I set my backpack

carefully on the floor next to the couch and head toward the kitchen. Surprisingly, there is a man I don't recognize hovering uncertainly near the back door. Vasel is here, as I thought he might be. When Carter sees me, he steps away from the counter and walks over to me.

"Hey," he says, and leans down to give me a quick kiss. This is one of my favorite things about Carter: his complete indifference to what other people might think about our relationship.

"Hi, how was practice?"

"Fine," he says, shrugging, and moving back to the counter where I see the evidence of smoothie making. "Do you want a smoothie?"

"Oh, sure, thank you. Hi, Vasel, how are you?"

"I am well, thank you for asking! Here is our new friend, Max." Vasel gestures to the other man, who raises his arm in a half-wave. There is something cautious about him, like he's positioned himself near the back door in case he needs to make a hasty retreat. "Max, this is Zeke. He is the best thing that has ever happened to Carter."

"Vas, shut the fuck up," Carter says, though the words lack any conviction since he sounds so happy.

"Hi," Max says to me.

"Hello!" I say, as cheerfully as I can.

"Max is new in this school year," Vasel tells me. "We are lucky to have him. He is a very talented hockey player."

I look over at Max, who has a hand cupped over the back of his neck and is looking embarrassed. There is something distinctly vulnerable in his posture—an innate sense of unease that makes me wonder about him. Carter starts the blender and nothing more is said for a few minutes.

"Well, welcome," I tell him, once the blender is turned

back off and Carter is busy passing around smoothies. "I hope you're enjoying it here."

"Yeah. My best friend transferred here to play baseball, actually. That's why I came. SCU has a better baseball and hockey team than the school we were at." He grimaces as he says this, sounding apologetic. "And I like it here fine, thank you."

There's something stiff about the way he says this, as though it might not be truthful. Carter looks at him and narrows his eyes, evidently picking up on the tone as well. He comes over to lean a hip against the counter next to me, brushing his fingers down my arm as he does. I see Max's eyes track the movement; when he catches me watching him, he smiles gently.

Later, after everyone leaves, I trail after Carter as he goes up to his room. "Your friend Max seems nice." He also seems sad, but I'm not sure that's something Carter would have picked up on.

"He's insane," Carter says, in a tone that makes it clear this is a compliment. "He can move the puck like nobody else. And don't even get me started on his slap shot."

I make a mental note not to get him started on Max's slap shot. "He seems pretty shy. It must have been hard, to switch schools and teams, and have to start over."

"Yeah, he doesn't say much. Did you get everything done that you wanted to do at the library?" He turns to look at me as he grasps the back of his shirt and pulls it over his head. *I've touched that*, my brain supplies helpfully, as I stare at his abs.

"Uhm...yeah, sort of. Jefferson came and hung out with me."

"You good?" he asks, squinting at me as he pauses undressing.

"Of course!" *I'm great, except for the fact that I'm freaking about the fact that we're going to have sex at some point.* "Uhm, so, what's the plan for tomorrow? You don't have a game, do you?"

"Nope! It's a free Sunday. Do you already have plans? Or, I thought, maybe we could do something?"

He sounds so hopeful. As always, there is that barely discernible worry underlying his words, as though he's expecting me to dash all his hopes away. I smile at him reassuringly and he relaxes.

"No plans. I was hoping you didn't have any, either. I thought maybe we could do something here. Set up on the couch and binge watch some movies."

"Eat junk food," Carter says, and his eyes light up at the prospect. He does well, usually, eating clean, but I've also seen him wolf down enough Mexican food to feed a family of four.

"Exactly!"

"Sounds great to me. You can pick the movies, since you know better than I do what's good and what isn't. I don't watch a lot of movies."

None, actually. Since I've lived here, I've seen Carter use the TV in the living for watching NHL games and playing video games—nothing else. Sitting down on the end of his bed, I watch the back of him as he strides over to his closet and starts getting dressed. It seems incredible to me that only a few months ago I was warning Carter that I might never become sexually attracted to him. *Ha! And look at me now, pondering the intricacies of anal sex.*

"Zeke?"

Oh Jesus, he was talking to me. "Yes, no, sorry. What did you say? Sorry."

"Are you sure you're okay? You look a little...off," Carter says, peering at me and frowning. "Are you sick?"

"I'm fine. Really, I'm totally fine. What were you saying?"

"I was just saying that maybe we should watch some of your nature documentaries during our living room campout tomorrow. Since that's your favorite thing to watch," he explains, looking down at his chest as he buttons up his collared shirt.

"Oh, sure. I mean, we can. But do *you* like documentaries?" I, too, am looking at his chest as I speak. I'm barely recognizable to myself right now—I've become one of those people who salivates over men's chests.

"I don't know, probably. I don't think I've ever watched one."

This effectively distracts me from admiring the way his shirt stretches over his shoulders. "I'm sorry, what?"

"Never," he says, smirking at the no doubt incredulous expression on my face. "I wasn't a TV kid, growing up. I was the run around outside and get muddy, kid. And now I just watch hockey."

"Oh, you poor, sweet, innocent boy. All right, we're going to watch *Planet Earth*. You're going to love it."

He finishes with his shirt and walks over to where I'm seated on the end of his bed. Planting his hands on either side of my hips, he leans down and kisses me. Reaching up, I put my hands on either side of his face and hold him at my level. He makes a small, pleased sound and presses his lips more firmly against mine. I really think I could die happy if I had nothing but a future of kissing Carter in front of me. I cannot fathom how sex of any kind could be better than this.

"I've got to go," he murmurs, mouth close enough to mine that I can feel his breath on my lips. "Bus leaves in thirty minutes."

"All right. Go win your hockey contest. I'll be here when you get back."

He kisses me again, once, and then twice. Sighing, he leans back enough to place a kiss to my forehead, too. I want to grab him and hold on; keep him here instead of watching him leave for the game. Instead, I watch as he goes and then head into my own room to get to work on homework. I make sure to have the livestream of Carter's game up on my laptop. I'm proud of the fact that I haven't missed a single one of his games, whether I go in person or watch the livestream. Every time I tell him that I watched, I can tell how happy this makes Carter. I have no intention of missing a game.

The game goes into overtime, but nobody scores. Groaning, I watch as the teams prepare to do a shootout. I *hate* shootouts. I can't imagine how Carter must feel, being the only one standing between his team and a loss.

"Yes," I whisper to the screen, as he saves the first one. He stops the second shot as well, and it must have been impressive because the announcers are going crazy. Pulling my notebook toward me, I write down 'poke-check' as a reminder to Google it later. Turning back to the screen, I whisper encouragement to Carter as the next skater comes forward.

"Ha!" I shout, when he blocks it. Vas is the next shooter that has to go on our team, and I cross my fingers for him. The opposing goalie stops it, which means Carter has to take *another* shot. Really, shootouts are a torture device. I'm not sure who thought this was a good idea, but my nerves have a bone to pick with them.

It takes another two rounds before SCU scores and wins

the game. I cheer into the empty house, arms held aloft. It'll still be a few hours until Carter gets home, but he shouldn't be too late. Deciding to wait for him in his room, I change into pajamas and grab a book. By the time I'm settled in on his mattress, he's texted me.

> Hey, no need to wait up, I'll be back late.

I laugh at this, shaking my head. I always wait up for him, or at least set an alarm to be awake when he gets home. It's another thing I've noticed about him: how much he appreciates someone caring about whether he made it home safe.

> I'll be awake. I'm going to read in your room. Good game! You killed that shootout. Why does that seem to happen so often? I hate them.

> Shootouts blow. Did you see Max's goal? Fucking FIRE.

> I did see, and yes it was impressive. Not as impressive as you stopping 27 shots on goal, but that's okay. We can't all be Carter Morgan III.

> Oh my god. Thanks for watching. I'll see you soon.

Soon comes a lot faster than I thought it would. In what feels like only minutes after we talked, Carter is here, hand on my shoulder, and a small smile on his face. I must have fallen asleep.

"Oh, shoot, did I fall asleep?" I sit up and my book falls to the floor with a thunk.

"You did," Carter confirms. He's half undressed—dress

shirt untucked and unbuttoned, hanging open over a white undershirt. His pants are undone and I can see the dark fabric of his boxers. Carter, either unbothered by my staring at his crotch, or unaware, turns away from the bed and begins to strip in earnest. "I'm exhausted. That was a tough game."

Bending down over the side of the bed, I pluck up my book and put it on his nightstand. Leaning back against the wall, I watch him undress and put on pajamas. Feeling my eyes on him, Carter looks at me.

"What?" he asks, and then rubs a hand over the bottom half of his face as though checking to see if he has food on his chin.

"Nothing, I'm just exercising my sacred right as your boyfriend to watch you undress."

He laughs, startled, and shakes his head. Pulling on pajama pants, but leaving his chest bare, he walks over to the doorway and turns off the light. The room is plunged into darkness for a few moments before a lamp clicks on on the other side of the bed from where I'm sitting. Carter tugs on the comforter.

"Move for a second so I can pull this back," he says, and I slide off the bed.

"I'll go back to my—"

"Oh, no, don't leave," Carter cuts in, climbing under the sheets and patting my recently vacated spot.

I hesitate. He just told me he's exhausted, so the likelihood of him wanting to have sex is probably low. Cautiously, I slide into the bed beside him. He's angled toward me, eyes soft and mouth in a frown-less neutral zone. There is a faint bruise coming up on his neck. Leaning over, I reach gentle fingers over to touch it.

"Please tell me you didn't get hit in the *neck* with a puck," I say, grimacing. I didn't see that happen while I was watching, but the game moves so fast it's possible I missed it.

"No," he says, but doesn't explain how he did get hit there. I'm grateful. I don't need to have nightmares of Carter getting seriously injured. "Do you want to stay here tonight?"

I stare at him, fingers clenched in the soft comforter. I *do* want to stay here tonight. I want to fall asleep to the sound of his breathing, and be kept warm by his body heat. Does his hair get messed up when he sleeps? Does he drool or snore? I badly want to know.

"Oh, well, yes, I could do that. Stay here," I stutter, blushing.

"Just to sleep, if that's okay," he says, kindly giving me an out. "Maybe a little snuggling, if you're up for it."

Scooting down and nestling into the covers, I lay on my side to face him. "I am absolutely down for it."

Mirroring me, he takes it a step further and comes so close to me our noses are almost touching. The arm he wraps around me is heavy and warm; it feels very, very good. I've never slept like this before—cuddled up with someone else—but I have a feeling it's going to be an enjoyable experience. Anything that brings Carter's face this close to mine is a worthy way to spend a night.

"Forgot to turn off the light," he mumbles, making me laugh. I push up onto an elbow and his arm slides down my hip. Leaning over him, I click the light off before settling back in the same spot as before. Reaching down, I grasp his wrist and pull his arm back to where it was lying below my ribs.

"Goodnight, Carter," I whisper, reaching a careful hand out to touch his bare chest, needing more contact.

"Goodnight, Zeke," he whispers back. I can feel the words on my face, close as we are. "Sleep tight."

I WAKE UP FIRST, which is delightful because it grants me uninterrupted staring at Carter's sleeping form. We managed to not move an inch all night—I've woken up in the exact position I fell asleep in, with his arm thrown over me and our feet tangled together. His lips are slightly parted, eyelashes fluttering with each breath.

Reaching out, I very carefully run a fingertip over the shaved side of his head. He makes a small noise but doesn't open his eyes. I do it again, but this time along the edge of the longer strands. Apparently, he does not experience bedhead. There isn't a single piece of hair out of place. When I trace my finger over the shell of his ear, he sighs.

"You're still here," he says, voice rough but discernibly pleased.

"I'm still here," I agree happily. "Did you brush your teeth when you got home last night? Before you woke me up?"

Carter cracks an eye open and looks at me. "What?"

"When you woke me up. You changed into pajamas and then came to bed."

"I came home, peed, and brushed my teeth in my bathroom," he says, propping himself up on an elbow to look at me. He angles his head to the left. "That bathroom. You sleep like the dead."

"Oh, good. Well, in that case—"

"Why?"

"Because I was thinking I might kiss you, but I wanted to make sure you didn't still have hockey breath."

"Hockey breath!" he exclaims indignantly. I laugh. Half of his face is sort of smooshed-looking—lines etched into his cheek from the pillow, and his eyelashes are bent out of shape.

"Yeah, like...mouthguard breath. And combined with morning breath? I mean...gross, right?" It's hard to get the words out without devolving into laughter. Carter is trying *very* hard not to smile. He's trying to look menacing but his mouth is too soft to pull it off.

"Okay, you're right," he agrees, but punctuates this with a roll of his eyes. "That would be gross."

He flops back down onto the bed and I smile, vindicated. He's flat on his back now, so it's me who rises up onto an elbow to look down at him. The bruise on his neck looks vivid. It crawls down over his shoulder and collarbone, visible even with the black tattoo ink coloring his skin. I wonder again how he got it, but am a little afraid to ask.

"So," he says, interrupting my thoughts, "I seem to remember there being talk of kissing? Unless *you're* the one who didn't brush their teeth last night."

Feeling daring, I lean down and press my lips to the closest part of him I can reach: his shoulder. He sucks in a sharp, painful breath, like I stabbed him with a knife instead of kissing him. I do it one more time, in a different spot. Scooting closer so that I don't have to reach as far and my front is pressed against his side, I skirt the bruise and kiss the center of his chest. His unmoving chest.

"Are you breathing?" I ask, leaning back to look at his face.

"Yes," he gasps. "Come here."

Reaching an arm up, he cups the back of my head and pulls me down to kiss him. I hum, happily, because I love kissing him. He turns his head and slides his tongue into my mouth; his hand is doing something glorious to my head that feels like a scalp massage. I'm distracted, so it takes me several long moments before I realize I'm somehow laying on top of him.

"Sorry," I gasp, using a hand on his shoulder to push myself up. I don't get very far, because he's holding me down with his free arm.

"Why the fuck are you sorry?" he asks. "Half of my fantasies start this exact way."

I snort a laugh and he smiles up at me. I wonder if I should take my shirt off, so that we'll both be shirtless. Before I can second guess myself too much, I lean down and give him a quick peck. "Let me up for a second."

His arms drop to his sides and I sit up. I'm straddling him —another thing I don't remember doing—which means he's lying below me half-naked and beautiful. A burning sensation starts low in my groin, as though my nerve endings are all zapping to life. I grasp the hem of my shirt and have it a third of the way pulled off when gentle hands stop me.

"What are you doing?" Carter asks, in a husky voice.

"Taking my shirt off," I say, and flex the hem of the shirt as much as I'm able with his hands on my wrists.

He sits up unexpectedly, causing me to slide down from where I was propped above his stomach. I gasp, startled by the sudden movement, and flush because now I'm essentially sitting directly in his lap. My entire body feels like it's on fire; Carter has a very noticeable morning wood. Politely, I ignore it.

"Zeke," he says, and releases my wrists in favor of putting his hands on my hips. The way he's sitting has his abdomen flexed in a *very* appealing way. "Do you *want* to take your shirt off? Because we can just keep making out. No pressure."

"I know. And I want to." With my hands free once more, I

reach up to cup his face and run my thumbs along the line of his jaw. He's got the darkest blue eyes I've ever seen—like the night sky just before full darkness descends.

"Okay. That's fine, obviously," he cocks an eyebrow, making me grin, "but I have one objection to make."

"Oh," I say, surprised. My hands are on his shoulders, now, and I resist the urge to clench them. I really hope he's not about to object to seeing me with my shirt off. He has to know by now that I don't look like him.

"I get to take it off," he says, grinning and leaning forward to kiss me.

I relax. *Of course, he's not worried about what you look like*, I chide myself. His fingers have crept up inside my shirt, hands careful against my sides. His thumb swipes across my abdomen, and the warmth in my pelvis becomes almost unbearable. Carter's still kissing me, gentle and slow, fingers creeping slowing across my skin. I wonder if he can feel my own hard-on.

Carter leans back, giving one more teasing swipe of his thumbs before he tugs the shirt up. I lift my arms and it's off, tossed to the side as his hands once more find my hips. I will myself not to blush as Carter's eyes blaze a very slow, and very heated path over my torso. He looks like a starving man being presented with a feast.

Suddenly, Carter flips us and I let out a huff of surprise as my back hits the mattress with a soft thump. Unlike me when our positions were reversed, he's holding all of his weight off of me—our chests are barely touching. The way he's looking at me makes it very hard to breathe.

"You good?" he asks, in a tight voice that sounds vastly different that usual.

"I'm good," I gasp, because he chose that moment to flick his tongue against the bottom of my jaw.

He follows the line of my throat, placing lingering kisses over every inch of skin. Adjusting the placement of his hands as he goes, he uses his lips and tongue to explore. If I thought my nerves were on fire before, it's nothing compared to now. My skin feels like it's melting off my bones. When he finds a sensitive spot between my ribs, he scrapes his teeth over the area. It makes me gasp, back bowing off the bed a bit and putting us closer together for a moment.

"I knew you'd be good at this," I say aloud, more to myself than him. He laughs against my stomach, vibrations rumbling through my pelvis. If he does that again, I'm going to come in my pants.

When he reaches my lower stomach, he traces his tongue along the waistband of my pajamas, but doesn't make a move to take it any further. Instead, he retraces his languid path back upward. By the time he reaches my mouth, I'm a mess of longing. When he kisses me, I lift my head to press harder into his mouth, and run my hands along the grooves of his ribcage.

"Do you want," I start, but lose the thread of my sentence when Carter nudges his face into my neck. "Do you want to keep going?"

"Well, I wasn't planning on stopping," he mumbles, and drags his teeth across my pulse point.

"No, I mean...do you want to keep going, and have—take our pants off." *Good lord, how is a man supposed to talk when Carter Morgan is licking his collarbone?*

"What?" Carter lifts his head, which is both a relief and a terrible loss. My skin tingles with the memory of his lips.

"Should we take our pants off?" I'm confused by the look

on his face. I'm not a virgin; I know for a fact the next logical step in this process is to lose our pants.

"No," he says quietly. "Not yet."

"Oh. You don't...you don't want to?"

"Mm, I want to. But let's just...go slow, okay? We haven't rushed into anything, yet. Let's not start now." He's smiling softly as he says this, the fingers of one hand teasing my hair. The look on his face is heartbreakingly tender.

"You like me," I marvel.

Carter frowns. "What the hell does that mean? Of course, I like you."

He rolls over onto his back, bringing me with him. For the second time this morning, I find myself splayed across his warm, muscular chest. There are worse places to be.

"Incredible," I say, laying my cheek against his chest. I can feel the beat of his heart in my ear. "I was a little worried you'd lose interest when you saw me without clothes on. Or, a shirt, in this case."

"That's dumb as shit," he says, and I laugh. He wraps his arms around me, hugging me to him. "I like you. Everything about you. I'm not sure when I gave you the impression that I *didn't* like the way you look, but I'm sorry if I did. I like your body."

My ears burn as my entire face flushes with heat. *I like your body* are words that have never been directed at me before.

"Thank you," I mutter, feeling disproportionately emotional. I've never put much importance into how others look, but I'm conscious of the level of importance others afford the superficial. And I'm painfully aware of where I fall short.

Carter stretches beneath me, his skin sliding against mine

deliciously. My face is still resting on his heart, so he can't see my expression and I can't see his. It's this, more than anything, that gives me the courage to speak.

"When I was in the library yesterday, I was doing research on how to have anal sex properly because I've never done it before."

He's silent for a long moment. His hands are splayed on my back, the fingers of one hand feathered across my shoulder blade. It dawns on me that he was probably wise to request that we continue to take things slow. I got carried away, which is ironic seeing as I was worried about *him* getting carried away.

"I didn't realize there was a library book for that," he says. Laughing, I turn my face and kiss the center of his chest.

"There's a library book for everything. No, I was on my computer."

"You know we don't have to do that, right? There are other things."

"No, I know," I say quickly. "But I want to do it. That's why I was researching. I didn't want to let you down. You're a lot more experienced than I am."

"Sweetheart," Carter says, and rubs a hand over my back. I squeeze my eyes shut.

"I know it's stupid, you don't have to tell me. But I feel better when I have all the information, and relationships are an area where I don't have a lot of first-hand knowledge."

"You should have just asked me. Not about the relationship stuff, but I could have helped you with the anal. Lube and fingers, that's all there is to it," he says, completely without inflection. I laugh, turning my face into his chest which is rising and falling with his own silent laughs. It takes us a long time to calm down, both of us breathing heavy as we try to tame the hilarity.

"Lube and fingers. I can't believe you just said that," I hiccup. *"Lube and fingers, that's all there is to it.* You are so ridiculous."

Chuckling, he leans down and kisses the top of my head. "It's true. I'll show you, sometime."

"Deal." Lifting my head, I wiggle my way upward until my face is hovering over Carter's. He groans, adjusting his hips. "Now. How about we make out some more?"

18

Carter

COACH MACKENZIE IS in his office, keyboard clacking audibly through the open doorway. He never closes his door, unless he's in a meeting; he always tells us we can come to him at any time, for anything. Yet here I am, standing in the hallway out of sight, nervous for some incomprehensible reason. Taking a deep breath and thinking about Zeke, I step into the open doorway.

"Hey, Coach," I say, rapping my knuckles lightly on the frame. He looks up, squinting at me across the room. There is a slight worry line between his eyebrows, like whatever he was looking at is displeasing him.

"Carter. Come in." He waves me forward, sitting up in his chair and resting his hands on the desk in front of him. This is one of my favorite things about Coach Mackenzie: he gives you his undivided attention no matter how important the work you're interrupting was.

I take a seat. "Can I talk to you about something?"

"Yes," he says quickly. I nod, reaching down and pulling my English notebook out of my backpack. Shuffling back through the pages, I find the notes Zeke and I had written down earlier.

"Uhm, I wanted to talk to you about..." I look down at the list we'd made. I'm so nervous I can't remember a single fucking thing I wanted to say. "I wanted to get your opinion about me being a free agent, and if you think I'm good enough to sign with a team in the NHL, and if you could help me find an agent, and—"

"Carter," he interrupts me. I look up at him. "Breathe."

I take a deep inhale without thinking about it. I'm a little lightheaded, and my fingers are clenched so tightly around the notebook they hurt. Coach pushes back his chair, standing and sliding carefully between the two desks. He perches on the edge of his, legs straight and ankles crossed; he holds a hand out.

"May I?"

Wordlessly, I hand him my English notebook. I'm grateful that Zeke is the one who did the writing—my own handwriting is atrocious and barely legible. Coach stares down at the list, reading in silence. I sit there, equally silent, and try not to fidget. Eventually, he rests the notebook down on his thighs and looks at me.

"Zeke helped me with that," I tell him, for no reason whatsoever.

"Things are going well?"

"Yeah. Great."

"You're happy?" he asks, and I gape at him. When was the last time an adult in my life asked me that question?

"Yeah. I'm really happy. This has been the best year I've had since starting school here."

This earns me the smallest of smiles. Coach Mackenzie once told me that he and I were alike. He'd meant it as a warning—a cautionary tale of what *not* to be. But I took it as the highest of compliments. He's the best role model I've ever had. I *want* to be like him.

"I'm glad to hear that. Now," he taps a long finger against the notebook, "I've had quite a few conversations with Anthony concerning your future in the NHL. I didn't want to pressure you, knowing that you've got family obligations to consider, but both of us think you've got a fair chance. I take it this means you've decided to pursue a career playing hockey?"

"Yeah," my voice comes out squeaky and several octaves higher than usual. Clearing my throat, I try again. "Yeah, I want to play in the NHL. Or the AHL, or wherever will have me."

"I'm glad to hear it. Anthony has been watching you—this season, in particular—and has been haranguing me about finding you an agent," Coach says, rubbing a temple with a finger. I fight a grin. "So, because of that, I've already prepared a short list and have begun sending a few feelers out."

"You...you have?"

"Yes. Just tentatively, seeing as I was still under the impression you were going to be moving on to your family's company after school."

"Yeah...sorry, I should have come talked to you sooner, probably. But I kept forgetting what I wanted to say, so Zeke helped me make that list, and...here I am," I finish lamely.

"Here you are," he repeats. "So, let's chat. Most kids—

such as your friend Max—will find representation when they are much younger. I believe he's been represented by the same agent since he was sixteen. We're coming into the game a little late, but I think I've got some good options for you."

Reaching behind himself, Coach Mackenzie grabs a leather folder and thumbs through it. When he finds what he's looking for he fixes me with a considering stare. He doesn't hand me the paper, but I can see a neat, handwritten list. There are a dozen names, at least. The band of worry constricting my chest loosens.

"I've got some good options," he repeats, "but my recommendation would be the last on the list."

He hands it to me. I read through it, quickly. "I have no idea who any of these people are."

"No. May I give you my opinion?"

"Fuck, yes. Just tell me what to do," I say, a tad desperately. I hold the list of names back out to him, but he doesn't take it.

"Last name," he says, and I look at the tidy line of writing. "Joel Street. He represents Anthony, who has spoken to him about you. Mr. Street has also been in contact with me. He's interested, if you are."

"Tony's agent? Hell yes, sign me up." I relax further. Maybe this will be easier than I thought.

"His phone number is written down there. Feel free to reach out to him, or, if you'd prefer, I can set up a meeting with the three of us."

"The three of us," I say quickly. Coach smiles, kindly, and nods. "If you...if you don't mind. If you're not too busy."

"I don't mind and I'm not too busy," he says brusquely. "I'll speak with him today and set up a meeting. I have your class schedule. Are there any other time constraints I need to work around?"

"Oh, uhm, no. Whenever. Can Tony come, too?" Coach's eyes visibly warm. The best way to soften him up is to talk about Tony.

"No, most likely not. He's on an extended road trip right now, as I'm sure you know. And I imagine Mr. Street is going to want to meet with you as soon as possible. You could get picked up by a team at any time. Which brings us to the next item on your list, here."

"My parents," I cringe, flopping back in my seat and looking away from him. My eyes snag on the photo of Coach with his AHL team and stay there.

"Would you like me to speak with them?"

Sighing, I look back over at him. "No, I'd better. Well...I don't know, maybe? What would you... I don't know, Coach. Maybe we should meet with this Joel Street guy first, and go from there. I have to go home for a few days on spring break, so maybe I can talk to them then."

"Excellent plan. The other thing you have written down is about school," he notes, running his fingers idly over the pages on my notebook.

"Right."

"I imagine the answer to that will depend on your visit with your parents," he says gently.

"Right."

"Keep your phone on you, and I'll reach out with details as soon as I have a confirmed meeting time with Mr. Street, okay?"

I stand and Coach hands me my notebook along with the shortlist of agents he made for me. I shove both haphazardly into my backpack and see him wince. Slinging it over my shoulder, I run my fingers over the strap. "Thanks."

"No need to thank me, that's my job." He rises to standing and makes his way back behind his desk to sit down. I turn to go, but halt in the doorway, turning back to see him watching me.

"Are *you* happy?" I ask him, and his eyebrows climb up his forehead. "You asked me when I first came in. You always ask how I am, but I just realized I never ask how you are."

I feel like a fucking idiot as soon as I say this. Being around Zeke has apparently put me so in tune with my feelings that I just spit out sentimental shit to anyone, now.

"Yes, Carter. I'm very happy," he responds. I nod, turning to go. "And thank you for asking."

I CALL Zeke the second I get out the door after my meeting with Coach and Joel Street. He answers on the first ring and I talk before he can even offer a greeting.

"I've got a fucking agent! I'm legit!" Several passersby look at me strangely. I glare at them until they look away.

"Yes!" He whoops. "That's amazing! I knew he'd take you on—you're a catch. What are we going to do to celebrate? We have to celebrate."

"You home? How about I pick you up and we go to dinner?"

"Deal. See you soon."

Zeke is sitting on the front step when I pull into the driveway. He's wearing my old SCU hockey hoodie that I gave him a few months ago, which sends my stomach pole-vaulting into my chest. He climbs to his feet when I put the car in park, popping the passenger door and grinning at me as he scrambles inside.

"You did it!" he exclaims, and leans across the center console to kiss me. His eyes are bright with happiness and he looks disproportionately proud of me. I cup a hand around his nape and pull him back for another kiss.

"How do you feel about oysters?" I ask him.

"I have no feelings about oysters. Never had them before."

"Willing to try?"

"Absolutely," he says, and clicks his seatbelt into place.

I wait until we've left the driveway and are on our way to the restaurant before I reach my hand out to him. He grasps it, lacing his fingers through mine and resting our linked hands in his lap. Zeke loves small displays of affection: holding his hand on campus, or kissing him outside of the locker room after a game. It's an easy desire to fulfill.

It takes a little bit to get seated at the restaurant; by the time our food arrives I'm starving. I give Zeke an oyster tutorial, and we dig in. He is so ridiculously excited about the whole thing, I can't help but watch him. He opens one and gasps, theatrically. I smile at him—his joy is contagious.

"Did you find a pearl?"

"Yes!" he exclaims. Plucking it out, he cleans it carefully on his napkin and examines it. I want to kiss him so badly in this moment, I can hardly breathe. He holds the pearl out to me, eyes shining with the lights of the restaurant. "Here. For you."

I hold out my hand and he drops the pearl into my palm. Brushing my thumb over it, I look up at him. "You don't want it?"

"I want *you* to have it," he says, reaching out to curl my fingers over it.

"Thanks," I mumble, carefully tucking it into my pocket. I'm far too pleased with this gift than is warranted.

"So, tell me about the meeting. Tell me about this Joel Street guy."

"Well, the fucker is huge. He's built like a linebacker. It was kind of funny, actually, watching him with Coach Mackenzie. They're, like, the exact opposite. But he seems like a solid guy, and if he's good enough for Tony, he's good enough for me," I say, shrugging and reaching for an oyster.

"But you liked him? It's important that you feel comfortable with him. Especially since..." He trails off, suddenly uncertain. Beneath the table, I press my knee against his.

"I told him I was bi, and that I was currently dating a guy," I tell him, and watch as he visibly relaxes.

"You didn't have to do that."

"I wanted to. I'm not ashamed of you, or being with you. If anyone has a problem with it, they can fuck off."

Zeke laughs, and then, as though the thought just occurred to him, he brightens. "So, that means you're expecting us to still be together. When you're off being a hockey star."

I think about this, for a second, not wanting to give him a throwaway answer. This is the longest running relationship I've ever had, and things are going good. Great, even. But if I get picked up by a team, I'll have to leave school. Will long distance work for us? Will Zeke even want to try? The pearl he gave me feels like a weight in my pocket.

"Yes," I say firmly. "I want us to still be together. In the future."

"Me too," he agrees, and hands me an oyster. "And I want you to succeed, and get signed by a team, and fulfill all of your dreams..."

"But," I laugh.

"*But*, I'm going to miss you so badly when you go. I miss you already, and you haven't even left yet."

I know what he means. When I think about the possibility of being signed by a team on the other side of the country, I feel sick. Hell, I could be signed by a Canadian team. We would go weeks, if not months, without seeing one another; he'll be tied to South Carolina until he finishes school and I'll be on the road. But if there is one thing, I know it's that we are solid, he and I. We've got what it takes to make it long-term.

When we get home, Zeke puts an arm around my waist as we walk up the stairs. Instead of peeling off toward his own room, he eyes the open doorway of mine.

"Want some company?" he asks.

"Always."

We go into my room and I go through the motions of getting ready for bed. This isn't the first night he's spent in my bed, so I don't read anything into it. It's not until I'm crawling under the sheets beside him that I note the look on his face.

"What?" I ask, settling on my side so I can look at him.

"Are you ready for butt stuff?" he asks, grinning suggestively. I laugh, and he scoots closer to me until our noses are nearly touching.

Instead of answering, I place a hand on the side of his face, fingers tangling in his hair, and kiss him. He makes a small sound and kisses me back, harder. It takes no time at all for my blood to get pumping, and yes, yes, I am very ready for butt stuff. Gently, I direct him onto his back without pulling our mouths apart. He makes another sound—closer to a moan this time—when I put my hand flat on his stomach. I'm already painfully hard, and it's been a long, long time since I've had sex. I want him *so bad*.

We tear our mouths away from one another long enough to sit up and shed our clothes. The sheets have been kicked down to the end of the bed. I rip my shirt off and toss it over the bed, intending to stop there until I see Zeke working his pants off as best he can from a seated position. He's left his boxers on, so I follow suit and do the same. My hands tingle with the urge to touch him. When he throws his pants over the side of the bed and looks at me, I damn near tackle him. His back hits the mattress with a soft *fwump*, and he laughs into my mouth. Reaching down, I put a hand to his leg and slide it up under the edge of his boxers until I can thumb at the juncture of his thigh. He moans and pushes his hips upward, erection brushing my stomach. I break my mouth away from his and suck in a much-needed breath of air.

"Jesus," I mumble. I'm so focused on where my own hand is that it takes me a moment to realize where Zeke's have wandered. He's got both inside my briefs, fingers trailing gently over the slope of my ass. I repeat: "Jesus."

I feel a little dizzy. Lack of oxygen from all the kissing, and the sudden exposure of so much of his skin have me faint with possibility. I feel like I've been waiting a very long time for this, and now that we're here I don't know what to do. I kiss him, pressing him hard into the mattress and using my hold on his leg to stretch my thumb just far enough that I can graze his dick. He pulls his mouth away from mine with a gasp.

"Naked," he says. His dirty blonde hair is fanned across the pillow and his face is flushed. "We need to be naked, like, right now."

Kissing my way down his narrow chest, I pause and look

up at him when I reach his waistband. He raises an eyebrow at me, as if to say *Well? Get on with it.* Another kiss to his navel and I step off the end of the bed as I slide his boxers off. I try not to make a big show of staring—not wanting to make him uncomfortable—but it's not easy. I tug my own underwear off, foot catching and almost tripping me up. I want to put my mouth on him so badly I'm salivating. Finally, after an embarrassingly long time, I get my briefs off and climb back on the bed.

"Breathe," Zeke reminds me quietly. I hadn't realized I'd been holding my breath; I suck in a lungful of air, and lean down to kiss him. He loves kissing.

"You're beautiful," I say, between kisses, and then immediately flush with embarrassment. Zeke makes a low humming noise, and arches his hips again. Without the cotton of his boxers between us, there is only the slide of his skin on mine.

Reaching a hand between our bodies, I wrap my fingers around his length in a gentle grip. I need him to tell me exactly what he wants to do, because I'll never be able to decide. I want to do *all* the things.

"What do you want to do?" My lips brush his as I speak, sending little tickles of pleasure zinging through me.

"I want your mouth on me and your fingers inside me, and then I want to do the same thing to you," he says, clearly and without a trace of embarrassment. I swear to god, I nearly come from the words alone.

Letting go of his dick, I shift so I can reach over to the nightstand and open the drawer. Reaching in for the lube, I jolt when I feel Zeke run his fingertips down my stomach and along the underside of my shaft. I look at him and he grins at me.

"Sorry. Just admiring."

"Admire away," I tell him, and he laughs.

We forget about the presence of the lube for a while, content to kiss and touch for an unmeasured time. I've never spent so much time on foreplay before. From the way I feel right now, I'm wondering if I've been having sex wrong all this time. It has *never* felt this good. By the time I reach for the lube, Zeke's skin is salty with sweat and his breathing is ragged. There isn't an inch of skin on either of our bodies that hasn't been touched. I feel like I'm on fire.

I lift one of his legs and straddle the other, still keeping the great majority of my weight off of him. I stop kissing him just long enough to coat a finger with lube, and then I'm back, tongue tangling with his as I slide my hand between his legs. I torment him a bit, running my finger along his crease to tease the nerves into action. Pressing the tip of my finger inside him, I get only to the second knuckle before he tightens around me.

I'm getting dizzy again from lack of oxygen to my brain, so I detour down his neck. There is a spot just below his jaw that is extra sensitive; I'm going to suck on it. He relaxes enough for me to inch my finger a little further, but the second I start moving he tenses up again.

"Did you know that, uhm, oysters can change their sex?" he asks. It takes me a long time to process the words, my brain already being pulled in multiple directions between the warmth of his body and the way his skin tastes.

"Mm," is the best I can manage in return. His hands are coasting along my back, the touch so light it tickles. He hasn't relaxed; if I pushed my finger any further inside him it would hurt, even with the addition of lube. I wait, teasing the sensitive skin of his taint with my thumb and biting lightly at his collarbone.

"Uhm, and a...," he breathes out hard, and his fingers tighten around my shoulder blades, "juvenile oyster is called a spat."

Lifting my head, I slowly remove my hand from between his legs. He's biting his bottom lip and looking at me out of wide, silver blue eyes. I narrow my own eyes at him.

"You're not having fun."

"Yes, I am!" he says, and widens his eyes further until they appear to take up half of his face. I move my still lubed hand to his hip, not caring about making a mess.

"Zeke Cassidy, you are a terrible fucking liar," I tell him, and then soften the words by kissing the corner of his mouth. "You have to tell me if you don't like what I'm doing. I'm a big boy—my masculinity will not be offended."

"Big boy," he repeats, and his laugh turns into a moan as I kiss him. "It's not bad, just sort of weird. Maybe we can try again some other time."

"Still want a blowjob, though?" I ask hopefully.

"Sure, if you want—"

"Thank god," I say emphatically, and drop another kiss onto his lips as I move back down his body. He's still laughing when I take him into my mouth.

I don't fuck around, because, quite frankly, I've been obsessing about doing this for a long time. I deep throat him, moaning when he hits the back of my throat, and use my lubed fingers to massage his balls. He arches his hips off the bed, and when I look up at him, I see he's already watching me. Arousal hits me hard; I rock my pelvis against the bed to try and relieve some of the pressure. I lose some of my rhythm and gag when I take him too deep, too fast. He breaks eye contact, resting his head back against the pillow.

"Oh, my god," he breathes.

He's rolling his hips steadily upward, matching his motion to mine. I close my jaw and scrape my teeth along his shaft—he gasps, fingers gripping the bedspread, and comes. I wait until he stops moving; easing him down, I slowly pull off of him. I had my eyes on his face the entire time, and I'm fucking thrilled. I know exactly what he looks like when he comes.

I move back up the bed, but slide off the side so that I'm no longer right on top of him. Trailing a thumb along his narrow jaw, I wait for him to look at me. I want to kiss him, but I also just swallowed a mouthful of his cum. He might not be into it.

"Sorry about that. I really thought I was going to last longer," he apologizes. I shrug.

"No worries." I tease his bottom lip with a fingertip and kiss his cheek.

"My turn?" he asks hopefully. I shrug, again.

"If you want." To be honest, all of my fantasies about having sex with him have centered around me making him feel good. I've been so desperate for the chance, my own pleasure hasn't even factored in.

He puts a hand on my shoulder and gently pushes me back until I'm lying flat. Leaning over me, he cups a hand over the top of my head and kisses me; my heart zings with pleasure. *He kisses after blowjobs!* I thread my fingers through his hair to keep him there. It's a shame his mouth will have to leave mine if he really does want to reciprocate.

"Where did the lube go?" he asks. I run my hands up and down along his flanks.

"Hell if I know."

Snorting, he sits up. When he locates the lube, he holds it up in triumph. He also takes a second to read the label. I smile, watching as he looks over the list of ingredients. Damn it all, I'm so obsessed with him.

"Hmm," he hums as he runs an appraising hand over my thigh. I've already got one leg propped up; my toes curl into the bedspread as his fingers inch closer to my dick. He skirts around it, dancing his fingertips over the crease of my hip and up the other thigh. Resting his palm on top of my knee, he looks at me and smiles. "Well, might as well get to it."

I laugh.

19

Zeke

It's very, very rare to see Carter so relaxed. There is a warm flush to his cheeks and the top of his chest, and when he smiles it comes easy. I think this must be why people so often confuse lust and love; having the opportunity to see someone like this is a heady, extraordinary thing. I run my hand down the inside of his thigh once more, because these legs are also extraordinary.

I've got the bottle of lube gripped in my other hand and turn it around idly. Carter is patiently waiting, watching me through lowered eyelids. His chest rises and falls in slow, measured breaths. Coming to a decision, I unclick the lube cap and coat one finger. Generously. Probably too generously, but better to use too much than not enough, I'm thinking.

"I'm starting with the butt," I tell Carter; his lips compress as he tries to contain his laughter. There's no hiding it, though—I can see it in his eyes. He doesn't say anything, just slides his foot across the bed to spread his legs wider. *Well, all right then.*

Dropping the bottle back onto the bed, I rest my lube-free hand on his hip. I mimic the way he touched me earlier, circling my finger around his entrance; it felt fucking good. He moves one of his hands off of the bed and rests it on my arm. I push my finger inside him slowly, marveling at how easy it is. Clearly, Carter is more relaxed than I was. No resistance, and he hasn't started babbling like an idiot, like I did.

I sit there for a second, knuckles resting against him. He's warm and it strikes me that this should probably feel a little gross, touching somebody here. It doesn't. If anything, it has my already satiated body perking back up, particularly when I turn my hand experimentally and hear a soft gasp.

"Yes," Carter says, and a little thrill shoots through me at the word. Watching his face, I rub my finger over the same spot, back and forth, until his eyes flutter closed and he arches his head back against the bed.

Adjusting my stance so that I don't fall over, I move my hand from his thigh to where his dick is laying hard and leaking on his stomach. The moment I touch him his hips arch upward and he groans. I'm going to be half-hard and ready for another round in record time if he makes another noise like that. Wrapping my fingers around him, I thumb his slit a couple times, smiling when he makes a noise that sounds suspiciously like a whimper. Realizing that I should have used lube on both hands if this was my intention, I keep my grip on him light enough not to chafe.

I set a slow pace. Tortuously slow might be a better descriptor, based on the way Carter is trying to push up into my fist. I time the slide of my finger across his prostate with each upward motion of my hand on his dick, and settle in to watch him come undone. He's panting, hips rolling upward and both hands back on the bed, clenched in the sheet.

"You're fucking killing me," he pants. I firm my grip, adding a little pressure, and he moans. I make no effort to speed things along—I want to see how sweaty I can get him.

We've worked ourselves into a steady tempo now, hips and hands working in concert. There is a distinct hitch in his breathing and a shimmer of perspiration coating his muscular chest. I press a little harder against his prostate and he whimpers, again.

"I'm..." He starts to speak, breaking off with a groan before trying again. "I'm going to come."

I don't put my mouth on him, because swallowing isn't something I enjoy doing if I can avoid it. When he comes, I'm not quick enough to catch it in my hand; cum spatters his abdomen as he groans through his release and collapses to the bed. I slide my finger out of him slowly, in case it hurts. He sighs, eyes closed and chest heaving as he works to bring his breathing under control.

Careful not to touch anything with my hands, I start to slide off the mattress. He cracks an eye open and lifts a hand out toward me, palm upward.

"Stay," he requests, and my heart does a slow, hard roll in my chest.

"I was just going to wash my hands. I'll come back," I promise.

He nods, dropping his hand back to the bed and closing his eyes again. Grinning, I walk to the bathroom and do a quick clean-up. Wetting a pair of washcloths with warm water, I pad back into the bedroom. I'm expecting to see

Carter right where I left him, dead asleep. I'm surprised to find him still awake, both eyes open and head turned toward the bathroom. When he sees me, he smiles. It's *my* smile. I've never once seen him gift one to anyone else.

When I get to the bed, I prop a knee up and sit down next to him. The moment I'm sitting, Carter rests a hand on my thigh and rubs a small circle with his thumb. I haven't yet put my clothes back on, and I'm pleasantly surprised to not be feeling self-conscious. I suppose once you've had your fingers inside someone's ass, there's not a lot to be shy about.

I pass one of the washcloths carefully over his abdomen, making sure to wipe up every bit of cum. Once I'm satisfied, I toss it back through the open bathroom door; Carter chuckles. I use the other cloth to carefully clean the lube from between his legs. I definitely used too much. When I've cleaned up as much as I can, I toss this cloth into the bathroom with the other. Carter's hand—still resting on my leg— makes a sweeping motion that brings his fingertips to my groin.

"Are you going to stay here?" he asks, a tad tentatively.

"Can I?"

In answer, he moves over on the bed, making room for me on that side. Once I'm sitting next to him, he reaches down to the foot of the bed and pulls the sheets back up. It makes me realize how cold I am, unclothed and coming down from the heat of having sex. I hope Carter is a post-coital snuggler, because that's something I would enjoy right now.

We settle down on our sides, facing one another with the comforter pulled up to our necks. I'm just working on extracting one of my hands when Carter beats me to it— he reaches over and curls his arm around my shoulders, tucking his fingers between me and the bed. I move a little closer, trying to make it a more comfortable position for him.

"Thanks for that," he says, and nods his head vaguely toward the bathroom.

"For what?"

"For...you know." There's a faint blush coloring his cheeks. "The towel. That was nice."

"Oh." I pause, wrong footed. "Isn't that, like...something people do?"

He snorts. "Not the people I'm usually fucking."

"Oh," I repeat, a little sadly. Further proof that quality is far more important than quantity, when it comes to sexual partners. I decide it's probably kinder if I keep this to myself. "Well, now that you're fucking me, you can expect the full-service treatment."

"Mm," he brings me in a little closer, tightening his arm. "Or the other way around."

I ponder this for a second, unsure if he means what I think he means. "You mean...you bottoming and me on top?"

This seems physically unlikely for many reasons. Not to mention he once told me he didn't like to bottom. He seemed to enjoy himself tonight, but even someone as inexperienced as I am knows there is a big difference between being fingered and fucking.

"Yeah," Carter says, completely unconcerned and unaware of the direction my thoughts have traveled.

"Okay, but you don't *like* bottoming, Carter. You told me that forever ago."

"It's you, though," he says, as though this is the most obvious thing in the world. "We're not going to have to worry about me liking anything. Trust me. It'll be fine."

"All right, but if it's not fine, I expect you to tell me," I say seriously.

"Scout's honor," he replies. "We need to turn off the light."

Both of us turn our heads and look at the light switch, over by the door. Grasping the comforter, I wiggle myself further underneath. Carter smiles like he knows what I'm doing.

"It's very cold, and I'm very small," I say, widening my eyes to look innocent. "And very, very naked."

Carter glares at me ineffectually, before slipping out of bed. I'm glad he's the one who got up—now I get a few moments to stare at the back side of a naked Carter. The light flicks off and a few seconds later the mattress compresses as he slides back in next to me. He scoots in close until I can feel his breath on my face in the darkness.

"Now *I'm* the one who's very cold," he says, trying and failing to sound harmless. "And very, very naked."

Smiling, even though he can't see it, I put an arm around him. "Yes, all right, come here."

He comes. His face presses against my neck and a heavy leg slides between mine. I'm not sure which of us falls asleep first, but it's the best sleep I've had in ages.

CARTER'S PARENTS' house is less of a house and more of an estate. There is a gate—manned by an actual security guard—who lets us pass through, up the winding driveway to the house. The closer we get to the house, the more freaked out I become. I'd known he was rich, but I hadn't known he was *rich*. When the building itself comes into view, I lean forward in my seat and shake my head.

"What the fuck," I mutter, and hear Carter scoff.

"Oh, just wait. The inside is worse. There is a pool out back, as well as a three-hole golf course and a tennis court. The pool is heated, too, so you can use it year-round." He sounds disgusted as he says this, and scowls fiercely at the house as he parks his car out front. I climb out of the passenger side just as Carter slams the driver's side door so hard I'm surprised the glass didn't shatter.

I walk around the vehicle to join him on his side. Reaching into the backseat, he pulls out the duffel bag of our stuff. Technically we have the entire week off for spring break, but we'll only be here for one night so we shared a bag. He slams the backdoor shut as well, slinging the bag over his shoulder. I wonder if we even have to knock on the door or if our presence was effectively announced with the door slamming. Carter holds his hand out to me and I grasp it, gratefully.

"Do you have a key? Or do we just..." For some reason, even though I know this is his family home, it feels strange to just walk inside. This feels like a place you have to be granted entry to, no matter who you are.

"Knock. Nobody but Mom and Jonesy will be here. I don't want to scare the shit out of them by barging inside. Half the time when I say I'm going to come home to visit, I don't bother showing up," he says, grinning wolfishly and pounding a fist on the front door. *Yes,* I think, *because that knocking won't scare anybody.*

The door is eventually answered by a man wearing a crisp button-up shirt and black pants. I squeeze Carter's hand a little tighter. *Is that a fucking butler?*

"Hey, Jonesy," Carter says, not waiting for an invite before stepping inside.

"Mister Carter. How nice of you to join us." The man's sharp eyes trail over to me and down my arm to where my hand is engulfed by Carter's. "And a guest. Your mother will be delighted."

"I can only imagine," Carter responds. "Same room as last time?"

"No, sir. There are some renovations being done, so you'll be in the pool house." Again, his eyes track over to me before settling back on Carter. "More privacy."

Carter grunts and the other man reaches for his bag. Carter jerks away from him, swiftly. "I got it."

He gives my hand a gentle tug and starts walking down a hallway to our left. From my vantage point by the door, I can see two staircases and four other doorways to choose from. The floor looks like it might be made of marble, and I can hear the tinkling of water as though there is a fountain somewhere inside. I'm horribly aware of the fact that I stepped in dog poop yesterday, and probably wasn't successful in scraping all of it off of my shoes.

"I'll let the kitchen know to prepare you some lunch, sir. I'm sure you're hungry from your drive."

Carter waves a hand over his shoulder, not looking back at the man. I shoot him a grateful smile over my own shoulder, but he's already turned away. The sound of our shoes on the marble floor feels ridiculously loud; I have the strangest desire to whisper.

"Uhm, who was that?" I ask. My voice echoes, slightly, even though I was talking low.

"Mr. Jones," Carter says, and I laugh. He smirks at me. "I know. He came to work here when he was really young, I guess, sixteen or something. My mom hired him to clean the pool or some shit. Anyway, he must have made himself useful and kissed my dad's ass just right, because they kept him around. He's worked for my parents for...twenty-five years? Maybe more. I don't fucking know how old he is."

"Huh. And is he a...butler? Manservant?"

"Personal assistant, maybe? To tell you the truth, I usually go temporarily deaf whenever someone is telling me the finer points about my dad's business and the family legacy."

I laugh again, squeezing his hand, grateful that my Carter wasn't left behind at SCU. It takes us fifteen minutes to get to the pool house, which ends up being an actual *house* that just happens to live by the pool and contain pool-related items. We bypass these and go upstairs where there are not one, but two bedrooms. Carter takes us into the larger of the two, throws the duffel bag on the floor and flops down on the bed.

"I'm ready to go home," he says. I lay down next to him.

"It's only one night," I say consolingly. He sighs. "I'm ready to go home, though, too."

"One night," he agrees, sitting up. "What do you want to do? We could hop in the pool, if you wanted. Or go eat. Jonesy said he was having lunch put out."

"I didn't bring a swimsuit," I tell him. I don't even own a swimsuit. He grins, and it looks twice as wolfish as before.

"We could swim naked."

I shove his shoulder, to no effect. "I'm not swimming naked here. Not with the personal assistant, butler guy walking around. Isn't your mom here, too?"

"Who knows," Carter shrugs. "I guess I could call her and find out."

He scrunches up his face as though smelling something unappealing. I grab his hand and twine my fingers back through his. "Okay, let's go get some lunch. Please don't let go of me. I don't want to get lost."

We make it to the kitchen without incident, and find that lunch was indeed laid out for us. It's so much food, in fact, that I wonder for a minute if other people will be joining us. Carter, unbothered by the sheer number of choices in front of him, sits down on a barstool and starts loading his plate. I follow suit and just grab everything he is grabbing.

"Who made all this?" I ask, and bite into a sandwich. It's some sort of fancy cucumber sandwich—delicious, but low on calories. Carter will probably have to eat his weight in these to feel full.

"There is a private chef who works and lives here full time," he says, and then smirks. "My mom *hates* to cook. The chef was the first person they hired once my dad's company took off. Dad says they used to live off of spaghetti, before."

"So...quite a few people live here, then? Not just your mom and dad?" I'm trying to work my mind around the sheer size of this place. A person could rattle around in this house and never see another soul if they didn't want to. It feels big and empty, and incredibly lonely.

"Mm," he hums around a mouthful of sandwich, thinking. "Not a lot. Jonesy, obviously, and whomever they have cooking for them usually lives on site. But I think that's it. Cleaners come twice a week to, you know, shine the golden candlesticks and whatever, but they don't live here."

I laugh. I haven't seen a single golden candlestick. "What about the grounds? I bet there is a lot of upkeep."

"Yeah, same as the cleaning crew. Twice a week. Fucking insane," he says, and gives me an apologetic little smile. I pat his arm.

"Absolutely fucking batshit insane," I agree. "You know, it's a good thing we're only staying one night. You would perish if you had to live off of this food."

He snorts. "No shit. Dinner will be better. A lot better, probably. Jonesy will have told them I brought a guest, which means they'll have to pull out all the stops to impress you."

"Uhm," I fidget with my fork, "I did bring my nice clothes, but you know I don't actually have anything *this* nice, right?"

I wave around at the house. I'm picturing his family having dinner around a massive dining room table, all of them wearing formal cocktail attire. Carter shrugs and pulls a face around a mouthful of sandwich.

"It's okay, really." He fiddles with his plate, turning it around on the marble countertop, eyes darting around the room. "Just, uhm...don't hate me for all of this. I know it's bad, and completely fucking ridiculous. I'm not this kind of person."

"I know," I say quietly. "There isn't a single thing you could do, or show me, that would make me hate you. You can't help it that you were born into a family with money, I know that."

"Yeah," he says, still fidgeting. "Still. I feel like a douche when I complain about it. You know, hard life and all, growing up with a personal chef and a tennis court in the backyard."

"Mm." He's trying to make a joke, but there's not a lot of heart behind it. Truthfully, I think it probably *was* hard to grow up here. The entire house feels cold and unwelcoming. I can't wrap my mind around the image of a child running through these halls.

We finish eating without seeing another person. Carter offers to give me a tour, which ends up being a seemingly endless journey of empty guest bedrooms and sitting rooms. One hallway is lined with painted portraits; I pause to look at one. He looks a little bit like Carter.

"Who's this?" I ask.

"That's my grandfather, Carter Morgan. Not to be confused with my father, Carter Morgan," he says seriously, and points to another portrait.

"Ah. I'll do my best to keep that straight," I laugh, shaking my head and peering around at the other paintings. "Where's yours?"

"Burned it," he answers proudly. "Fucker lit right up. Had a nice little bonfire."

I tip my head back and laugh, the sound echoing up into the vaulted ceilings. "I think we need one of these above the mantle, at home. We can commission one of the both of us."

"Shut up, no."

"It'll be nice," I say, trailing after him as we leave the hallway. "Oh! How about a themed portrait? We can dress up as Victorian men."

"I beg you to stop."

Laughing, I move up next to him and he puts an arm over my shoulder. We finish the tour with the grounds, which ends up being more fun than the house, if only because we get to walk around outside. By the time we get back to the pool house, we're pink-cheeked with cold and it's time to get ready for dinner. While Carter digs our clothes out of the bag, I stand at the window and look up at the main house. Nearly all of the lights are on, even though the majority of the rooms are empty. I wonder if that's for our benefit.

"Here," Carter says, and I turn to see him laying my clothes onto the bed. "Too bad we don't have time for a shower. Warm us up a little bit."

He waggles his eyebrows at me, making sure I understand what he's really suggesting. I peek into the bathroom and look at the massive, walk-in shower. Neither of our bathrooms at home have a shower big enough for two to fit comfortably. We've tried.

"Mm. Something for later, perhaps."

"God knows I'll need something to look forward to in order to get through dinner," he says, yanking off his pants and dropping them to the floor.

There's soft music playing when we get back to the main house. I nearly ask if there is a pianist who lives here, but Carter points a finger at the ceiling and mutters *speakers* before I can. The dining room is far more inviting now than it had been earlier, during the tour: there is a fire going in the fireplace and candles on the table. Only half of the table is set, meaning we'll all be seated together. I'm grateful—I hadn't been looking forward to shouting down the length of the table to speak to Carter's parents.

His mom is the first to arrive, and she looks almost exactly the way I'd pictured her: shoulder-length blonde hair, Carter's eyes, and a smooth, Botox-ed face. She's slim and shorter than Carter, but she makes up for it by wearing painful looking heels. She is also—as he warned me she would be—wearing a form-fitting cocktail dress, and a full face of makeup. When she greets Carter, she gives him a light kiss on his cheek and a small smile.

"Hey, Mom," he says, and for some reason my heart breaks a little bit. I greet Jefferson with more warmth than his mother just afforded him. "This is my boyfriend, Zeke."

"Hi, Mrs. Morgan," I hold out a hand to her and she grasps it, smiling benignly at me. If she's surprised by the word *boyfriend*, she doesn't show it. Perhaps nothing about Carter could surprise her anymore. "I like your house; the grounds are beautiful."

"Thank you," she says, and then adds: "I've recently taken

up gardening. Unfortunately, I mostly end up making a mess of it all and the real gardeners have to come and fix it. Did you happen to make it down to the tennis court?"

"Yes, I got the full tour." Her smile grows a little wider. Beside her, Carter is standing back on his heels, hands shoved into his pockets as he listens.

"I planted those rose bushes along the north side of the court. They were tiny little things at the beginning," she cups her perfectly manicured hands to show me, "but are growing quite nicely, now."

"They're beautiful," I tell her, even though I can't remember even seeing rose bushes. It had been hard to care about anything other than Carter's warm hand around mine, and the way his laugh would echo across the grounds when I teased it out of him.

She waves this away. "Oh, thank you, but it's just a little hobby. Let's have a seat, your father will be here shortly."

This last is directed at Carter. He scowls, but shrugs and moves toward the table to pull out a chair. He looks over at me, patting it. As I move to sit down, I notice his mom is watching us. When she catches me staring at her, she gives me another of her small smiles. She hands them out more freely than her son, although they seem less genuine. Carter flops down in the chair next to mine, scooting it close enough that we won't be able to maneuver silverware without bumping elbows.

"He's never brought somebody home to meet us," she confides to me.

"Nope," Carter confirms.

I'm saved from answering by the appearance of Carter's dad. At least, I'm assuming it's his dad since I doubt any member of the staff would be wearing a suit that fancy.

Again, I applaud myself on my ability to correctly guess what Carter's parents look like. His dad is the same height as his son, but a good deal less bulky. He fills out the suit, but most certainly isn't hiding any hockey muscles underneath it. His hair is a darker blonde and his eyes a slate blue behind wire glasses. There is almost nothing of Carter in his face, beyond the shape of his jaw.

"Dad," Carter says, not bothering to stand up. "This is my boyfriend, Zeke Cassidy."

I do stand up, because I'm meeting his parents and I want to make a good impression. His dad sighs at Carter's introduction, but shakes my hand with both of his. The look he gives me is kinder than the one he sends Carter's way.

"Nice to meet you, Zeke Cassidy. How was the drive? It can be rough this time of year." As he sits down, he unbuttons his suit jacket in a practiced motion. As though summoned, a man appears in the doorway wearing a crisp white shirt and black slacks.

"I'll bring in dinner then, Mr. Morgan?" he asks, and Carter's dad nods but doesn't look over at him.

"It was fine," Carter answers, shrugging. He's slouched down in his seat as though he'd like nothing more than to slide beneath the table and disappear. If he did, I'd join him.

"Good, good," Mr. Morgan says, and then pauses as the man from before starts putting food down in front of us.

I look over at Carter, uncomfortable. It's a strange feeling, being in what is obviously someone's home but being served like it's a five-star restaurant. I miss the casualness and comfort of our home back at SCU. We might not have a gourmet chef cooking and serving our food, but I'd take anything over this. He grimaces at me, correctly reading my expression. When a plate is set down in front of him, he looks up.

"Thank you," he says, and I do the same. The man nods but says nothing as he leaves. *Jesus Christ, this is so awkward.*

"So, kids, how are classes? Having a good semester?" Mr. Morgan asks. I feel Carter stiffen beside me. I wonder if calling him a *kid* was done to purposely rile him up.

"Fine," I answer quietly, as I cut into my food. I have no idea what it is. Probably duck, or whatever sort of meat rich people eat for dinner. Beside me, Carter hasn't done anything more than fidget with his fork. He makes no move to start eating.

"Classes suck, I hate them," he says baldly. "But that's not why I'm...we're...here. I need to talk to you about something."

I glance at him. I suppose I shouldn't be surprised—Carter isn't exactly known for his subtlety. His mom, who also hasn't touched her food, smiles at him. His dad doesn't even look up from his plate; there's no acknowledgment that Carter spoke to him at all.

"What's that?" his mom asks, politely curious.

"Coach Mackenzie helped put me in touch with an agent, and I'm going to pursue a career in the NHL," he says in a clear, ringing voice that fills the mostly empty room. His dad looks up at him, dabbing idly at his lips with a cloth napkin. He looks amused.

"Carter, isn't it about time we finished with this dream?"

I flinch at the tone. It's the tone adults use to explain something to children—at once cajoling and derogatory. It's not the tone you'd use with your adult son. And certainly not if your adult son was Carter, who will most certainly take offense.

"No," Carter answers, fist clenched around his fork.

"I've indulged this fantasy for long enough. I let you play hockey—paid for it, I might add—and now it's time to join the real world. Enough is enough." He cuts a hand through the air as he talks, his voice hard. I can practically feel the rage radiating off of Carter; he's going to bend that fork in half if he grips it any tighter.

"I'll pay you back," he says, and his dad sighs.

"The money isn't the problem."

Carter makes an aggrieved noise in the back of his throat. "Then what's the problem? If I fail, I fail, but at least I tried. It's what I *want* to do."

"It's not about whether or not you'll succeed. You're going to graduate and come work for me, as you promised."

"That wasn't the deal. I play hockey for SCU while I get my degree and then we *revisit the conversation*. That was the deal, and this is me revisiting the conversation. Just, listen to me for a second—"

"No," Mr. Morgan's voice cuts through the room like a blade. Carter is so still beside me, I don't think he's breathing. As though remembering that I'm in the room, Mr. Morgan clears his throat and tries to smile. "Perhaps your friend might take his meal in the kitchen; give us the privacy to have this conversation?"

"His name is Zeke, he's my boyfriend, not my friend," Carter says, before I can even move to stand up, "and he can stay. I need him."

Carter's dad pulls off his glasses and rubs at his eyes with his thumb and forefinger. I try not to look too pleased with myself; below the table, I put my hand on Carter's knee. *I need you, too.*

"Can you not listen to me one time? Must you fight me on everything?" his dad asks, exasperated.

"If you wanted obedience, you should have gotten a dog."

I snort, and then hastily cover it with a cough. Carter helps me with the charade by lightly patting my back. His mom reaches across the table and nudges my water glass toward me. I could almost swear I see a glint of amusement in her eyes.

"We're not having this conversation, Carter," Mr. Morgan doubles down, annoyance peeking through the calm veneer. "Hockey is not a career. It's something you can use to pad your resume. It is *not* a suitable choice for your future, which is something you would understand if you ever listened to me."

"You don't listen to me!" Carter explodes, before closing his eyes and breathing out hard through his nose as though visibly reaching for calm. "I don't want to work for you, Dad. *I don't want to.*" He enunciates each word carefully, voice wavering in anger and frustration. "Doesn't what I want count for fucking anything?"

"Yes, honey, of course it does," his mom answers, swiftly. She sends a silently communicative look at her husband, who sighs again. I'm getting sick of the noise. He looks away from the table, staring sightlessly out the dark window. The room is uncomfortably silent, absent of even the clink of silverware. Nobody is eating.

"Look, Carter. The bottom line is, I haven't paid three years of tuition at that school for you to play a game. I did it so you could earn a degree that would be *useful* in the real world. I understand you want to play hockey; I'd like to play golf all day, but that is a *dream* and not a *reality*. Every kid wants to be the football player, or hockey player, or NASCAR driver. The difference is most kids grow out of that and realize it's time to grow up."

The sharp inhalation of breath from Carter sounds like knives in his lungs. Before he can say something he regrets, I speak; it's the first words I've said since dinner was served. "It's not the same thing."

Everybody looks at me. Mr. Morgan looks shocked by my presence at the table for the second time tonight. I divide my attention between Mr. and Mrs. Morgan, since the words are for them. Carter already knows.

"Perhaps the reason you don't play golf for a living is because you weren't good enough to play golf professionally. Carter *is* good enough to play hockey professionally. His dream is the reality."

A ringing silence follows. I glance over at Carter to find his gaze already on my face.

"Passions don't pay bills," his dad says.

"His will," I retort quietly. Another sigh, this one accompanied by the scratch of chair legs across the floor. Carter and I break eye contact and look over at his dad, who has risen to standing.

"You've never even seen me play," Carter says to him, voice raw, almost pleading.

"I've made my position clear. You will do whatever you want to do, as always, but I will not continue to pay for it. If you want to pursue a career in professional sports, I will not continue to waste my money for you to attend that school. You have until the end of this year, Carter. After that, you are on your own."

My jaw actually drops. I know Carter was worried about this exact thing, but it felt so unbelievable. His dad buttons the front of his suit and leaves the room without a backward glance. I turn to watch him go, confused. *Did he really just walk out in the middle of the conversation?* Appalled, I turn back to Carter.

"What...He's coming back, right?" Offense colors my tone on his behalf. Carter shakes his head.

"Nope. He always has to have the last fucking word. He can't just have a conversation like a normal goddamn—"

"Carter," his mom breaks in smoothly, before he can pick up too much steam. She dabs carefully at the corner of her mouth, even though I didn't see her eat anything. "We've never gone to one of your games, because we didn't want to see you get hurt. Hockey is a dangerous sport."

Carter stands, tossing his napkin down onto his still-full plate of food. It occurs to me that he is probably starving. Cucumber sandwiches at lunch time is not enough of a caloric intake for an athlete. I rise as well, placing my napkin on my chair and waiting to see what Carter wants to do.

"I'm the goalie, Mom. Which—if you'd ever bothered to watch—you would know means I'm pretty much untouchable. I don't get hurt," he says, holding his arms wide in frustration. "We're leaving early tomorrow, so I think we'll call it a night and go to bed."

She nods and Carter needs no further permission. He swings around, jaw clenched tight, and gestures for me to proceed him through the doorway. His hand is gentle on my lower back.

"Carter," Mrs. Morgan's soft voice has us turning back around. She's still seated at the table, somehow looking cool and collected despite the tumultuous evening. Perhaps she's used to it, after living with the Morgan men for so long. "I'll speak to your father."

He inhales, deeply, and lets it out slowly. "Goodnight, Mom."

"Goodnight. It was nice to meet you, Zeke."

I murmur a response and allow Carter to lead me from the room. We don't speak as we walk through the equally silent house, but it's a comfortable silence. I can tell he's mad, but it's not directed at me. His hand has left my lower back and crept around to my hip, hugging me to his side. I can't tell if he's comforting me or himself. When we get to the pool house, he squeezes me to his side and presses kisses the top of my head.

"Thank you," he says into my hair.

"For what?"

"Everything you said to my dad. That was...it was a nice thing to say, that's all," he says stiffly. "I just wanted you to know that I appreciated it."

"It was true. And, you're welcome." I sit down on the end of the bed and scrub my hands over my face. I'm exhausted. "That did not go as I thought it would go."

"Went exactly how I thought it would go," he mumbles, undoing half of the buttons on his shirt before giving up and pulling it over his head. He strips out of his pants and stands there in briefs and an undershirt, looking at me. Despite myself, I remember his suggestion from earlier about the walk-in shower. He holds a hand out to me, pulling me to my feet.

"What do you need? We could go to sleep or you could strip and lay there," I say, pointing at the massive bed, "and I could just...lick you all over. Whatever will make you feel better."

"Oh my god," he laughs. I beam, happy to hear that noise and see that look on his face. "While that does sound like a good time, let's put a pin in that one. I want to leave as early as humanly possible tomorrow, so we should probably get some sleep."

Nodding, I change into pajamas and join him in the bed. He's quiet and it's dark in the room; I'm unable to see him. Reaching out, I place my palm on his chest. His worry feels like a third person in the room. After a few moments, he puts his hand on top of mine and sighs.

"What should I do?" he asks.

"I don't know," I admit. It was easier to convince him to pursue a hockey career when I thought his parents wouldn't pull the rug out from under his feet. "What are the chances that you'll get picked up by a team before next year?"

"I have no idea. I mean...there's no guarantee that any team will sign me, let alone when."

"So, essentially, you're good through the rest of this school year, but if you weren't signed by the next term, you'd be on your own. You'd either have to cover tuition yourself or drop out," I summarize, feeling sick to my stomach. "That's not a forgiving timeline."

"No. But you don't have to worry," he says suddenly, and increases the pressure on my hand. "Dad owns our house, it's not like he's paying a mortgage. So, you'll still have a place to live next year, no matter what."

This is, quite literally, the last thing I was worrying about. I move closer to him and kiss the first part of his body I can find in the dark—his shoulder. "Carter, I wasn't worried about that."

"I was. I don't want to cause problems for you. But he won't make us leave, Mom would never let him."

"I like your mom," I tell him. She's clearly the softer of the two, though not by much.

"Me too," he says, and I chuckle. "I didn't know about the

gardening thing. Do you even remember seeing fucking rose bushes when we went for a walk?"

"Not a single one," I answer, and we devolve into laughter.

"I can't wait to go home," Carter says, after catching his breath. "I have some ideas about how we can spend our spring break."

"Homework and studying," I put in and he groans, dramatically.

"Okay, sure," a pause, and I can hear the smile even though I can't see it, "but we're also going to do that licking thing."

20

Carter

WHEN WE PULL into the garage, Zeke and I look at each other with identical expressions of relief. We're home far later than I had originally anticipated, given a surprise storm that decided to pass through on our drive. We hop out of the car simultaneously and head inside. I check my phone on the way and note I've got two missed calls from my mom and a single missed call from Coach Mackenzie. There is also a text message from Vas, asking how things went this weekend. I ignore everyone but Vas—shooting him a quick message I toss my phone on the kitchen counter and decide to forget about it for the rest of the evening.

"Ah. I feel so much better," Zeke says, coming out of the downstairs bathroom and wiping his hands on his thighs. "If we'd been stuck in traffic even five minutes more, I swear I would have peed on your car seat."

"Or," I say, leaning against the counter and watching him,

amused, "you could have just peed in one of our empty water bottles. Instead of, you know, on my seat."

He throws up his hands. "Figure of speech."

Laughing, I look at the time on the oven. "So, what should we do to kick off spring break? You hungry? Want a shower? Gym?"

"Hmm. I'm still pretty full from lunch; I'm not even going to respond to the gym suggestion. But a shower does sound good." His eyes light up and he steps closer to me, sidling into my personal space until our shirts brush. "Together?"

"Yeah? Last time wasn't too much of a deterrent?" The last time we showered together we kept knocking our elbows into the wall and bumping into each other. What had started as sexy had ended with the bathroom ringing with laughter.

"Nope," he slides his hand into mine and we amble up the stairs.

Other than some planned workouts and the quick visit to see my parents, I've got nothing going on for the entire week. And although Zeke was right in saying that we'll need to do some studying, I'm hoping that the majority of the time is spent together. We've never had so much time uninterrupted by hockey or school—the possibilities feel endless.

Our shower is exactly that—a shower. Zeke is quiet, for once, so we wash mostly in silence. We take our time, and since he doesn't try to turn this into shower sex, neither do I. I do, however, take the opportunity of a well-lit room and a small space to look my fill of him. He's so slim; the line of his clavicle is severe—a narrow shelf of bone, trailing to equally narrow shoulder blades. I'm a little bit obsessed with how he looks.

Because he's right there, I run my fingertips over the top of his shoulder, down along his collarbone, and over the other shoulder. On the way back, I stop and trail my knuckles down the center of his chest. His stomach is perfectly flat, framed by slender hips. Watching my hand, I trace those too. Eventually, I become aware of how still Zeke's standing. I glance up at his face. He's watching me, a small smile playing at the corners of his mouth.

"Sorry," I clear my throat and drop my hand.

"Nobody ever looks at me like that," he says.

"They better not. Only I can look at you like that," I tell him, and the smile grows. I reach a hand out to brush the wet hair out of his face, rivulets of water trailing down his cheeks. I am suddenly very, very horny.

Zeke's eyes leave my face and coast down my body until they settle on my pelvis where I am sporting a semi. He looks back up at me, humor dancing in his eyes, and crowds me until our wet chests are pressed together. He tips his chin up. I lean down to oblige him, putting a hand to the back of his head to hold his lips to mine.

"Clean enough?" he asks against my mouth. In answer, I reach around him to turn off the water. Grabbing a towel, I throw it over his shoulders and give him a vigorous rub. He laughs, like I knew he would. He's like my own personal ray of sunshine.

I don't give him the opportunity to put clothes on, but slide the towel off and walk him backward toward the bed. I turn us around and then pull him down on top of me. He smiles into my mouth, our teeth bumping together in sloppy kisses that neither of us are willing to break. I'm only half on the bed, with Zeke mostly on top of me, our still damp skin warm against one another. My knee twinges where it's twisted at an odd angle. I can't really bring myself to care.

"So impatient," he mumbles, and moves to pull away. I try

to grab him but he gives me a playful shove. "Scoot up before you hurt yourself."

I slide up toward the head of the bed; Zeke follows and this time lets me pull him back down on top of me. Holding his head with both of my hands, I kiss him fucking senseless. We stop when my lungs burn from lack of air, and I gentle my hands. He rests his forehead against mine, fingers coasting down my ribs. Confidently, he stretches an arm out and pulls the lube from my bedside table.

"Grab a condom, too," I tell him, and he looks at me.

"Are you sure?"

"Yes." I wish I'd never told him that I don't like to bottom, because he's assigned more meaning to it than it deserves. What I should have said is I don't like to bottom when I can't see the other person's face. I don't like to be held down, and I don't like it rough. Somehow, I don't think any of these things will be a problem with Zeke.

"Okay, but are you *sure*," he says, grabbing my chin and looking hard into my eyes like he's trying to see into my soul.

"Do you want it in writing?"

"Don't joke, I'm being serious," he says sternly. I sigh and close my eyes, because I don't think I'm going to be able to say these words with his face that close to mine.

"I don't mind being the bottom, as long as there is enough prep. I'd prefer to not be on my hands and knees, and I'd prefer not to be...like...drilled into the mattress."

There is a very long silence following these words. I keep my eyes closed. I'm not sure why saying any of those things is embarrassing, but it is. Even to Zeke, whom I should be comfortable saying *anything* to. He's still got ahold of my chin, and uses the grip to reach up and catch my lower lip with his thumb, gently.

"Hey," he says quietly, as though the room is full of people but he's speaking to me alone, "look at me."

I open my eyes. He's got one hand planted on the bed and has shifted so that his face is further away, hovering above mine. My eyes skim over his face and find it contemplative, not critical. I relax.

"We don't have to do this," he reminds me.

"I know. I want to. Just...not the way that I said."

"Of course. To be honest, I think I lack the physicality needed to drill you into the mattress." This startles a laugh out of me, which seems to be happening more and more often of late. Zeke smiles, tenderly. "And I don't think I'd like the hands and knees thing, either. I mean, I want to *look* at you. You've got a very nice back, but your eyes are better."

"Exactly," I sigh. "Exactly."

"Thanks for telling me that. And while we're on the subject, I'll just go ahead and let you know that I've given exactly one blowjob in my life, and I think it might also be my last."

This time, when I laugh, I curl upward to kiss him. I have no idea how I was able to survive so long without Zeke Cassidy. I think if he ever left me, I'd die.

"Giving head can be awful," I agree. He sits back against my stomach to give his shoulder a rest; I put my hands on his thighs and admire the view I now have of his dick. "I usually don't like it either. Except, apparently, with you."

"All right, so we've covered blowjobs." Zeke makes a motion of ticking off a checkmark in midair. "This is turning into a very informational naked chat. What else haven't we discussed?"

"No more talking for today. I can only take so much." I

swipe my thumbs along the crease where his thighs meet his groin and he gives me a stern look. I try to look innocent.

"You win. I'll allow you to distract me this one time. But we're going to circle back to this conversation. I need to know your thoughts on rimming and—"

I cut him off with a kiss, tangling my tongue with his and rocking my hips upward to grind against him. He groans, fingers tightening where they are pressed against my pecs. He mimics me, rolling his pelvis and rubbing his dick against mine. I swear I almost come from the noise he makes alone. Clamping my hands on his hips, I direct him to repeat the motion. He does, frotting against me in a slow, even motion. I've never, in my entire life, been so turned on from doing so little.

Gasping, Zeke pulls his mouth from mine and blindly reaches for the lube. "Jesus," he mutters.

"Do the condom first. Before your hands get messy."

"Smart," he says, and leans down to kiss the hollow of my throat.

He situates himself down near my feet; I lift my legs without prompting and watch as he opens the condom with trembling fingers.

"You okay?" I ask, narrowing my eyes on his hands.

"What? Oh, yeah. Nervous, but, like, good nervous. Where's the lube?"

I hand it to him and watch as he coats the condom before looking at his hand, perplexed. "We should have brought a towel over."

"You can wipe your hand on the bed, if you want. I can do laundry," I tell him, and then laugh when he scrunches up his nose. "Or just grab one of the towels we used in the bathroom."

He brightens. "Good idea. Wait right here."

Patting my knee with his clean hand, he goes to the bathroom to bring back one of the bath towels. Climbing back between my legs, he looks at me and adopts a serious tone.

"Are you ready for your prostate exam?"

We're still laughing when he passes a lubed finger between my raised legs and traces it around my hole. As he preps me, he runs the fingers of his free hand over my legs and occasionally drops kisses wherever he can reach. It's easily the best prostate exam I have ever received. Zeke works me open slowly and methodically which ensures that I am prepped well enough, but also that I am going to bust a nut if he doesn't fuck me soon. I'm sweating and my feet are tingling so much it feels like I've got a tens unit hooked up to them.

"Zeke," I say, and then groan when he takes another pass of my prostate, "I'm good. You could fit your whole arm in there at this point."

He does a few more slow strokes before carefully pulling his hand away. He wipes his fingers on the towel again; I make a mental note to remember to grab one for him next time. I wait for him, watching as he looks me over appraisingly. One of his hands is resting on my ankle, his fingers moving idly. He sighs.

"All right, I'm not a big porn guy. You're going to have to give me a little direction."

"You can just come here." I hold a hand out to him through my raised legs. When he's close enough to do so, I pull him down to kiss him, resting a palm on his chest as I do so. His heart is beating fast.

Pressing a thumb to the bottom of his jaw, I angle it upward and pull my mouth away from his. I hold him to me, fingers spread wide across his back, and lavish attention to his neck. He moans, softly, and lowers down further. The blood is pounding in my groin—helped by the slight friction of Zeke's stomach against my dick. I can feel myself leaking against my abdomen. I'm probably going to come the second he's inside me, like this is my first time being touched.

The kissing has served it's intended purpose; his pulse has calmed and he's far more relaxed against me. Raising my feet off the bed, I nip lightly at his jaw and slide my hands down to his hips.

"Knees on the bed," I tell him. "A little wider than that."

"Okay," he breathes, ducking his head to look between us. "Hey, did you know that cats have penile spines?"

Thrown by this completely random and disturbing fact, I'm distracted. "What?"

He looks up at me. "The male cats."

"Yeah, I was able to puzzle that part out for myself."

A small giggle bubbles its way up his throat. "Sorry. I was just looking at *your* dick and it popped into my head. I knew you'd want to know, so I thought I'd share."

"I'm glad neither of our dicks have penile spines," I say seriously, and he bites his lip to keep from laughing. "Come here."

I reach one hand between us and keep the other on his hip. He's ducked his head again, watching. Directing him, I apply gentle forward pressure to his hip; he comes easily until I've brought him in enough for his tip to push inside. He balks, halting right as I can feel the stretch. I can't see his face—he's still watching where our bodies are now connected. I give his hip a squeeze.

"You can move," I tell him, voice tight. I *need* him to move. He looks up, wide eyes locking on mine.

"Okay," he says, and he sounds every bit as strained as I feel.

I put both hands on his hips as he rocks forward experimentally. *Oh, thank god.* I groan, pulling my knees back into my chest and closing my eyes. He's moving painfully slow—I can feel every millimeter of movement as he tunnels inward until he bottoms out. I realize I've got a death grip on him and loosen my fingers. The last thing I want is to leave bruises on his skin. He's completely immobile; I open my eyes to find him watching me.

"You can move," I repeat. I'm about to say more when he gives one fluid thrust and hits my prostate perfectly. Groaning, I arch my back and use every bit of my goalie flexibility to bring my legs up and back. I want him deep. I want to *feel* him.

"Oh my god," he murmurs, dropping his forehead down to my shoulder.

I'd agree with him if I wasn't focusing all of my attention on trying not to blow my load too early. He's barely moving, his hips rolling languidly and his dick dragging across my prostate so slowly it's torturous. He's experimenting, trying to figure out his positioning and rhythm. I'm going to explode long before he does.

The buzzing in my extremities picks up as he moves faster. Sliding one hand down to cup his ass, I squeeze and he gasps. He kisses his way up my neck and then fuses his mouth to mine, moaning. He lowers down enough that his abdomen brushes across my dick every time he thrusts. *Yes, yes, yes,* I think as I kiss the breath from his lungs.

Heat steadily climbs my spine, release building with Zeke's every push into my body. I come first—cum painting both of our abdomens with heat. He gasps into my mouth, surprised, and his thrusts become a little more frantic as though me coming eroded some of his control.

"Don't stop," I pant, when he shows signs of wanting to slow down, "don't stop."

Moaning, he presses his mouth to mine and continues moving. Neither of us can devote much attention to kissing— it's little more than lips brushing as we move together. I've got both hands on his ass now, pulling him in every time he rocks forward, trying to tunnel him deeper. My entire body is buzzing from the sustained pressure against my prostate and my cum is tacky between us. I'm in fucking heaven. He gasps when he comes, tucking his face into my shoulder and dropping on top of me almost immediately. I wait until the movement of his hips stops completely before I carefully lower my feet back to the bed.

Feeling ridiculously emotional, I wrap my arms around him; one hand on the back of his head and the other on his back. I really, wholeheartedly think that if he were to pull away from me right now, I might actually cry. Taking several long, deep breaths, I try to get ahold of myself. The last thing I want is for him to see my face and worry that he hurt me. *Don't mind me, just having an emotional crisis after getting boned, like a goddamn amateur.*

Eventually, since this is Zeke, the continued silence becomes worrisome. His face is lodged firmly in the crease of my neck, warm breath coasting over my throat and making me shiver. He hasn't moved or said a word; the only indication that he's even awake is the flutter of his eyelashes across my skin when he blinks. I clear my throat.

"Zeke?"

"Mmfph," he makes an incomprehensible noise. One of his hands moves, fingers toying with my earlobe.

"You okay?"

"I have a lot to say, but I don't know how to say it," he says, voice muffled. He adjusts himself, slightly, and the press of his mouth against my neck has me relaxing. He wouldn't kiss me if something was wrong.

"That's a first," I tease. I know what he means, though. I have a lot to say as well, although I'm pretty sure everything I want to say is eventually going to boil down to three words. I should probably feel more freaked out by that than I do; mostly, I just feel content.

"Was that good for you?"

I smile up at the ceiling. Nobody has ever asked me that before. I open my mouth to say something flippant about how I've never come so hard in my life, but bite the words back at the last moment. Now's not the moment and he deserves honesty, even if it's hard for me to spit it out.

"Yeah, that was good for me. Actually, I've never, uhm… that was the best sex has ever felt, for me. Probably because it was with you." He breathes out hard, against my neck, and kisses me again. Turning my head, I rest my cheek on his hair.

He adjusts again, moving his leg so it's in a more comfortable position. I'm surprised he hasn't gotten up to take care of the condom and the mess between us. "Hey, Carter?"

"Yeah?"

"I really like you. And I'm really glad that you're the first person I've done that with." He turns his face further into my neck, muffling his voice. "And it probably would have made more sense for us to shower *after* we did this."

Smiling, I kiss the top of his head. His hair is wet and messy; he smells like me. "Yeah, probably. Want to get up and take care of it?"

He lifts his head. "Yeah," he says, grimacing apologetically.

Gently, I guide his mouth to mine with a hand on the back of his head. I can't get enough of the taste of him. "All right, let's get up."

He climbs off of me, and goes immediately to the bathroom to dispose of the condom. Giving him time to clean up, I strip the bed. Truthfully, it wouldn't bother me to sleep on the soiled sheet, but I don't think Zeke would appreciate rolling over in the middle of the night and touching a wet spot from stray lube. Easier to just get a clean blanket.

Shoving everything into the laundry basket, I toss a clean sheet over the bed and call it good. I'm walking into the bathroom just as Zeke is coming out. He's got a towel in his hand and smiles when he sees me, tipping his chin up to look at me. Holding out a hand for the towel, I lean down to kiss him despite the fact that my lips are sore and swollen from all the kissing we've been doing today. Totally fucking worth it.

I have to tug on the towel to get him to let go of it. I raise my eyebrows at him and he huffs. "I was going to do it."

Propping a foot up on the toilet seat, I clean between my legs first. Zeke, worried about doing harm, used way too much lube. I glance over to see him standing in the doorway, leaning against the wall and watching me. My stomach takes less effort to clean; when I'm done, I wash my hands and eye his reflection in the mirror. He's watching me *very* closely.

"Zeke." He stops looking at my ass and brings his gaze to mine.

"Sorry. I was just making sure you were moving okay."

"I'm okay," I tell him, exasperated. Turning around, I let him lead the way back into bed.

"Yeah, you say that, but last time you bottomed, you came

home and very obviously was hurt. So, sue me for being concerned." He pulls the clean blanket over us and looks at it, startled and temporarily distracted. "Oh. Did you change the sheets?"

"Yes. And last time was...different. You didn't hurt me. Thank god you don't have a barbed penis." He gives a hoot of delighted laughter, elbowing me in the ribs. I grin. Nobody finds me as funny as he does. He snuggles into me, pulling my arm over the top of him before I can do it myself.

"Do you want another penis fact?" He sounds delighted, already excited to tell me.

"Oh lord. Yes, all right, hit me with a penis fact. God help me."

"Echidnas have a four-headed penis." He drops this bomb and then pauses, grinning maniacally. "Only two heads are used at a time, though. The females have a dual branched reproductive system. And then the next time the little guy mates, he uses the other half of his penis."

"I don't even know what an echidna is."

"It's a spiny little thing." He cups his hands, showing me it's size. "They're cute."

"Except for their monster dicks."

He snorts. "Google it."

"I'm not going to Google echidna penis, Zeke. Can you imagine the sort of spam I'd get after that?"

He devolves into delighted laughter. I smile, watching him. I'm feeling pleasantly sleepy, after the long drive and the evening activities. Perhaps I'll try and convince him to sleep in tomorrow; spend a little time warm in bed in the morning, instead of going our separate ways to the gym and the library. Abruptly, I think of the missed calls waiting for me on my phone, downstairs. I feel bad for leaving Coach waiting.

"What is it?"

"I need to go grab my phone," I tell him, thinking regretfully of the fact that I'll have to leave the bed. "Coach Mackenzie called me. I should probably text him."

"You should," Zeke says immediately. "He might be worried, if you don't."

Sighing, I slip out of the bed and lean over him for a quick kiss. I head downstairs, snatching up my phone and noting that there are now two missed calls from Coach. Cringing, I listen to the first voicemail.

Carter. You should be heading back by now, so call me once you get home. I want to make some changes to your training schedule; nothing major, just a few things Anthony suggested for you. I hope everything went okay with your family. Call me.

The second voicemail is more terse, and I can perfectly envision the look on Coach's face as he left it.

I'm assuming you haven't called me back because your generation is allergic to speaking on the phone. So, if calling is too hard for you, send me a text message, or a smoke signal, or a damn carrier pigeon.

Smiling, I head back upstairs. Flicking the light off on my way into the room, I fit myself back against Zeke and replay the voicemail for him. He bites his lip.

"You're in trouble," he remarks.

Coach answers on the first ring when I call him back. "Carter," he snaps.

"Hey, Coach," I respond, blithely. Sliding an arm underneath him, I pull Zeke toward me until his head is pillowed on my shoulder.

"Thank you for calling me back. I'm glad to see that you didn't get into a car accident on the way back to campus." He sounds pissed, even though it's clear he was worried about me.

"Yeah, sorry. The drive took a lot longer than expected and then I was getting laid." There is a sputter of indignation from Zeke, and a hard poke in the ribs. On the other end of the line, I hear Coach muttering something about needing a new job.

"How did it go with your family?" he asks.

"It was shit. Went exactly how I thought it would go. Dad won't pay my tuition if I plan on moving forward with hockey." Scowling up at the ceiling, I try to keep an even tone. It's not Coach's fault my dad is an asshole. "I won't qualify for any sort of aid, so unless I get picked up by a team this summer, I'd have to find a job and make enough money to pay my tuition for next year out-of-pocket and I've never had a job in my life, so I—"

"Carter," he interrupts, and I snap my jaw shut. He sounds less angry than before. "Let's take this one step at a time. Your parents phone numbers are the same as you gave me your freshman year, correct?"

"Yeah," I say, confused. Weird fucking question.

"Okay. I'll call them. Now, when you come to the gym tomorrow morning, stop by my office first. Anthony had some good suggestions about—"

"You're going to call them?" I hiss, interrupting him mid sentence. He's silent for a moment and when he continues it's in the same tone one might use to calm a startled animal.

"Yes, Carter, I am going to call them. I think perhaps I might be able to offer some insight that they'll appreciate."

It won't work. Nothing Coach Mackenzie has to say will sway my father, who's hated my love for hockey since the day it was born. I tip my head sideways so that my cheek can rest on the top of Zeke's hair.

"Okay." My voice sounds small, even to my own ears. This whole situation is so ridiculous; I'm disgusted with myself.

"Okay," Coach echoes. "My office, tomorrow morning. Have a good evening."

Hanging up, I let my arm flop down onto the mattress. I wish life wasn't so complicated, and I could just play hockey and have sex with my boyfriend for the rest of all time.

"Coach is going to call Dad," I tell him, and feel his head bob in a nod.

"Good."

"It won't work."

"It might, you never know. And if not, we'll figure something else out. Maybe your dad is bluffing," he adds, hopefully.

"He's not. This is so stupid. I should just get a job and figure out how to pay my own way. God, if only I could quit school and just play for the team, that would be perfect. I don't even want this stupid degree."

"Mm. But even if you do play in the NHL, it would be nice to have the degree as a backup. Or for when you aren't playing anymore, right? It would be a terrible loss to quit now, after you've come so far. And while, yes, you could get a job over the summer and save up some money, I'm not sure the kind of job you'd qualify for would be enough. You'd have to cover tuition but also basic needs like food and gas and things. And during the season the hours you'd be able to work would be drastically affected by class, practice, and game schedules..."

"You do it, though. You have a job and a heavier class

schedule than I do," I point out. He sighs, tracing a finger along my collarbone and down my arm.

"Yes, but I'm a tutor, which means I have an unusual amount of control over my schedule. And sure, I have more classes than you, but hockey is a huge drain on your time. You're gone for entire weekends at a time, on some occasions. It's just...it would be a lot for you to take on, that's all I'm saying. And I'd hate to see your play suffer because you're trying to pull yourself in a dozen different directions."

"We'd see each other less, too," I realize, and my stomach clenches in pain.

"Sure," he says, not sounding as though this is a big obstacle, "but that wouldn't change anything. I'll still like you the same, even if I see you less. If you got signed by an NHL team, you'd be gone a lot, right? Or, even in another state?"

"Right." My skin prickles with unease, cold sweat dotting my upper lip. I'd hoped to have another year. Another full year playing hockey at SCU and living with Zeke, before I joined the league. But I'm not going to have a choice of when or who picks me up—I'm going to have to take whatever I can get. Which means Zeke and I are now living on borrowed time.

"But we're not going to break up. Distance would be hard, but it would be harder to not be together at all, right?"

"Right."

"Carter," he huffs, sitting up so he can look me in the eye. "You're stressing out about this now, aren't you? I'm trying to make you feel better, not worse."

"I'm not stressed out," I lie, scowling.

"Yes, you are! You're not going to break up with me, are you? If you get signed by...I don't know, Colorado or something, and have to leave?"

"No," I say, vehemently, "of course not."

"Well! Then everything will be fine. You'll have your hockey, I'll have my math, and we'll have each other. Simple." He settles back down against me, completely at ease. *Simple*, he says. I try to think about it in a way that makes it so.

"We could fly to meet each other when I've got a couple days off in a row," I say slowly, thinking it through as I speak. "And over the summer I could come back here."

"Sure, exactly. And every day in-between we will talk on the phone. But you know we're getting a little ahead of things. Maybe South Carolina will need a new goalie and they'll sign you."

"You bite your tongue," I admonish, gently pinching his butt. "Tony is the goalie for South Carolina. I don't want him to get hurt, or something."

Zeke huffs. "Well, there's more than one, isn't there? He needs a backup, right? That could be you!"

In a perfect world, I muse, but quickly smother the warm feeling that burns in my chest at the thought. Best not to get my hopes up for *that* eventuality. I'll only be setting myself up for disappointment.

"Or somewhere near here," I add, because that's really the best we can wish for.

"Either way, we don't really need to be worrying about this right now. One problem at a time. Let's figure out what you're going to do for next year, before we get ourselves worked up about a long-distance relationship that may never happen."

"Yeah. No, you're right. Sorry." I shake my head and reach over to put my phone on the nightstand.

I stay on my side, back to Zeke, who burrows against me. When he slides an arm over my middle, I tangle our fingers and use our linked hands to bring his chest flush against my back. The way he tucks his face into my neck sends shivers skittering down my spine; my skin feels like it's on fire where his mouth is resting. Pulling his hand up to my lips, I kiss his palm.

"Goodnight, big spoon." There is a flurry of warm air against my neck when he laughs.

"Oh my god," he mumbles, shifting and pressing his face deeper into my shoulder.

It takes me a long time to fall asleep. Zeke's snoring softly, his arm lying limp across me and held in place largely because I've still got ahold of his hand. Eventually, it's the thought of having an entire week to spend with Zeke that chases away the worries about the future and finally allows me to fall asleep.

21

Zeke

I PULL Carter's SCU Hockey hoodie over my head and give my hair a cursory pat to put it back into place. Downstairs, Jefferson is in the kitchen singing nonsensically and clattering around the kitchen. I check my phone, making sure there aren't any messages from Carter, as I jog downstairs to join my friend. He turns when I enter the room. He's wearing his own, brand new SCU Hockey sweater, which was purchased in honor of all the games we go to now.

"You ready to go?" he asks, checking the time on his watch. It's the first home game after spring break, and Carter told me that the game sold out.

"Yeah, I—" A brisk knock on the front door interrupts me. Jefferson and I both look in the direction of the front door, bewildered. "Uhm. Should I answer that?"

Even though I live here, I don't feel like I live here in the way that entitles me to answer the door. Another knock sounds, a quick three beat staccato. Jefferson's car is parked out front—we'll have to leave through the front door, which means there's no way to sneak around whomever is standing out there knocking. I look at Jefferson.

"Well, I'm not going to answer it," he says, fairly.

Sighing, I walk toward the front door and reach it just as another trio of knocks come. Peeking through the peephole, I gasp. Jefferson, who followed me over, looks as well.

"What? Who is it?" he whispers, clearly not recognizing the woman on the other side of the door. Shaking my head, I motion for him to step back so I can open the door.

Carter's mom stands on the threshold, looking like she just stepped off of a Hollywood movie set. She's wearing a long, camel colored peacoat that's belted across her slim waist, and heels that make my feet hurt just looking at them. Her hair shines gold in the sunlight, exactly the way Carter's does. Jefferson lets out a low whistle behind me, and I bite back the urge to try and surreptitiously stomp on his foot.

"Hi, Mrs. Morgan." It takes me a full thirty seconds and a throat clearing from Jefferson to remind me of my manners. "Uhm, do you want to come inside?"

"Hello again, Zeke. Yes, thank you." She takes a step inside, but doesn't move far from the door. She gazes around the room with a vaguely interested air, her purse dangling between both of her hands. "This is very nice."

"Oh, uhm, yes. Have you not been here?" I ask, and there is another throat clearing behind me. I flush. "Oh, and this is my friend, Jefferson."

"Hello," Mrs. Morgan says, shaking his hand politely before returning her fingers to the purse strap. "No, I haven't been here. I try to give Carter his independence, and I doubt he would have appreciated his mother coming and decorating his house."

She smiles at me and I do my best to return it even though I think she's wrong. I think Carter would have grabbed ahold of any overture from his mom and held on tight with both hands.

"Did you want something to drink, Mrs. Morgan?" Jefferson asks, and I throw him a grateful look.

"Oh, no, thank you." She stares at me, eyes skimming over the ill-fitting hoodie. "Are you going to Carter's game?"

"Yeah, we are. We go to all of the home games."

She smiles again, adjusting the front of her coat. "That's nice. Would you mind if I rode with you? I've never been before, and I feel it might be prudent of me to go with someone who's familiar."

"To the *game*? You want to ride with us to the...to the hockey game?"

"If you don't mind. I'd like to sit with you, as well, if possible. Maybe you and I can get to know each other a little better."

I gape at her. *Is this the fucking Twilight Zone? What is happening?* Jefferson—bless him—saves me once more. "Of course. The more the merrier. Do you have a ticket? Otherwise, you can take my ticket and go with Zeke."

"Oh, yes, I have a ticket. Nico Mackenzie left me one at will call, I believe."

A few puzzle pieces slot into place. "Well, in that case, we'd love you to join us. Are you...will you be comfortable in that or are you going to change...?"

Jefferson makes a choked noise and I blush even more. I stand by the question, though. She's wearing *heels* for fuck's sake.

"Oh, no, I think I'll be all right." She smiles at me, a touch wider. "Are we leaving now? I'm looking forward to watching

Carter play. Mr. Mackenzie told me he'd be playing tonight. I take it they switch out, usually? The two...goalies?"

"Yeah, that's...they do, you're right." I nod, encouragingly. There is no way Carter knew she was coming; he would have said something to me before he left for the game.

I gesture for her to precede us through the door. As soon as her back is turned, I look at Jefferson, helplessly. He shrugs, grimacing. Neither of us planned on being joined by Carter's mom. This is going to be the most awkward threesome of all time. I try to get her to sit in the shotgun seat, but she refuses and slides into the back before I can argue. Feeling distinctly uncomfortable, I sit, hands clasped in my lap, and allow Jefferson to fill the car with meaningless chitchat. It's not lost on me that 'meaningless chitchat' is usually my forte.

While Jefferson is regaling Mrs. Morgan with an in-depth explanation of his degree path, I slip my phone out of my pocket and text Carter. We always meet up right after the game. Jefferson calls it the trade-off: we meet at the locker rooms and I ride home with Carter instead of Jefferson. I hope he thinks to check his phone before meeting me, or he's going to be *very* surprised by my guest.

As expected, we attract a lot of stares as we move through the crowds at the rink. Usually, Jefferson and I slink through all the bodies, jostled on every side by elbows. Not today. Today, the crowd parts like the red sea as Carter's mom stride's purposefully down the hallways, heels clicking on the concrete floor. When we sit down—me seated between them —Jefferson looks like he finds this whole thing hilarious, and Mrs. Morgan merely looks curious.

"It *is* cold in here," she muses, untying the belt on her

coat but leaving it on. "Mr. Mackenzie warned me it would be."

She smiles benignly, idly scanning the crowd of students and the team warming up on the ice. I wonder if it's necessary for me to point out Carter. She might not know what his number is. Clearing my throat, I lean a little closer to her. She smells like flowers.

"Mrs. Morgan? That's Carter," I point to one of the goalies down on the ice, stretching, "right there. Number seventy-seven. Do you see?"

"Oh! There he is. Thank you." She pats my knee and watches, eyes narrowed.

The first period goes well. Jefferson and I both leap to our feet, cheering, when Vasel scores the first goal of the game. Carter's mom stays seated, but claps politely. I'm not actually sure she saw the goal happen, since her gaze hasn't really wavered from Carter the entire game. He's playing well, of course, and made some truly spectacular saves. A couple times, she's leaned over to me and asked, "That was good, wasn't it?". Jefferson turns his head away and laughs every time this happens—the hockey blind leading the blind.

During intermission, Jefferson strolls off to get us food while Mrs. Morgan and I keep our seats. With the absence of hundreds of bodies around us and the distraction of the game, I'm nervous once more. What am I supposed to talk about with her?

"Are you...are you having fun?" I ask her. She turns in her seat, trying to face me, and crosses one ankle behind the other. She looks like the First Lady, slumming it with the peasants.

"I am! Thank you for letting me sit with you. You know, I

was worried when Carter wanted to play hockey. It's a particularly violent sport, isn't it?"

"Yeah, but luckily he's the goalie. There is this weird, I guess unspoken rule in hockey that you can't touch the goalies. One time, someone stopped too close to Carter," I mime a slanting motion with my hand, meant to illustrate the angle of the skate blade on the ice, "and a bunch of ice flew up into Carter's face. They have a word for it...frosting? Icing? No, that's the other thing...snowing! It's called snowing. So, anyway, that happened and our team pretty much lost their minds. Huge fight. And Carter was fine, but I guess it's rude, or something."

I shrug, the tops of my ears burning. I feel unbearably self-conscious talking to her even though she's only been kind thus far. She nods, looking contemplative.

"Snowing. Interesting. Well, I am glad to hear that, at any rate. Now, tell me, what are you going to school for? Are you from South Carolina or did you come here for university?"

Her hands are resting atop her bag, settled in her lap, and her blue eyes are unwavering on mine. She gives me her full, undivided attention as I speak, and doesn't interrupt a single time. It puts a pang in my chest. She's a good listener, just like her son. When I pause, she asks thoughtful questions, and the twenty-minute intermission passes by so fast I'm surprised to see Jefferson slide back into his seat. It felt like barely five minutes.

We eat shitty concession stand food as we watch the last two periods of the game, and the air feels distinctly easier than it did at the start. I don't have to strain myself to envision this version of Mrs. Morgan on hands and knees, getting her hands dirty in a garden. We end up winning the game and she stands with us this time as we applaud, watching the team line up and hug Carter. She's smiling so wide it's crinkling the corners of her eyes.

"That's nice, isn't it?" she says, as the team all pat Carter on the head. Vasel gives him a hug, rocking them from side to side.

"It's my favorite part," I admit, and share a grin with her. She nods.

"Yes, me too. Where do we go from here? Mr. Mackenzie indicated I could meet Carter after the game, but I'm not sure I know where to go."

"I can show you. I always wait for him at the locker room so that we can ride home together."

She beams. Jefferson says his goodbyes, still looking amused, and I lead Mrs. Morgan slowly toward the locker rooms. I'm nervous again, unable to stop my fingers from fidgeting with the strings at the neck of Carter's hoodie. I don't know if he received my message about his mom being here; my guess is no, seeing as he hasn't replied. I feel like the unwitting accomplice in an unwanted surprise.

As usual, I can hear the locker room long before we actually arrive in the hallway. Usually, I just wait, leaned against the wall and as out of the way as possible. Carter never dawdles, and I rarely have to wait long. Tonight, however, I text him again to let him know I'm here and have company. *Check your phone, check your phone, check your phone,* I chant to myself, just as the door to the locker room opens.

"Oh. Hi, Max." The wild noises are louder for a moment, before the door closes behind Max. He looks at me and then at Mrs. Morgan. He probably doesn't remember me. "I'm Zeke, we met a few weeks ago, Carter's—"

"Boyfriend," he fills in. "Yeah, I remember you. Are you waiting for him? I could go get him."

"If you could tell him I'm out here with his mom, that would be great." *And please make sure to emphasize the mom part, while you're at it.* "Thanks, Max."

"Of course," he murmurs, already turning around to go back inside.

"Well, they're sure having fun," Mrs. Morgan notes, as the volume swells once more. There is a rap song playing on the speakers, and in the five minutes we've been standing here I've heard the words *pussy* and *ass* far more than I would have liked, given my present company. I don't need a mirror to know my face and ears are burning.

As I knew it would be, the door is flung suddenly open so violently the bang off the wall is audible even over the rap song. Carter, who has eyes only for me, smiles and steps out. He'd obviously been mid-change, because he's wearing only his base layer of clothing. Everything is *very* tight, and *very* revealing.

"Zeke, hey, Max said some crazy shit about you being here with my—" His words grind to a halt as he finally notices his mom. He couldn't look more shocked if he tried. I see his eyes flick away from her, back down the hallway, as though looking for someone else. His brows furrow in confusion, and the smile is swiftly replaced with a frown. "Mom?"

"Hi, sweetie," she says, smiling at him. "Congratulations on your win. Zeke tells me it's quite an accomplishment to earn a shutout and that you have quite a few this season."

He stares at her. "Uhm. Yeah. Right, that's...Is Dad here? What's going on? Did Grandma die?"

"Not that I'm aware of," his mom answers dryly. "And no, your father couldn't come."

Silence falls between us, weighty and uncomfortable.

Carter looks at me, helplessly confused. I open my mouth to explain, but Mrs. Morgan beats me to it.

"I spoke with Nico Mackenzie on the phone last week. He was quite complimentary of you, I have to say. Spoke very highly of how hard you work and how dedicated you are to the team. He said he's never seen someone progress as quickly as you did after your freshman year. He said you'd made *friends*." She places a particular emphasis on this last part. "I have to admit, I spent a great deal of the conversation wondering if he was confusing my son with another."

Carter gives a bark of laughter. His mom smiles and the discomfort eases, slightly.

"He also said that you've struggled a great deal with your classes, but have managed to pass them all, regardless." She eyes him, expression turning serious. "He said that you've spent much of your time here miserable. That the only thing that makes you happy is being on the ice."

"And Zeke," Carter says quietly.

"Yes," she smiles at me, "and Zeke."

"So..." Carter rubs a hand over his chest and then over his hair. "Coach asked you to come to a game?"

"He did. He thought it might be beneficial for your dad and I to see you play, so that we might better understand the difficulty of your position, and the skills you possess to manage it."

"But Dad didn't come," Carter says, not sounding disappointed but resigned.

Just then, the tall form of Coach Mackenzie materializes at the end of the hallway. I sag with relief. There is another man with him, walking just a step behind, strolling casually with his hands tucked into his pockets and a smirk on his face. Hearing the footsteps, Carter turns and the world is treated to the second of his smiles this evening.

"Tony! Holy shit! I didn't know you'd be here, tonight."

Seems to be a lot of that going around. Tony—whom I remember is Anthony Lawson, Coach Mackenzie's partner—smiles broadly at his welcome and pulls Carter into a one-armed hug.

"Nice game," he says, and I swear I can see Carter swell with pride.

"Thanks. This is Zeke—Coach Mackenzie already met him so maybe he told you. And this is my mom. Dad didn't come."

Tony winks at me and reaches a hand out to shake Mrs. Morgan's. Beside him, Coach Mackenzie is watching the proceedings vigilantly. It's hard to picture him as one half of a couple with Anthony Lawson, even with them standing right next to each other.

"Mrs. Morgan, I'm glad you were able to come." Coach Mackenzie says, politely. Next to him, Tony has leaned a shoulder against the wall next to Carter, lounging as though he's perfectly at ease. He watches Coach Mackenzie as he speaks, a small smile playing at the corner of his mouth. Perhaps it's not *that* hard to picture them together.

"Of course," Mrs. Morgan responds.

"I don't suppose you'd mind stepping with me into my office for a moment? I won't keep you long. Carter, I imagine you'd like a shower."

I almost laugh at the look of relief on Carter's face at the obvious dismissal. Before I can get roped into accompanying everyone into the office, I volunteer to stay behind.

"I'll wait here for you," I tell Carter, and Tony turns his face away from the group to hide his smile.

"Certainly," Mrs. Morgan says to Coach Mackenzie, adjusting the front of her coat. She smiles, glancing between Carter and I. "You'll wait for me?"

"Of course," I say, at the same time that Carter responds: "Sure, Mom."

"This way," Coach Mackenzie says, and gestures her forward with an outstretched arm. He goes to follow, shoulder almost colliding with the wall as he turns. Tony, moving so quickly I hardly see it, reaches out and grasps his elbow. He lets go of him just as fast as he grabbed hold; as he passes, Coach Mackenzie brushes his hand across Tony's stomach. Carter and I watch them all go. The second they're all out of earshot, he turns to me.

"What the fuck?" he asks, and I laugh. He gives a strained chuckle and shakes his head, turning to look at where his mom disappeared down the hallway. He holds his arms open and I step into them, gratefully.

"You always smell *so* bad," I tell him, hugging him tight around the middle and trying to ignore how wet he is. He vibrates with laughter. "I take it you didn't get my text messages? I tried to warn you about your mom. She just showed up at the house, right as Jefferson and I were leaving. She was wearing *heels*, did you see? To a hockey game."

"Honestly, she probably wears heels to garden." We break apart and I take a moment to admire what he's wearing. Hockey really is a lovely sport.

"I can't believe she's here," I tell him.

"I know. And did you hear all that stuff she said? About Coach? I thought when he called them he was going to…I don't know…give them basic information. Stats and shit. I didn't think he'd say all that stuff. And then he got my mom to come to a game? Fucking incredible."

He laughs, incredulously, and reaches a hand out to touch the side of my face. It's an unthinking gesture, sweet and gentle. It makes me want to hug him again.

"It was really nice," I agree. "Do you think he asked Anthony Lawson to come to talk with her? Maybe provide some insight into the NHL?"

"I bet you're right," he agrees excitedly. Shaking his head, he plucks at the front of his shirt. "I better go shower though. You cool to wait out here?"

"Of course."

"All right. Be right back," he says, reaching out and brushing a thumb over my jaw again.

He's back in less than ten minutes, hair wet and pulled back in its usual bun. His cheeks are flushed from the heat of the shower, and his shirt is clinging to his chest as if he didn't bother trying to dry off properly before he dressed. The smile that graces his face when he steps back into the hallway and sees me waiting nearly sends me into cardiac arrest. *My Carter, my smile. Mine, mine, mine.* I smile back and step forward to hug him again.

"Do I smell better?" he asks.

"Mm. Much." Several of his teammates pass us on their way out of the locker room, barely sparing us a glance. I step back from Carter, but he slings an arm over my shoulders and pulls me to his side. He leans back against the wall, dropping his bag to the floor. I tuck myself into his side and mimic his pose. Apparently, we're going to wait for his mom right here.

Max leaves the locker room, eyes catching on us. He nods politely, hitching his bag up his shoulder and turning to walk toward the exit. Carter calls him back before he can get too far.

"Max, hold up."

The other man turns, apprehension clear on his face. The fingers of his right hand are clenched right around the strap of his bag. "Yeah?"

"You busy tomorrow? Vas and I were going to have an NHL tournament on the Playstation at my place. You should come."

Max stares at him, silently. Two other teammates leave the locker room and pass us before he speaks. I can't tell if he's trying to figure out a way to tell Carter no without being rude, or if he's weighing the sincerity of Carter's offer. Either way, he thinks things through before responding.

"Yeah, all right, sounds fun." He fiddles with his bag. "Just the three of us? Or will there be a lot of people there?"

I look up at Carter and see him pulling a face. I grin—Carter hates parties.

"Hell no, just us. And Zeke, obviously," he jostles me, "although he usually ditches me to go to the library."

I roll my eyes at Max, bringing him in on the joke. He smiles, faintly, but perks up slightly at the confirmation that it will be a small crowd at Carter's. He runs a hand through his hair, causing the damp strands to stick out haphazardly.

"Okay, great. Yeah, I'll be there! Just text me the details."

"Sure. See you, man."

Leaning heavily against Carter, I watch Max stroll off down the hallway. There is something strange about Max that I can't put my finger on. Something vulnerable and sad, like a puppy who's been left outside in the rain. I don't have long to ponder the mysteries of Carter's new friend, however, because we're joined once more by Carter's mom, Coach Mackenzie, and Anthony Lawson. Carter straightens, but keeps his arm around my shoulder.

"Thank you for waiting," his mom says, as though we would drive off and leave her stranded here.

"Sure," Carter says, eyes bouncing between the three of them and a scowl on his face.

"You'd better get out of here," Coach Mackenzie says, eyes narrowed on Carter. "Make sure to ice and stretch tonight, okay? We'll speak tomorrow."

"But—"

"Tomorrow," he repeats. Carter nods, biting back whatever else he wanted to say. "Thank you again, Mrs. Morgan. It was a pleasure speaking with you."

"Likewise. Thank you for reaching out. And you, Mr. Lawson. I appreciate what you've both done for my son."

Carter and I exchange a loaded glance, but say nothing. I can tell he's dying to know what was said in that office, but too afraid to ask. Coach Mackenzie's face is carefully blank, and next to him, Anthony Lawson is wearing a benign smile that gives even less clues. I squeeze Carter's hip, out of sight of all the adults, and he looks down at me.

"Time to go home?" I ask, and he nods.

"Yeah. You ready to go, Mom? Or do you want to see if the concession stand is still open—maybe we can get you a corndog?"

Anthony Lawson and I both laugh, while Coach Mackenzie and Mrs. Morgan both look at Carter with identical quelling expressions. I have to turn my face away. It only makes me want to laugh harder. Corndogs notwithstanding, we say our goodbyes and head off toward the exit and Carter's car. Neither he nor his mom speak, and I can tell from the tightness of his grip on my hand that he's tense.

"You can sit in front," I tell her, when we reach the car.

She shakes her head, already adjusting the bag on her arm so she can reach for the rear door.

"No, that's all right. You two sit together."

Everyone is silent on the drive home. Carter looks up into the rearview mirror so often, it appears that he has a tic. I want to pull one of his hands away from the steering wheel and trace soothing circles on his palm. I want to say things with our skin that can't be said out loud with his mom in the car. Instead, I reach across the console and put my hand on his leg.

"Dad didn't say anything about me bringing a guy home?" Carter asks suddenly, and at a volume totally inappropriate for the close confines. I jump. His tone matches the scowl on his face as he stares defiantly at his mom in the rearview.

"No," his mom responds, simply. Carter scoffs. "You can bring whomever you want home."

Carter drums his fingers on the steering wheel, frowning out the windshield as he mulls this over. It's clear he thought there would be more of a fight where his sexuality was concerned, and isn't certain what to do now that there isn't.

"Okay," he says finally, "thanks."

We get home and the discomfort grows until the air feels heavy with it. Carter is jangling his keys in his hand as we walk inside, eyes darting to and from his mom rapidly.

"You're not driving home tonight, are you Mrs. Morgan?" I ask, suddenly realizing how late it is and how far away she lives. Carter looks downright terrified at the realization that she might be expecting to stay here. I spend the majority of my nights in Carter's room, so technically there is an extra bed available, but neither of us were expecting company in the form of his mom.

"Oh, no, I'll head back tomorrow morning. I've got a hotel

for the evening." Carter visibly deflates and his mom's lips twitch. "I'll get out of your hair, shall I? Thank you for letting me spend time with you, Zeke. I hope I'll be seeing more of you."

"Of course," I answer quietly. "Anytime."

She turns to Carter. "And I'm going to try and come to more of your games. Your father, too. Perhaps when you play teams closer to us we could go to those games? I'll have a look at the schedule and let you know."

She waves a hand and then sets about tying the belt of her coat. Carter is staring at her like she's an alien life-form that just strolled into his kitchen.

"Okay," he says, sounding unsure as to whether he means this as a question or not.

"Oh, and if you do get an offer through your agent, you should send it to your father to have the lawyers look over. It can't hurt to have as many people look it over as possible, make sure you're getting a fair deal."

"What the fuck is happening here?" Carter asks succinctly, looking around as though hoping for somebody to pop out and explain the situation to him. His mom raises an eyebrow at his tone, but doesn't scold him for the attitude. She's probably used to it.

"I'll speak to the registrar's office on Monday, make sure that everything is squared away for next year."

"Mom, seriously, what is—"

She interrupts him, voice firm and eyes hard. She looks more like Carter in this moment than she ever has. "I wasn't under the impression that when you came to speak to your father and I, you were asking for permission. You were asking for support."

"And money," Carter adds, honestly.

"We aren't going to take away your tuition. Even with a long, full hockey career you are going to need something to fall back on. A business degree will do that for you, even if you aren't using it for the purpose we had originally intended." She sighs, brushing her hair out of her face and softening her tone. "Carter, you're twenty-one years old. Your father has spent every one of those years living under the assumption that you and he would one day be working together. I won't lie, this isn't the future he wants for you, but neither will he—we—actively do anything to jeopardize it. You're going to finish school and you're going to play hockey; you'll probably still butt heads with your father, but we love you all the same."

I look over at Carter, who'd probably be less surprised if she pulled a gun from her purse and shot him. He opens his mouth, closes it, shakes his head and looks at me. He stares at me for a long, silent moment, before looking back at his mom.

"Thank you," he says, and then in a halting, uncomfortable tone: "I love you, too."

She's not quick enough to hide the look of surprise that crosses her face. It makes me wonder if this is the first time those words have been shared between them in a long while. No wonder Carter acts like he's getting teeth pulled whenever I try to have an emotional conversation with him, the poor guy hasn't had any practice.

"Well," she says brusquely, "I'll talk to your dad when I get home tomorrow. And I'll let you know next time I come for a game, shall I?"

"Okay," he says in a strangled voice.

"I'll get going then." She smiles and turns toward the front door. Carter trails after her, uncertainly, looking at me over his shoulder before reaching around her to open the front door.

"You're sure you don't want to stay here?" he asks nervously.

"Positive. You boys have a good night." She brushes a hand across his and then she's gone.

Carter stands in the open doorway, watching as her headlights sweep out of the driveway. Once she's gone, he slams the door and turns to look at me, one hand rubbing at the shaved side of his head.

"Okay, what the actual fuck," he says, sounding flummoxed. I laugh, helplessly.

"Did she really just stroll in here and solve all of your problems?"

"I mean...fuck me, I guess. I don't know!" He flops down on a kitchen stool, fingers still dancing over his skull nervously. I reach out and grab his hand. "I can't believe Coach got her to come. Seriously, I can't fucking believe it. I stopped asking my freshman year because I figured I'd never get them here."

I grimace, heart twinging with pity at these words. "Yeah, he really pulled a fast one on you, didn't he? Even got Anthony Lawson involved."

"Goddamn Tony," Carter mumbles. "They swung it for me, for sure."

He blows out a hard breath and brings our linked hands upward to kiss the back of mine in a mindless gesture of affection. I tug, pulling him to his feet and heading toward the stairs. He follows without complaint, letting go of my hand in favor of an arm around my waist. He's been doing this a lot more, of late: touching me or pulling me to him whenever we're together, as though he craves contact. When we reach his bedroom, he drops his arm and flops onto the bed, one leg dangling over the side.

"I'm so freaking tired," he groans, "but I also feel like I've got a vat of caffeine flowing through my veins."

I laugh, pulling his hoodie off before laying down next to him. He turns his head to look at me, lifting a hand to trail his knuckles down my bare arm.

"Me too. That was nice of you to invite Max over."

"What? Oh, right." He shrugs. "No big deal. He's pretty chill."

"Mm." I rest my palm on his chest. I'm pretty sure the invitation *was* a big deal to Max. "So, lots of pent-up energy that needs to be expelled, huh?"

"Yeah. Might have to go downstairs and tire myself out on the treadmill." He sighs, gustily. "It's too bad there aren't any other ways of getting spent and sweaty, you know?"

"Yes," I say seriously, and run my hand down to his abdomen, "I wish there was a way I could help you with this particular conundrum."

The words are barely out of my mouth before he's on top of me, mouth against mine as he catches my laugh with his teeth and kisses it away.

22

Carter

ZEKE IS at the motherfucking library, which makes no damn sense. Who goes to the library on the *last day of class?* Sighing, I peek out the front window again, hoping to see his familiar figure walking down the sidewalk. No luck. Annoyed, I turn around and continue pacing a hole into the floor. The piece of paper I've got tucked into the pocket of my basketball shorts burns like it's on fire. If he takes any longer to get home, I'm going to have talked myself out of this.

I've been going around and around for weeks, writing down what I want to say before scratching it out again. I've convinced myself this is stupid and I should keep it to myself, only to turn right back around and convince myself of the opposite. I worked myself into such a frenzy one night, I had to go into the bathroom and hover over the toilet, uncertain whether I was going to puke or not.

I pull out my phone to text him—see if he wants me to

pick him up—when I glance out the window again and spot him.

"Fucking finally," I mutter, tossing my phone down on the couch and throwing open the front door. It bangs satisfyingly against the wall and bounces back toward me. I catch it with my foot and lean against the doorframe with a casualness that I do not feel. I watch as Zeke meanders down the sidewalk, kicking nonchalantly at rocks and totally unaware that I've been in a tailspin, waiting for him. When he catches sight of me in the doorway, he beams.

"Carter," he calls, and picks up his pace. I raise a hand back to him in greeting. He's wearing the same thing he always wears—old, faded jeans, and a plain black shirt—but still my mouth feels dry and my stomach clenches at the sight of him. I don't know how anyone could possibly be that cute and get away with it.

He steps up onto the front step and immediately leans forward for a kiss. Palming his hip, I pull him in and keep him there, enjoying the sun on my face and his lips warm against mine. He makes a small, happy noise and rises up on his tiptoes to deepen the contact. I'm probably going to die from the way this sends my nervous system firing.

"Were you waiting for me?" he asks, delighted. He's grinning as he falls back on his heels, face tipped upward as he looks at me. I roll my eyes dramatically.

"No."

Zeke snorts, putting a hand on my abdomen and gently pushing me backward so he can come inside and close the door.

"How was the library?"

"Good! What were you up to? Other than pining away for me." He shoots a teasing look at me over his shoulder as he heads toward the kitchen, dropping his backpack on the floor by the stairwell on his way.

"Just the pining," I say, as my fingers find the pocket of my shorts. "Hey, do you mind if I talk to you for a second?"

"Sure, what's up?" he asks, closing the refrigerator and looking at me. His smiles drops a couple octaves as he gets a good look at my face. I wonder if I look as strung out as I feel. "What's wrong?"

"Nothing's wrong, I just want to talk to you. In here." I point to the living room, directing him to have a seat in one of the chairs.

"Carter," he says carefully, but I wave a hand and shake my head.

"Just give me a second." I pull the folded piece of paper out of my pocket. I'd thought I would just stand here and say what I want to say, but now that the moment has arrived, I'm feeling a little shaky. Compromising, I pull the coffee table over toward Zeke's chair, and sit down on it so that I'm facing him. He stays quiet for all of a minute, watching as I unfold the notebook paper, before he can't hold himself back any longer.

"What's that?"

"Talking points," I mumble, looking down at my suddenly illegible handwriting. I should have typed this. The paper has been folded and unfolded so many times, it's worn and ragged. I have to hold it carefully, so as not to accidentally tear it down the middle with my trembling fingers.

"Right," Zeke says, looking flummoxed.

"I'm going to start here," I nod my head at some writing that he can't see, "and I have to read it word for word so don't interrupt, okay?"

"Okay," he says, and knots his fingers together in his lap,

like this will keep him from talking. I clear my throat. *Here goes.*

"I want you to know that this has been the best year of my life, and most of that is because of you. You remind me that life doesn't have to be so serious all the time; you are always teaching me new things, and you make me laugh more than I've ever laughed before. I wish I'd posted an ad for a roommate years ago, because we might have met sooner." Stopping, I clear my throat. I can't look up at him, though, so I keep my eyes firmly on the paper. "Whenever I used to picture my future, it never included anybody else with me. Now, you're the *only* part of my future that I'm certain of. I..."

Fuck me, I think, looking down and trying to discern my handwriting. My hands are full on shaking now and if I don't get this out soon, I'm not going to make it through.

"I...sorry, I can't read what I wrote... I just wanted to say that I don't care about anything else that happens in the future, as long as you're in it. Hockey, no hockey, I don't care. I just want you." I suck in a deep breath. This part I can read just fine. "And, I love you."

I look up, now. Zeke is watching me, eyes wide and tender. He scoots to the end of his chair and leans forward, putting both hands on my knees and bringing our faces closer together. I breathe a very heavy sigh of relief. He doesn't have to say it back—I can see it in his eyes and the soft, upward tilt of his mouth.

"I love *you*," he says, and okay, so maybe I *did* need to hear it. My hands are really trembling now, the paper crinkling as I hold it aloft.

"I'm not quite finished," I tell him.

"Okay," he says, and rubs his hands across my legs.

"Just two more things. One, will you move in with me?" I

look back up at him, already seeing confusion writ across his face. "I mean, like, for good. Today is the last day of school so I don't know if you were planning on going back home or not...but I wanted to ask if you would want to live here, with me, and to also sleep in my bedroom. You know, not have separate bedrooms. Like we do now."

Oh for the love of all that is holy, shut the fuck up Carter. I knew I should have written *everything* down that I wanted to say, word for word.

"Yes. Yes to all of that," Zeke says, voice breaking slightly before he clears his throat.

"Okay. Thank god," I respond and he laughs. Some of the tension breaks, and I smile at him, gratefully. "And the last thing was—"

My phone rings, startling both of us. Scowling, I turn to look at the offending device. *Are you fucking kidding me?*

"Who is it?" Zeke asks, so I reach over and grab it. The name *Joel Street* flashes across the screen. Zeke inhales, sharply, and his hands tighten where they're still on my legs. "Holy shit. Answer it."

23

Zeke

"Answer it!" I repeat, grasping Carter's arm. He looks at me like I've completely lost my mind.

"I'm not done, though," he tells me, eyes tracking down to where his notebook paper is clutched in his hand. I can make out his messy scrawl, but can't read any of the words.

"You have to answer." I reach over and slide the green button, grinning when Carter scowls at me. I mouth *love you* at him and watch as he lifts the phone to his ear.

"Hey, Street," he answers, voice clipped and rude.

"Carter!"

I jolt at the booming voice of his agent. He's practically shouting, as if him and Carter are trying to converse from opposite ends of a football field. Carter lowers the volume on the side of his phone, smirking at me.

"What's up? No offense, but you're sort of cock blocking me right now. I was in the middle of something important."

"Carter," I hiss, nudging his ankle with my foot.

Joel Street laughs so loudly Carter has to pull the phone away from his ear, regardless of how low he turned the volume. It's like he's in the room with us, bellowing into our eardrums.

"Christ, you've got a lot of attitude for a fucking rookie. All right, you sitting down?" A pause. "I'm looking at an offer for a one-year entry level contract for South Carolina's AHL affiliate."

I gasp loudly, and then clap a hand over my mouth in apology. Carter makes a face, pulls the phone away from his ear and puts the call on speaker. He gestures for me to speak.

"Street, you're on speaker and my boyfriend is here. Zeke Cassidy."

"Fantastic, so what I was saying—"

"Oh, we heard you loud and clear," Carter says, making another face at me. I bite my lip to keep from laughing out loud. He scuffs his foot back and forth on the carpet, looking uncertain. "So...you're serious? They offered me a contract?"

"Well, I sure as shit ain't going to call and lie about it," Street says indignantly. "Listen, kid, I'm not going to lie—the contract isn't great. It's the best you can hope for given you're fresh off college ice and didn't go through the draft, but it's not great. One year and low pay. I doubt you'll start even a third of the regular season games."

"I don't care about the money," Carter says immediately.

"Well, good, because this is as good as it's going to get for a while. This season will be a contract year if you sign this. That means you go out there and play your fucking heart out. You play like every game is a Stanley Cup Final and maybe, come the following year, they offer you an extension. Best case scenario."

Carter looks a little bit like someone hit him in the

stomach and he's not yet recovered the ability to breathe. Leaning around him, I scrabble for my own cell phone and pull up the notes app. I type out a quick message and hold it out to him. He nods, giving me permission to speak.

Clearing my throat, I lean closer to his phone.

"Hello, sir, Mr. Street? This is Zeke. May I ask you a couple questions?"

"Hit me."

"How long does he have to look over the contract and decide? Also, were he to sign, when would he be expected to..." I trail off, looking at Carter. What I want to know is when he'd be expected to be there, but I honestly have no idea where the AHL affiliate team is located. Maybe he won't have to leave at all.

"I asked for a week. It's the offseason so we were able to buy a little bit of time. The contract is in your inbox—read it over, sleep on it, read it over again. Have Nico Mackenzie read it. Don't bother asking Lawson to read it because I'm not convinced he can."

Carter snorts, earning an echoing chuckle from Street before he continues.

"As for after you sign," he says, like it's a sure thing Carter will, "you won't be expected to report until a couple days prior to training camp. That being said, I'd recommend getting a jump on living arrangements. The housing market in Florida isn't great, and you don't want to fork out the cash for a long-term hotel."

Florida. My stomach sinks all the way to the floor. I fix my eyes on Carter's fingers, wrapped around his phone, and try not to let my disappointment bleed through. *Florida is better than California*, I remind myself, *it could be worse.*

"Okay. And what about school? He has another year left

before graduating," I say, glancing back up at Carter. He nods at me and gives me a small, grateful smile. "He can't be the first athlete to still be in school. What would be your recommendation on how to navigate that?"

"Another good question. You looking for a job, Zeke Cassidy?"

I laugh and then wait for him to answer my question. When he doesn't, I realize his own question had been serious.

"Oh, uhm, well, no. Thank you," I stammer. Carter snorts again so I give him another nudge with my foot.

"Too bad. To answer your question, I'd utilize the summer. Knock out as many summer classes as you can. Once the season starts, you can probably manage one or two online courses, but your first year in the league is going to be tough. Don't bite off more than you can chew."

"All right," Carter says, clearing his throat and looking at me. I shake my head to indicate I can't think of anything else right now. Not until I see that contract, anyway. "I'll have to look at my degree requirements and see what they offer for the summer. Anything else?"

"Not on my end. You know how to reach me."

Carter hangs up the phone and tosses it onto the couch; it bounces onto the floor, making me wince in sympathy. Before I can pick it up and put it on the couch *gently*, he looks me hard in the eye and says: "I fucking love you."

Laughing, I abandon the phone and pull him to standing so that I can hug him. He's big and warm, solid and mine. His hand on the back of my neck kneads gently, tracing along the fine hair there.

"What was the other thing on your list?" I mumble into his chest, putting the phone call on the back burner for now.

"Mm?"

"You said there was two things you need to talk about. One was living together. What was the other one?"

"Oh," he says, pulling back slightly and looking down at me. "I was going to suggest we offer to let your grandma live here...we have the extra room—or we could even convert the basement into an apartment— so that she wouldn't be living all alone so far away. More cost effective, too, for her. I doubt social security checks are great, you know?"

He's rambling, arms still wrapped around me and eyes bouncing all over my face as he tries to read my expression. I hope my face conveys: *you are the kindest, most generous person I know and I love you.*

"Uhm, and also, now that I'll probably be in Florida for half of the year, it might be nice for you to have someone here with you. That way you wouldn't be all alone when I'm gone. But no pressure, it was just an idea. Whatever you want to do."

"Carter."

"Yeah?"

"I love that you thought of Grandma. Not many people would have, so thank you." He moves his head in an embarrassed gesture. I tighten my arms around his waist. "But I don't want you to think you have to offer something like that. This is your house, and—"

"Ours," he corrects immediately. For a second, I can hardly breathe around the burning in my chest. Resting my head back against him, I close my eyes; he cups the back of my head again, kneading gently.

"Okay, ours. But Carter, I know you like having your own space. It might be too much to have me *and* my grandma here. And that's okay—I don't expect you to adjust your entire life for me."

He huffs. "I wouldn't mind, Zeke. I already feel bad, thinking about being gone for half of the year and you being here alone. I also feel bad that she lives in a trailer and I live in a house that's way too fucking big for a college student."

He scowls and waves an arm, indicating the massive living room and vaulted ceilings.

"We can ask her, but she's going to be stubborn about it," I warn him. Rising up onto my tiptoes, I angle my head back and wait for him to lean down and kiss me.

"Will your grandma care if you sleep in my room?" he asks against my lips, pausing before adding a clarification: "With me?"

"No," I laugh, giving him another quick peck before I lower back down onto my heels to give my calves a rest. "She knows I'm planning on keeping you."

He smiles at that. Stepping back and away from me, he picks up his phone and tucks it into his pocket. The motion gives me a clear view of the coffee table and the raggedy piece of paper he'd written his notes on. I lean over and snatch it up.

"Oh," Carter says, holding out his hand. I shake my head and back away from him.

"No way, I'm keeping this," I tell him, looking down at his chicken scratch writing and beaming. He looks embarrassed.

"I would have forgotten what I wanted to say," he admits. I nod.

"Talking points," I repeat, grinning at him and laughing when he rolls his eyes. "Hey, let's print out that contract and read it. You should also email it to Coach Mackenzie. And then we should celebrate!"

"Celebrate, huh?" He perks up, grinning and stepping closer.

"Oh my god, not like that." Laughing, I sidestep him and walk toward the kitchen. "We should celebrate with your friends. Invite everyone over."

"Sure. Just Vas and Max, though."

I turn to look at him, reaching behind me for the refrigerator handle. I'm starving, and Carter never says no to food. He has a bottomless pit for a stomach. "You could invite the whole team if you wanted. There's enough space here for everyone."

"They're the only two I'm friends with," he replies, shrugging and sliding onto one of the barstools to watch me. "Besides, Max won't come if it's a big group."

"Really?"

"Nope. He gets invited to shit all the time, but the only time I've seen him say yes is when it's just Vas and I."

"Oh." I fiddle with the package of spinach in my hands, the bag crinkling as I think. "Do you think he has social anxiety or something? He always seems sort of...lost? I don't know, Carter, I just have a bad feeling."

"About Max?" he asks, sitting up straighter and narrowing his eyes at me.

"Yeah, I think something is really wrong. I can't explain it, it's more of a...vibe, I guess."

Carter looks away, drumming his fingers on the island as he thinks. He's scowling so hard there is a deep groove carved between his eyebrows.

"I don't know him well," he admits. "We don't sit around and talk about feelings when we're together. We just talk about hockey."

Snorting, I grab a few more ingredients from the refrigerator. Carter loves enchiladas, so that's what I'm making.

"Well, maybe just keep an eye on him. And give him a hug every now and then. He looks like he might need it."

Carter's nose scrunches up adorably and I laugh. I was joking about the hugging, hoping I'd tease that expression out of him. "I'm not going to hug him, Zeke," he says, and I laugh again.

"I know. Now," I point a wooden spoon at him, "email that contract to Coach Mackenzie and print it off. I want to read it."

I THINK Carter might be coming down with a cold. Turning over as carefully as I can and trying not to dislodge the heavy arm thrown across my middle, I watch him sleep. His face is lightly peppered with golden scruff, somehow making his jaw seem sharper. I like the way it feels, and how it leaves small burn marks on the sensitive skin of my thighs. I hope he keeps it.

Gently, so as not to wake him, I rest my fingers against his forehead. He's not any warmer than he usually is first thing in the morning, but I still don't like the sound of his breathing. I wonder if he's prone to upper respiratory infections. I should make sure to keep enough nasal decongestants in the house, just in case.

"Hey," Carter whispers sometime later, eyes still closed. No longer dead weight, his arm tightens and his hand slides up to splay over my shoulder blades. I smile at him even though he can't see it, when he pulls me across the bed toward him.

"Good morning." Helping him along, I snuggle a little

closer. Carter isn't much of a cuddler when he sleeps, but he likes to do it in the morning. "How do you feel?"

Cracking an eye open, he looks at me and smiles. There is a very short list of Carter smiles, and this one is my favorite. This one is private, only for us; soft and cozy like sleep-warmed bedsheets and early morning light through the window.

"Fine," he says, clearing his throat to try and expel the gravel. Because I'm approximately two inches away from his face, I see the flinch. "Little bit of a sore throat, actually."

"Sounds like you might have a stuffy nose, too," I point out, tucking my hand against his chest. It's the first week of June in South Carolina and by all accounts too hot for snuggling, but this is my favorite part of the day and I want to enjoy my fill before he's gone in the fall.

"I'm not sick," he says, like saying the words out loud will make them true.

"Maybe you're starting to come down with something though. I'll get you some medicine, just in case. And this morning you should drink some hot lemon water with honey."

"Sure," he agrees, adjusting his face and rubbing the sleep out of his eyes. The eyelashes on his left eye are all crinkled from sleeping on that side, and pillow lines mar his cheekbone. Carter is the most beautiful in the morning, before he cleans himself up and puts on a scowl. He catches me watching him. "What is it?"

"Love you," I whisper, and am treated to another Carter smile. This one is the dizzying relief of falling in a dream, only to wake up and find yourself safe on solid ground. This is the smile that's half joy and half surprise at his own good fortune.

"Love you," he repeats back.

I lean forward to kiss him. If he is sick, there's no way I haven't already been exposed so there is no reason not to exchange a few more bodily fluids. His hand slides up from my shoulders to cup the back of my head, and he sighs. When he rolls on top of me, I laugh into his mouth, wiggling as he kisses his way slowly down my neck. He must not be feeling *that* badly.

"Max and Vas are coming over around midday," I remind him, grinning when he groans and slumps down on top of me. It's hard to breathe, but it's also hard to care.

"We could just stay in bed all day. I'm sick," he says happily, like that will convince me to engage in an all-day sexathon.

"Thirty more minutes." Lifting my chin, I give him more room and laugh when he mutters *I can work with that* against my neck.

Nearly an hour later, we finally make it out of the bedroom. After fixing Carter a mug of lemon water and honey, we tag team a quick clean-up of the house. Neither one of us are particularly messy, but we've learned from past experience that if things are left out when Vas arrives, he will clean it up for us.

"Max is on the driveway," Carter calls from where he is leaned against the wall and looking out the front window.

"He's just sitting there?" I press against Carter's side and look out. Max is indeed on the driveway, sitting in his car. "He's probably waiting until closer to one, since that's when we told them to get here."

"He's only fifteen minutes early," Carter huffs, gently moving me to the side so he can violently fling open the front door. He waits for Max to open the driver's door before calling out to him. "Come inside before you die of heat stroke."

"Sorry," Max says, walking up and rubbing a hand over the back of his neck, "I'm a little early."

"Fifteen minutes early is right on time," I quote my grandma and Max smiles at me. He looks exhausted, face pinched and bruises beneath his eyes. He looks like he hasn't slept in days. My gaze tracks over to Carter, who's staring at Max through narrowed eyes.

Before we make it back inside and close the door, Vas pulls into the driveway. He's smiling as he gets out of the car, holding a bouquet of flowers and a helium balloon. Max laughs softly and Carter mumbles a string of obscenities.

"Vas, what the hell is that?"

"This is the last balloon the store had," he explains, glancing up at the *It's a girl!* balloon. Holding out the flowers, Carter accepts them with a frown that makes Max cover up another laugh with a cough. "Congratulations on becoming a professional goalie!"

"This is the weirdest thing you've ever done, Vas," Carter tells him.

"You're welcome!"

When the pizza comes, we take it outside to eat in the backyard. Once Carter is seated in a chair, Max quietly ties Vas' balloon to the back of it, lips curved up in a small smile. I wait until Carter is looking at me, mouth turned down in a frown and pink balloon bobbing behind him, before I snap a picture. It's adorable, so I put it as the background on my lock screen.

"Have you talked to any of the coaching staff yet?" Max asks Carter, a plate balanced on his lap with an untouched slice of pizza on it. "The assistant coach was one of my coaches in the juniors. He moved up last year."

"Just the head coach and a few of the guys have reached out."

They devolve into hockey talk, so I sit back in my chair and eat while I listen. Max and Vas hold most of the conversation, with Carter chiming in every now and then between slices of pizza. As I watch, Carter and Vas finish off an entire pizza before Max has made it through a single slice.

"You are not hungry, Max?" Vas asks, apparently noticing the same thing I did. Max's cheeks pink as he looks down at his plate and picks up the slice.

"Oh, no, I had...I had a big breakfast," he says, and takes a bite. The expression on his face is almost resigned, like going through the act of chewing and swallowing is painful. I glance over at Carter to find him watching Max as well, brow furrowed.

"You can take leftovers home for you and your roommate," he tells him, gesturing to the stack of waiting boxes. "We won't eat all of this."

Eventually, we find ourselves back inside and I somehow get roped into playing a spirited NHL tournament on the PlayStation. Carter sits next to me on the couch, pressed against my side with an arm thrown around my shoulders. He kisses the top of my head before explaining the teams.

"You and I will play together because you suck and I'm good. Max and Vas will be together because Vas sucks, too."

"True," Vas sighs, fiddling with the joystick on his controller.

We end up playing long into the afternoon, everyone sprawled out in the living room with cold pizza on the coffee table for anyone who needs sustenance. The sun is setting by the time Vas stretches his arms over his head and groans as his neck pops. Carefully placing the controller down, he slumps back against the couch and sighs.

"I must leave. I have a very early flight tomorrow."

"You're going back to Germany?" Max asks.

"Indeed. My brother will also be visiting, so it will be nice." He glances over at Carter. "I suppose we will not be seeing each other before you leave for Florida, yes?"

"Probably not."

"You shall have to hug me when I leave so that I have something to remember you by," he says wistfully. Max laughs, rolling his head along the back of the couch to grin at Carter, who is doing his best to maintain a glare.

"I'm joining the AHL, Vas, not the military," he says, standing up as the others rise and bending to pick up one of the several uneaten pizzas littering the room. Carter has yet to master the science of ordering the correct amount of food based on number of guests. He holds the box out to Max, who looks embarrassed.

"That's okay," he says, but reaches out and takes it.

"Maybe your roommate is hungry," Carter says, and Max smiles gratefully.

"Yeah," he mumbles. "Thank you."

Carter stares at him, his glower slipping just enough to show a hint of worry. His eyes bounce to me and back to Max; I can practically hear my earlier words playing through his mind: *give him a hug now and then, he looks like he might need it.*

I'm fairly certain the only person Carter has hugged in recent years is me, but still, he gamely pulls Max into an awkward side hug, patting his back and looking miserable. Max flinches before leaning into it, hands clenched tight around the pizza box. *Jesus, now I want to hug Max, too.*

"Thanks for coming," Carter says gruffly, letting him go and stepping back.

"Of course. Maybe we can hang this summer."

"Yeah. It'll be more fun without Vas bringing down our NHL scores."

"That is rude, but I shall forgive you because I am nice guy," Vas says, yanking Carter into what appears to be a bone-crushing hug. Huffing in annoyance, but nonetheless looking pleased, Carter returns it. After rocking them back and forth a few times, Vas lets him go and hugs Max before making his way over to me. "I shall miss you most of all, Zeke. Keep Carter out of trouble, yes?"

"I'll do my best," I say into his shoulder, because all of these hockey guys are fucking ginormous.

Carter looks relieved that the hugging portion of the goodbye is finished, and leans against the doorframe to watch as Vas and Max leave. When I stop next to him, he raises his arm immediately and pulls me into his side. He smells like pizza and fresh air. Suddenly, I feel a little sad. In a couple months, Carter and I will be spending most of our time with several state lines between us.

"How's your throat?"

"Fine."

"Are you feeling congested?"

Gently, he pulls me back inside and closes the door after watching Vas' taillights disappear down the road. He looks down at me for a second, before cupping my cheeks and kissing me. Something in me settles at the touch— there's no sense in missing him when he's right here in front of me, shoulders warm and solid beneath my hands, and lips soft on mine.

As we go through the motions of cleaning up and getting

ready for bed, I have a sudden clarity of how my future will look. I'll finish school while Carter makes a name for himself on the ice. I'll graduate and find a job nearest wherever Carter is playing.

I'll ask him to marry me one day, to save him the anxiety of doing it himself.

"Love you," I tell him as we crawl into bed and settle on our sides, facing each other. He looks pleased. He *always* looks pleased, no matter how many times I've said it.

"Love you more," he returns.

Impossible, I think. He loosely links the fingers on his left hand with mine in the space between us on the bed. Closing my eyes, I fiddle with his ring finger as I fall asleep, dreaming about one day.

THANK YOU

As always, I need to thank my partners in crime, Chelsea and Koma, without whom nothing would ever get published.

Thank you to everyone who has messaged me about their excitement for Carter's story; I hope I didn't let you down, and you had as much fun reading it as I did writing it.

The biggest thank you of all to Ivanna for the beautiful cover. If it's possible for them to get any better, you'll be the one to manage it. I can't wait to see what you do with the next book.

ALSO BY J.J. MULDER

The Offsides Series

Changing the Game

Square to the Puck

Between the Pipes